ANNJA KNEW SHE NEEDED HELP

"I'm trying to identify this," she said.

Mr. Kim took the picture. "This looks very old. The artwork is Scythian," the antiques dealer said.

Impressed, Annja nodded. "I thought so, but I also thought the work might possibly be Chinese."

"Why?" he asked, surprised.

"I took it from a Chinese man," she said.

Kim regarded her carefully. "Up in Volcanoville?" he asked.

Annja decided to be as honest as she could. Kim's personality inspired that, and she'd learned to trust her instincts about people. She nodded in answer to the old man's question.

"The man you were with—the one who killed those young men—he was the one who wanted this belt plaque?"

"Yes," Annja said.

"But you still have it?"

Annja nodded.

Kim studied the photograph intently for a moment. Then he looked straight at Annja. "This is a very dangerous thing to possess Miss Creed. This belt plaque carries a terrible curse."

Titles in this series:

Destiny
Solomon's Jar
The Spider Stone
The Chosen
Forbidden City

ROGUE Angel

Alex Archer

FORBIDDEN CITY

A GOLD EAGLE BOOK FROM

WORLDWIDE®

TORONTO • NEW YORK • LONDON
AMSTERDAM • PARIS • SYDNEY • HAMBURG
STOCKHOLM • ATHENS • TOKYO • MILAN
MADRID • WARSAW • BUDAPEST • AUCKLAND

First edition March 2007

ISBN-13: 978-0-373-62123-1
ISBN-10: 0-373-62123-X

FORBIDDEN CITY

Special thanks and acknowledgment to
Mel Odom for his contribution to this work.

Printed in U.S.A.

The
LEGEND

...THE ENGLISH COMMANDER TOOK
JOAN'S SWORD AND RAISED IT HIGH.
The broadsword, plain and unadorned,
gleamed in the firelight. He put the tip against
the ground and his foot at the center of the blade.
The broadsword shattered, fragments falling
into the mud. The crowd surged forward,
peasant and soldier, and snatched the shards
from the trampled mud. The commander tossed
the hilt deep into the crowd.
Smoke almost obscured Joan, but she continued
praying till the end, until finally the flames climbed
her body and she sagged against the restraints.

Joan of Arc died that fateful day in France,
but her legend and sword are reborn....

PROLOGUE

Loulan City, China
184 A.D.

Everyone in the city hated Emperor Ling's tax collectors. Times were hard. Spring floods had ruined crops and dwellings. Families struggled to make ends meet while still having enough left over to fill the imperial coffers. The Han Dynasty, though, remained unsympathetic to the needs of its citizens. Rebellions had begun around the kingdom.

Occasionally, when angry men grew tired of the heavy tax burden, they killed the royal collectors and took back their taxes. The emperor then had to employ more warriors to protect the tax collectors, and that raised the taxes again.

Of all the emperor's tax collectors, Tsui Zedong was the most hated.

Fat and arrogant, Zedong enjoyed throwing around the emperor's power. It was said that were he not able to add sums so quickly in his head he would have been executed for being a thief.

Dressed in brocade robes, he traveled the countryside inside an opulent carriage. Six armed warriors on horses escorted him and protected the emperor's gold from bandits. All of the warriors were experienced and scarred from many battles.

When the carriage slowed that late spring morning, Zedong slid the rice paper shade from the carriage window and peered out. Loulan City was small, filled mostly with farmers who barely eked out an existence. But there were a few skilled artisans and craftsmen. Most of them had shops on the street he presently traveled.

The driver pulled the carriage to a stop, then got down and opened the door.

Holding his robes together, Zedong heaved his bulk up from the padded seat and got out to do the emperor's collecting. Zedong smelled food in the air. When he stepped down from the carriage, he saw a tavern three shops down. The carcasses of ducks and geese hung from a rope out front, ready for purchase by those who worked inside the city and didn't raise their own livestock.

All of the shops ran in straight lines on either side of the street. Most of them had existed for years, put together by families and trained carpenters. A well in the center of the square provided water for travelers. Several shopkeepers stopped their work and came out to look at the carriage. Most of them wore looks of dread.

The warriors, bristling with swords and bows, tied their horses to the back of the carriage. They took the chest from inside the carriage. Two of them carried it between them.

Several murmured curses echoed along the street. The shopkeepers knew what was about to occur.

Unrolling the scroll the emperor's tax keepers had prepared listing the shopkeepers and the amounts they were to pay, Zedong reviewed the listing for the jeweler he planned to visit first. Zedong rolled the scroll back and entered the small shop.

The jeweler's establishment was small and tidy. On the surface, he appeared to be a poor man, but Zedong knew from years of collecting that many shopkeepers and tradesmen disguised their wealth.

An old woman sat in a chair holding a fat cat in her lap.

"I have come to collect the taxes for the emperor," Zedong announced.

The old jeweler looked nervous. His back was bent from years of hunching over his tools, creating settings and pulling thin gold wire. With a trembling hand, he handed Zedong a cloth bag that clinked.

Zedong knew from the feel of the bag that it didn't contain enough gold. He could have told the shopkeeper that without opening the bag, but he opened it anyway and spilled the contents across his hand.

"There is not enough," Zedong accused.

"It is all we have," the jeweler whispered.

"Nonsense. You have a fat cat. If you have enough to keep your cat fat, then you have enough to pay the emperor his taxes."

"No, I swear to you," the old man said. "It is all we have."

Zedong dropped the bag into the emperor's chest. Then he looked around the shop. "You have gold ingots and jewels."

"Please," the old man begged. "We do not have many

of those. Hardly enough to stay in business. If you take those, we cannot make items to sell. Then the emperor's new taxes won't be met."

"If you don't meet the taxes," Zedong promised, "things will go badly for you." He turned to the warriors. "Seize the gold and gems."

The warriors went about their assignment. Screaming in outrage and pain, the old jeweler grabbed one of the warriors by the arm and yanked. Without hesitating, the warrior shoved the old man away and thrust a dagger through his throat.

The jeweler fell and his blood stained the wooden floor. He clasped his throat and kicked helplessly as his life ebbed.

Wailing, his aged wife abandoned her chair and rushed to her stricken husband. She called on the gods and for help from anyone, but no one came. No one dared.

The old woman's pain didn't touch Zedong. He'd ordered the deaths of many others. This one had been easy because he didn't have to think about it. Furthermore, with one man dead, the other shopkeepers would readily pay.

As her husband died, the old woman turned to Zedong. "May the gods curse you," she moaned. "May your life end soon and in painful agony. May you throw up your own entrails and take days to die."

Zedong knew he couldn't afford to allow such an affront. He was the emperor's tax collector. An insult to him was like an insult to the emperor. If he did not avenge it, the emperor would have him executed.

"Kill her," Zedong ordered.

The nearest warrior drew his sword instantly, then slashed down into the old woman, cleaving her from shoulder to heart. With a last gasp of pain, she fell across her husband.

Zedong looked at her and hated her even in death. He kicked her three times, getting madder each time because she wasn't alive to feel pain.

He wished he'd killed her before she'd cursed him. Curses were powerful things.

At his order, the warriors looted the shop. Zedong stood and watched. The fat cat stared at him with its unblinking green gaze. Zedong walked toward it, slipping a dagger from inside his sleeve. When he was close enough, he struck.

But the feline moved at the last moment, leaping over Zedong's knife, landing on his arm and leaping up again. The cat's claws struck Zedong's face above his right eye. Blood dripped onto his cheek and fire stung his flesh. He swung the knife again, but the cat vaulted through a window and vanished.

Zedong wiped the blood from his face and kicked the dead woman again. He didn't think she had the power to properly curse him. The cat was merely bad luck.

Still, he wished he knew for sure.

THAT EVENING, AFTER FULL DARK had finally draped Loulan City and all the shopkeepers had paid, Zedong left town. With two people dead, Loulan City wasn't safe for him. He wouldn't have admitted that to the emperor, though.

Eating roast duck from the large basket of food he had seized from the vendor, Zedong listened to the emperor's gold clinking in the trunk at the back of the carriage. He relished the spicy meat enough to lick the flavor from his fingers.

The carriage took a sudden hard turn to the right. Zedong cursed the driver as he reached into the basket for one of the pastries he'd claimed.

The carriage dodged again.

Cursing more, Zedong slid the window shade aside and took a deep breath to better yell at the incompetent driver. Likely the man had gone to sleep. He had complained of fatigue for himself and the animals when ordered to leave town.

Before Zedong could remember the man's name, the driver's corpse suddenly sprawled over the side of the carriage. The man's dead face slapped against the window. Only the long arrow through his throat kept his head from entering the carriage. A fearful look was frozen on his face.

In a moment he was gone, dropping to the road beneath the whirring wheels of the carriage. The vehicle rose sharply for an instant as it rolled over the dead driver.

Zedong grew afraid. The horses ran faster, thundering over the road as fear filled them.

"Help!" Zedong called out. "Help me!"

Inside the carriage, he bounced vigorously, slamming against the walls and the cushioned seats. He fumbled the door open and gazed outside, thinking of trying to climb up to the driver's seat.

Twenty feet ahead, one of the warriors toppled from his mount with an arrow deep between his shoulder blades. Only then did Zedong see two other riderless horses running after the carriage.

One of the warriors in front of the carriage wheeled his mount around and spurred the animal to speed. "Get back inside the carriage!" the man yelled.

Zedong wanted to retreat to safety, but he wished to

know what was happening. Gazing behind the carriage, he spotted a slim rider dressed in black. The rider drew back an arrow and let fly.

The warrior who'd gone to engage the enemy gazed down at the arrow that suddenly jutted from his chest. While he still seemed lost in his astonishment, he slid from the saddle. His right foot didn't clear the saddle straps and his body was dragged across the broken terrain.

The surviving two warriors approached more carefully, riding low over their horses. They closed on the rider in black.

Ignoring them, the rider urged his mount on. He slid the bow over one shoulder and pushed himself into a crouch on the horse's bare back, balanced one foot in front of the other.

Before Zedong realized what the rider was doing, he'd vaulted from his mount to the top of the carriage. Zedong screamed shrilly and dodged back inside the carriage. Glancing through the back window, he watched helplessly as the final two riders went down to arrows.

Seconds later, while Zedong quivered in fear, the carriage came to a stop.

The rider was at the side of the carriage. He held a sword in his hand as he opened the door.

"Out," the rider demanded.

Certain that he'd been held up by one of the many thieves that made travel so dangerous in the area, Zedong obeyed. He tripped on the step and fell to his hands and knees. Before he could stand, a blade was pressed to his throat.

The clouds cleared the face of the full moon in that moment. Surprise filled Zedong when he realized that the thief was a woman. A fox mask covered her facial features.

"Who are you?" Zedong demanded, using the imperious voice that he employed whenever he was on the emperor's business.

She didn't answer. The sword never moved.

"I represent the emperor," Zedong threatened. "Your life is forfeit for killing the imperial guardsmen."

"One more life," the fox-faced woman said, "won't matter, then, will it?"

Zedong had time to think only briefly of the curse the old woman had called down on him. It took a moment more to realize that the woman before him might not have been wearing a mask at all and might have been one of the legendary fox spirit women who drained men of their lives.

His throat was cut before he knew it. Then blackness filled his vision.

1900 A.D.

Huddled beneath a thick wool blanket that stank of wet donkeys, Dr. Heinrich Lehmann, a university professor at Berlin University, cursed in the four languages he knew.

"Steady on, Lehmann," one of the older men at the dig site advised, shouting to be heard over the roar of the storm. "We'll be out of this shortly."

Lehmann ignored the man. He hadn't cared for any of the men Dr. Hedin had employed for the dig. All of them were coarse and vulgar, nothing like the educated men he'd gone to school with.

The windstorm howled and dirt thudded against his blanket.

"Have you ever seen anything like this before?" Lehmann asked.

"Every now and again," the man yelled. He was American, thick and swarthy from equatorial digs. He spat on the ground at their feet. "It's worse in Egypt."

Long minutes later, the windstorm passed.

Lehmann threw the heavy weight of the blanket off. Dust obscured his spectacles. He removed them and cleaned them with his handkerchief. Tall and lean, he was in his twenties, his body stripped of any spare flesh by hard work. He wore jodhpurs, boots and a khaki shirt that was wet with sweat.

Only a few feet away, Hedin doffed his own blanket and looked around. With his glasses and hair in disarray, coated in dust, the Stockholm professor looked like some kind of rodent burrowing out of the dry lands.

"Look!" Hedin pointed.

Staring off to the left where the professor was pointing, Lehmann was amazed. Where piles of loose earth had been, the broken remnants of a city stabbed up at the dusty sky.

"I knew it was here." Hedin's voice barely contained the excitement that filled him.

Lehmann couldn't believe it. Even though Hedin had already achieved several finds in China, in fact had been one of the few Western archaeologists to be allowed into the area, Lehmann had begun to think that Loulan City was nothing more than a fictional reference.

But that would have meant the gold was fictional as well. Lehmann couldn't accept that. He knew about the City of Thieves. Hedin didn't. The Swedish professor had been assigned to map out Asia and to trace the history of the Silk Road, the trade route used for centuries to ferry silk out of China and import Western goods.

"I see it, Dr. Hedin." Lehmann smiled in acknowledgement. The Stockholm professor was only in his midthirties, not much older than Lehmann.

Gazing into the sky, Hedin shook his head. "We need to move quickly. In case Mother Nature decides to take back what she's so freely given."

Lehmann reached for his pack and shovel. Dust and grit rubbed his skin under his clothes, promising yet another uncomfortable day. He pushed the discomfort from his mind, remembering only the legend of the gold and the fox spirit that had stolen the emperor's gold nearly two thousand years before.

1

"Do you do this often, Miss Creed?"

Taking her eyes from the thick expanse of the Eldorado National Forest ahead of her, Annja Creed glanced at her hiking companion. "Not often," she admitted. "Generally only when someone has piqued my curiosity."

"And I have done that?"

Annja Creed smiled. "You have." She'd only known the man for a handful of hours. They'd met briefly in nearby Georgetown, California, to arrange for the hiking trip. Before that they'd had conversations online for almost three weeks.

Genealogy wasn't Annja's field of study. When Huangfu Cao had first approached her about trying to find the final resting place of his ancestor, Annja had decided to turn the man down. As a result of the cable network show she co-hosted, she often received cards, letters, and e-mail requests to help strangers track down family legends. The death of Huangfu's ancestor—

though a brutal and interesting story—was too recent to warrant her attention or expertise.

At least, that was what she'd thought until Huangfu had sent descriptions of that ancestor's prized possessions. One of them had caught her eye enough to draw her to California on a cold day in March to go traipsing down old roads that had once led to gold mining towns long gone bust.

Huangfu Cao looked like he was in his early thirties, but Annja didn't bother to guess. She was wrong more often than not. He was five feet ten inches tall, matching Annja in height. But he was thin and angular, contrasting with her full-figured curves. His khaki pants held crisp creases. He wore a dark blue poly-fill jacket against the wind and dark sunglasses to offset the bright afternoon sunlight.

Dressed in a favorite pair of faded Levis tucked into calf-high hiking boots and a black long-sleeved knit shirt under a fleece-lined corduroy jacket, Annja was comfortable in spite of the March chill that hung in the afternoon air. She wore her chestnut-colored hair under a baby blue North Carolina Tar Heels cap she'd fallen in love with at one of the airports she'd passed through in her recent travels. Blue-tinted aviator sunglasses took the glare out of the day. Her aluminum frame backpack carried numerous supplies, as well as her notebook computer, but it was well-balanced and she hardly noticed the weight.

"I'm glad you were interested," Huangfu said.

"Let's just hope we get lucky," Annja said as she scanned the forest before her, barely able to make out the old mining trail they followed.

A century and a half earlier, wagons had carved deep ruts in the land and left scars that would last generations.

"You're in very good shape." Huangfu adjusted his backpack. When he spoke, his breath was gray in the cool air for just a moment until the breeze tore it away.

Huangfu was in good shape, as well. Annja knew that because the pace she'd set had been an aggressive one. The man hadn't complained or fallen behind. When she'd realized what she was doing and that she should have been going more slowly, she'd expected to find him out of breath and struggling to keep up. Instead, he'd been fine.

"I have to be in good shape in my profession." Annja rethought that. "Actually, I don't *have* to be, but I want to be. It comes in handy." *Especially when someone's trying to kill me.* That had occurred far too much lately. Ever since she'd found the last piece of Joan of Arc's sword in France.

Before that, before Roux and Garin had entered her life, Annja had never once considered the possibility that she might ever have been connected to Joan of Arc. The sword, or maybe it was Annja herself these days, seemed to draw trouble like a magnet.

That was the downside, however. The upside was that whatever karma she presently lived under was taking her places she'd only dreamed of.

"I didn't think television people actually needed to exercise. Only that they look so." Huangfu smiled, showing that he meant no disrespect.

"Television isn't exactly my profession." Even though she'd been hosting spots on *Chasing History's Monsters* for a while now, Annja still felt embarrassed. But doing the show allowed her to go more places than she would have been able to on her own as an archaeologist. Television shows tended to be better funded than the universities that would have hired her as a professor.

Likewise, the show had given Annja more international recognition than the hundreds of articles, monographs, and couple of books she'd written. She knew many of those publishers wouldn't have considered her work if she hadn't had the large underground fan base *Chasing History's Monsters* had provided. And more of those published pieces had been for laymen than for professionals.

Unfortunately, the recognition was a double-edged sword. Many people tended to think of her as a television personality first and an archaeologist second. Annja never thought of herself that way. What she often gained in access she lost in credibility.

"It wasn't the television personality I asked to help me—it was the archaeologist," Huangfu said.

Annja smiled a little. She still wasn't sure if Huangfu was flirting with her or simply being disarming. She was wrong about that more often than not, too. "Thank you," she finally said.

They walked for a time. Annja took out the GPS device in her coat pocket and checked their location.

"Do you get many offers to do something like this?" Huangfu opened his canteen and took a sip of water.

"To go looking for someone's ancestors?" Annja replaced the location device and uncapped her own canteen. "I do get a number of offers."

"Do you answer them all?"

"No. I wouldn't have time," Annja replied.

Huangfu smiled. "Then what was it about my offer that interested you?"

"The family heirloom you're looking for. That interested me."

"Because it is a—" Huangfu paused, reflecting.

English was not his native language, and he wasn't as skilled as Annja had expected for someone who worked in international trade circles. He shrugged and shook his head. "I can't remember what you called it."

"I was fascinated because of the Scythian art," she said as she started walking again.

"Yes. You said the Scythians were a nomadic people."

"They were. In all probability, they were Iranian, but they were known by different names. The Assyrians knew them as the Ishkuzai. The Greek historian Herodotus of Halicarnassus described them as a tribe called the Kimmerioi, which was expelled by the Ishkuzai. The Kimmerioi were also known as Cimmerians, Gimirru in the histories left by the Assyrians." Annja smiled. "Some people think Robert E. Howard borrowed the Cimmerian culture for his hero, Conan the Barbarian."

Huangfu shook his head. "I don't know those names. My ancestors were Chinese." The words came sharply, edged with barely concealed rebuke.

Evidently Huangfu was, if not somewhat prejudicial, somewhat race conscious. Annja was aware that a number of Asian cultures looked down on each other. Regionalism divided civilization as surely as skin color, religion, and wealth.

"I didn't mean to infer that they weren't," she said.

For just a moment Annja wished she'd passed on the offer to act as guide for Huangfu. She'd spoken the truth when she'd said she regularly got offers to investigate all sorts of esoterica people thought might end up as an episode of *Chasing History's Monsters*.

If it hadn't been for the Scythian art, she'd have passed on this. Looking for dead ancestors didn't make her Top Ten List.

"The Scythian people traded with the Chinese beginning in the eighth century," Annja went on. "Probably before that. But archaeologists and historians have been able to track the gold trade to that time period. All I was suggesting was that the design you found in your ancestor's journals might be older than you think it is."

Huangfu nodded, mollified to a degree. "Ah, I see. You think helping me find my ancestor might give you more information about the Scythian people."

"I hope so. It would be a coup if I do. I hope I don't sound insensitive."

"Nonsense. I'm here for a man I've never met. If it weren't for my grandfather, I might not be here at all. Are these people you hope to discover more about important?"

The grade went down for a while and became a minefield of broken rock and low brush. "There is a lot we don't know about the Scythians. Located as they were in Central Asia, trading with China, Greece, what is now Eastern Europe, Pakistan and Kazakhstan—probably other nations, as well—there's a wealth of history that archaeologists, historians, and linguists are missing."

Annja took another GPS reading, then corrected their course. She'd confirmed the directions she'd gotten over the Internet with the local Ranger station and with the people in Georgetown, which was a small town only a few miles to the west.

"What do you hope to find?" Huangfu asked.

"The same thing that you do. Some proof that your ancestor was—" Annja stopped herself from saying *murdered in Volcanoville* just in time "—here."

Annja followed a small stream through the fringe of the Eldorado National Forest. According to her map, they weren't far from Otter Creek. Paymaster Mine Road was supposed to be only a short distance ahead.

Tall pines mixed with assorted fir trees. All of them filled the air with strong scents. Sunlight painted narrow slits on the ground. Powdered snow covered patches of the ground. Squirrels and birds met the spring's challenge, foraging for food in the trees, as well as on the ground.

"He is here." Huangfu's face looked cold and solemn. "I intend to bring my ancestor's bones home, if I am able, and see him properly laid to rest. It is my grandfather's wish to gather all of our family that we may find."

Scanning through the forest, Annja found the trail she thought they wanted. The trail rose again with the land.

Everything is uphill out here, she thought.

The park rangers she'd talked to over breakfast in Georgetown had assured Annja the path she planned to trace was an arduous one. Only hikers, horses and bicycles were allowed into the protected areas.

The muddy land was sloughing away under the melting snow. Rainfall for days had turned the ground soft in places. They'd have struggled on bikes and Huangfu had said he wasn't a horseman so Annja had elected to walk to the location.

"Are we close?" Huangfu asked.

"I believe so. Another mile or so should put us there." Annja kept walking.

VOLCANOVILLE WAS ONE of the hundreds of towns and mining camps that had sprung up in California after James W. Marshall, an employee of John Sutter's lumber mill, discovered gold flecks in the tail race in January of 1848. By the end of that year, word had spread and hundreds of thousands of people from around the world had flocked to the most recent member of the United States.

The mining camps and towns had risen up like dandelions, springing full-born almost overnight, then dying in the same quick fashion when the gold ran out or was never found. Hell Roaring Diggings, Whiskey Flat, Loafer's Hollow, and others had each left behind something of a history in the area. But separating the true stories from those that had been embroidered later, or from the lies they'd been mixed with from the beginning, was almost impossible. As with any history, murder, betrayal, success and failure were all part of the tapestry.

Huangfu gazed at the ramshackle buildings that stood under a thick canopy of trees. Many of the trees showed signs of repeated lightning strikes. Broken limbs, shattered trunks, and places bare of bark were scattered around the site.

Not exactly a place to inspire hope, Annja thought as she turned to Huangfu. "It's not as bad as it looks."

The man offered her a faint smile. "That's good. Because at the moment it looks impossible."

"If we were just going off the journal you found, maybe it would be. Fortunately the California Historical Society, as well as dozens of other branches and genealogists in the area, collected stories, journals, and newspapers."

"I trust your expertise in this matter." Huangfu smiled. "That's why I hoped you would help me."

Annja slid out of her backpack and placed it beside the nearest building. The wind picked up and caused the branches to rattle against the roof. No trace of paint remained on the weathered boards. It was possible the exterior of the building had never been painted.

Working quickly, she paced off the dimensions of the buildings. Most of them appeared to have been constructed roughly the same. She guessed that the building she was searching for would be similar. When she finished, she returned to the backpack.

Huangfu didn't say a word.

Crouching, her back against the building, she took a bound journal from the backpack, as well as two energy bars, offering one of them to Huangfu. The man took the snack and crouched beside her.

"What's that?" He pointed at the book.

"A journal I made for the search we're going to conduct here."

The journal contained hand-drawn maps Annja had created from topographical surveys she'd found of the Volcanoville area, as well as ones she'd found in newspapers and letters collected in the historical societies she'd visited. Tabs separated sections on known facts, rumors, and stories she'd gleaned from her research. All of the notes were handwritten, and she'd made the sketches, as well.

"You have maps?" Huangfu sounded doubtful.

"I made them, based on geological surveys of the area, as well as stories I found. The forest and the stream, they're there in the right places. The map of the town is purely guesswork."

"I thought you'd arrived in Georgetown only this morning."

"I did." Annja smiled at him. "The Internet is a wonderful tool."

"You do this for all of your projects?"

"When I can. I like to have an idea of what I'm getting into before I arrive. Usually time at dig sites is limited. You have to know what you're looking for and where to look for it. Not all nations welcome archaeologists with open arms." Annja flipped through the maps she'd created. "A lot of that has to do with the fact that in the early twentieth century a number of archaeologists served as spies for the Western world."

Huangfu laughed. "Have you ever been a spy, Miss Creed?"

"No," Annja said flatly.

"Would you be one if you were asked?"

"I guess it would depend on the circumstances. That's not what I'm about. I'm an archaeologist." Annja looked around at the buildings, trying to see through the present into the past that had existed over a hundred years ago.

Huangfu drank water from his canteen and sat silently. From the man's relaxed posture, Annja believed he could have sat that way for hours. She hadn't yet gotten a fix on him and that left her feeling a little unsettled.

When she'd first connected with Huangfu over the Internet and then the phone, Annja had guessed he was a corporate worker. But from the money involved in his quest—and the fact that he'd generously arranged her flight out and her bed-and-breakfast accommodations in Georgetown—she'd figured he was near the top tier. A background check on him had confirmed that Huangfu Cao worked for Ngai Enterprises, a Shanghai-based international pharmaceutical company.

Bart McGilley, the New York homicide detective who was one of Annja's closest friends and who had done the background check on Huangfu, had wanted to dig deeper. But Bart tended to be overly protective where Annja was concerned. She hadn't wanted to wait any longer. Huangfu had volunteered to pay her expenses, and he'd said he only had the next few days to attempt to locate his ancestor's remains. She'd assumed he'd taken leave to attend to the matter.

Annja was all too aware that her own free time turned on a dime and was often gone before she knew it. She'd already turned down a *Chasing History's Monsters* assignment to track down the legend of a vampire living in Cleveland. Vampires were perennial ratings winners on the television show, and her producer, Doug Morrell, had a special interest in them that she hadn't quite figured out. Given her options, she'd jumped at the free trip to California.

Within minutes, Annja found the few remaining landmarks she'd identified from the stories and the geographical maps. Once she was oriented, she grabbed the straps of her backpack, hoisting it to one shoulder.

"Let's go," she said.

Huangfu fell into step beside her. "Do you know where the building we're looking for is located?"

"I think so." Annja pointed. "Chinatown was up on that ridgeline. Mining towns were usually segregated by race. Chinese immigrants poured into California in the 1850s and 1860s."

"For the promise of gold. I know."

"Not just for the promise of gold." Annja started up the incline, grabbing an exposed tree root as she leaned into the ascent. "They were also escaping the Taiping Rebellion that occurred after the British defeated the Chinese in both Opium Wars to force British trade."

"I'll take your word for that, Miss Creed."

Annja was surprised that Huangfu wouldn't know that. Those times had been hard on the Chinese people. The British had usurped the emperor's control and spread opium throughout Shanghai and other provinces through gunboat diplomacy.

The Chinese had invented gunpowder for fireworks, and had even used it somewhat for cannon and flame-throwers, but they had never mounted cannons on ships for use in war. The British had done that with success unmatched by any other nation.

Reaching the summit of the rise, Annja looked down, orienting herself again. She tried to imagine what the town had been like when it had been booming with the promise of gold. In San Francisco, which had been in its infancy when the Gold Rush had started, sailors had abandoned ships and left them sitting crewless in the harbor, chasing after the elusive promise of sudden wealth. Only later, after some of the prospectors had struck it rich and others had returned looking for work, had San Francisco grown into a huge port city.

Men had lived and fought, chased possibilities, drowned sorrows and died in a microcosm fuelled by dreams. Annja felt the history almost come alive around her.

She relished opportunities to go places and see them for herself. She'd never been to an abandoned mining town before. Even though it was only a hundred and fifty years old, not centuries or a millennia as many of her studies were, the history of the place touched her more than she thought it would.

She let go of the city and focused on the man she'd come there to find. She turned to face Huangfu.

"Your ancestor, Ban Zexu, arrived in San Francisco in 1872. I confirmed your research with my own. Most of the Gold Rush was over by 1855, but several strikes kept happening. Some of them took place here in Volcanoville." Annja walked west along the ridgeline, seeing the layout of the buildings in her mind's eye.

Huangfu followed her.

"He lived up here in Chinatown, overlooking Volcanoville proper. The Chinese immigrants weren't allowed to mix with the white population."

"But the shopkeepers took their gold for things they needed," Huangfu said.

Annja nodded. "All of these towns were violent. Too many men were looking for too little gold, which had gotten harder and harder to find. In 1874, Chinese miners found a ten-ounce nugget at the Cooley Mine. Drunken miners locked over a dozen Chinese in the cabin at the mine and burned it to the ground with them inside. The men who escaped the fire were gunned down."

"Was that where my ancestor was murdered?"

"No." Annja walked along, studying the ground. "Ban Zexu was killed here. A few of the buildings in Volcanoville had root cellars where they kept potatoes and other perishable goods. Fewer still of the Chinese structures up here did. Your ancestor died in a house two houses down from one of the houses that had a root cellar made of rock according to the information I was able to find."

Dropping her backpack to one side, Annja reached inside and took out an Army surplus trenching tool that snapped together and a metal rod with a handle. She pulled on a pair of leather work gloves.

"First we'll find the stone foundation of the root cellar, then we'll find the house where Ban Zexu died."

She thrust the metal into the thick loam and got started, searching for stone. Thankfully, the early spring thaw had left the ground soft and easy to work.

She only hoped the root cellar had truly been made of stone and wasn't too deep to reach with the tools she was using.

IT TOOK LESS THAN AN HOUR to find the root cellar. Stepping off the measurements of the house, assuming that the cellar was under the center of the building and was entered from the back, Annja quickly located the area where she believed the building Ban Zexu had been murdered in had once stood.

She had stripped off her fleece-lined coat, finding it too hot to work in. Huangfu had divested himself of his jacket.

"Make sure you get plenty of water." Annja uncapped her canteen and drank. "Cold will leave you as dehydrated as heat."

Huangfu nodded and drank. Despite his exertions, he didn't look any the worse for wear. One of his shirt sleeves crept up and revealed the red, yellow and blue ink of a large tattoo. It had scales, so Annja guessed that it was a dragon or a fish. Self-consciously, he pulled his sleeve back down, looking at Annja.

She acted as if she hadn't seen the tattoo, but dark suspicions formed in her thoughts. She suddenly didn't feel as comfortable and confident as she had.

"Here?" Huangfu pointed at the ground in front of her.

Annja nodded, capped her canteen, and picked up her trenching tool.

"How deep, do you think?" Huangfu shoveled like a machine.

"A foot or two at least. This far into the forest, foliage and dead trees are going to compost and add to the humus layer. If you leave anything on the ground long enough, nature has a tendency to pull it deep and cover it over."

They dug rhythmically. The shovel blades bit into the earth and turned it easily.

Ban Zexu had suffered a harsh death that had mirrored the men who'd worked the Cooley Mine. Jealousy, fired by desperation, had turned the white miners against everyone else. Chinese and Mexican miners had become targets.

In 1875, little less than a year after the murder of the Cooley Mine workers, Ban Zexu and his small group of miners had been burned out, as well. The stories varied. Some said it was over a slight made by one of the Chinese miners, and others insisted it was over a woman. There was even a story that Ban Zexu and his friends had struck it rich, though no gold had ever turned up. Locked inside the building they'd lived in while working different claims, the Chinese miners had had no chance when the building had been torched.

As Annja worked, she tried not to think about that horrible death. Or about the tattoo she'd seen on Huangfu's arm. She still wasn't sure what that meant; only that Huangfu was more than he seemed, and that waiting for Bart to conduct a deeper background check might have been a good idea.

LATE INTO THE DAY and almost three feet down, the light was fading fast and Annja's certainty about her calculations was ebbing away as the dirt piled higher and higher. Suddenly her shovel struck burned wood. She saw the black coals stark against the lighter colored dirt.

Rotting wood would have been absorbed back into the earth. But the burned wood had been carbonized and would take longer to leach back into the soil and break down.

"Huangfu," Annja said.

He looked at her. Although he hadn't said anything, Annja had felt the wave of exasperation coming from him. He wasn't a man used to failure.

"We've found it." Annja pointed at the coals left from the fire over one hundred and thirty earlier. "We must go slowly now."

Huangfu nodded. "What about the belt plaque I showed you?"

Is that what this is really about? Annja knew she couldn't ask, but she was certain that retrieving the bones of his ancestor wasn't the man's real goal.

"If it's jade or steatite, it'll break easily. Just go slow."

Huangfu looked at the sky. "I would like to finish tonight."

So would I, Annja thought. "If it's possible, we will. But hurrying and ruining everything we might find isn't the answer."

Reluctantly, Huangfu nodded.

"Shovelful by shovelful. Feel your way into the ground, then shake it out so you can see anything you might have found. When we reach a body, we'll work with our hands." Annja showed him, slowly scooping up the earth and spreading it out across the hill she'd created.

Huangfu did as she directed, and they continued digging.

FORTY MINUTES LATER, Huangfu found a body. "Here," he said. Excitement tightened his voice.

Tossing her shovel onto the dirt hill beside the hole she'd dug, Annja joined him. Enough light remained that they didn't need flashlights, but they would soon. The air was turning colder and their breath showed constantly.

Dropping to her knees, Annja looked at the rib cage Huangfu had uncovered. Carrion beetles had stripped the bones of flesh before the earth had claimed the body. Soot still stained the ivory.

Removing her digital camera from her backpack, Annja took several pictures. Huangfu stood by impatiently.

"We'll take pictures as we go," Annja explained as she replaced the camera in the backpack. "We can search through them later. They might help us discover if we missed anything."

Annja slipped her gloved hands around the bones and gently began disinterring them. She placed them carefully beside the hole, keeping them together as she found them.

Huangfu watched her. "Do these bones belong only to one man?"

"So far." Finding the pelvis, Annja headed in the other direction, searching for the skull. More bones created a skeleton on the ground.

"I can help."

"Keep the bones in order as we find them." Annja handed over the collarbone.

"Why?"

"We'll learn more if we do. How many people were in here. Maybe who they were. If we post this on the Internet, we might find others who are looking for lost family members. Information works best if it's keep neat and arranged."

Annja found the skull and lifted it free of the earth. "Your ancestor might have escaped that night."

"According to the journal that came into my possession that did not happen. Ban Zexu died here."

"Judging from the roundness of this skull, and the

arched profile, and widely spaced round eye sockets, this person was of Mongoloid decent."

"Chinese?"

"That's one possibility. Pathology isn't an exact science when it comes to race. We can identify the three different racial characteristics of Caucasian, Mongoloid, and Negroid."

Annja handed Huangfu the skull, noting that the man took it without hesitation. That wasn't a normal reaction for most people when they were confronted with such a situation. She knew beginner archaeologists who took years to get over the queasiness of handling dead bones fresh from a dig.

Huangfu placed the skull at the top of the skeleton they were building.

Annja continued digging, going back toward the pelvis now. Noting the narrowness of the pelvis and the sciatic notch that allowed the sciatic nerve and others to go on through to the leg, she also knew the remains were male. Pathology was more exact about sex and age.

Below the pelvis there was a leather bag that hadn't yet rotted away. But her attention was riveted on the rectangular shape she'd spotted. Even with the gloves and though the rectangular shape looked more like a clod or a rock, she knew what it was.

Excitement filled her as always. Every discovery she'd made affected her the same way. She hoped that would never change.

"Is that the plaque?" Huangfu asked.

"I think so." Annja breathed out and started brushing dirt from the piece. With the shadows in the hole they'd dug, she couldn't clearly see the piece, but she saw enough of it to note the stylized tiger poised with its ears flattened to its head and one clawed paw raised to strike. Scythian art stylings, picked up by some of the people they traded with—including the Chinese, often showed fierce animals.

"Let me see," her client said.

Annja was loath to let go of the prize. The memory of the tattoo hidden on Huangfu's arm disturbed her thoughts and took away some of the joy of discovery.

The unmistakable ratcheting of a rifle bolt seating a round in the chamber caused Annja and Huangfu to freeze. Glancing up toward the sound, Annja saw three armed men emerge from the gathering darkness.

2

All three of the men looked scruffy. Patched jeans, hoodies, dirty boots and coats clothed them and lent them the sameness of a predatory pack. They were young, barely into their twenties.

But old enough to point a gun at you, Annja thought as she remained frozen. Looking into their eyes, she noticed how red and glassy they were. It wasn't a huge leap of logic to guess that they were under the influence of something. In the thin cold air, she smelled the acrid odor of marijuana and the cloying stink of horse sweat.

Beside her, Huangfu shifted slightly, just enough to get his footing and redistribute his weight. The three young men didn't notice.

"I told you I saw somebody out here, Dylan." The speaker was the thickest of the three. He carried the extra weight around his middle, looking like a football player gone to seed.

Dylan was bearded and had kinky black hair that looked like he hadn't brushed it since he was a teenager.

He aimed the rifle in his arms with grim authority, pointing it at Huangfu.

"Shut up, Beef," Dylan said. "I can see them. I got eyes."

"Do you think they've been out to the patch?" the third young man asked.

"Shut up, Neville," Dylan ordered, then spat foul curses. "I swear, neither one of you has any sense."

Annja looked at the semiautomatic Beef carried and the revolver Neville held. She'd been in similar situations of late. She was afraid she was starting to get used to life-threatening situations.

"What're you doing out here?" Dylan demanded.

"We're archaeologists." Annja gestured to the bones gathered at the side of the hole. "We were sent here to find these bodies."

Beef walked away from the other two, closing in on the bones. He kicked the skull with the toe of his boot and sent it rolling a few feet away.

"Cool." Beef grinned and went after the skull. "Think I'll put this in my room. Get some black light action going on this. Candles for the eyes. It'll look awesome."

"Why are you out here looking for skeletons?" Dylan asked.

Beef picked up the skull, hooking his fingers through the eye sockets and his thumb through the mouth. He mimed swinging it like a bowling ball, then laughed uproariously.

Annja kept her voice calm and soft. "These people were Chinese. Their families found out they were murdered here and want them back." She felt another slight shift in Huangfu's stance, aware of it only because she'd been involved in martial arts for years.

"That's all you're doing out here?" Dylan asked.

"Yes."

"You aren't, like, police?" Neville looked suspicious.

"No."

"That was a dumb question." Beef snorted derisively.

Neville looked irritated. "Why? All I asked was if they were police."

"Well, for one, they could lie to you."

"Uh-uh. Police have got to tell the truth."

Beef cursed and juggled the skull in one hand. "Dude, I don't know what planet you're from, but my brother is a cop, and they can lie to everybody. Ain't no law against lying for police."

Neville shook his head. "That don't seem right. I mean, a police guy has gotta tell you he's a police guy."

"And two," Beef went on, "now they know we got a reason to worry about police up here." He looked at Dylan. "We gotta kill 'em now, dude. They've seen our faces. Anybody finds out we're growing pot up here, we're gonna go to prison this time."

Dylan didn't say anything for a minute. Then he shrugged. "They already dug the hole, I guess. Kill the guy first." The rifle shifted to center over Huangfu's chest.

Unable to stand by while the man was killed, Annja surged up from the hole. Controlling the fear that vibrated within her, she stayed low, diving toward Dylan because she believed the other two would fire their weapons after he did. Catching Dylan around the waist in a flying tackle, she spilled to the ground with the young man in a tangle of arms and legs as the rifle went off.

Three other reports cracked almost simultaneously, all of them different timbers.

Rolling, Annja came up in a crouch, taking in the

scene before her in disbelief. Beef collapsed only a few feet away, his face covered in blood. Huangfu, low to the ground and in motion, held a small black pistol in his fist. The weapon cracked, spitting fire twice more.

Neville staggered back, gazing down at his chest in astonishment. Two tiny flowers blossomed bloodred over his heart. "Very uncool, dude." Then he dropped, sprawling across the ground.

Stunned, Annja didn't notice Dylan's kick until his foot was only inches from her face. By then it was too late to avoid the blow. She twisted her head in an effort to deflect the impact and succeeded, but the side of her face suddenly felt like it was on fire and her vision turned blurry for a moment.

Dylan was cursing and scrabbling for a pistol in the waistband of his pants when Huangfu took aim and fired again. Two bullets caught Dylan in the chest, staggering him but not knocking him down. He brought his pistol up in both hands and fired.

The bullet sheared a tree branch only inches from Huangfu's head. The loud detonation filled the ridge for a moment, but it relented when Huangfu fired three times in a rapid string of explosions.

Huangfu pointed the pistol at Annja as Dylan's knees buckled and he fell face first onto the ground.

Time slowed for Annja as she tried to assess what had happened. Huangfu had acted only to save them. Having the gun he'd obviously carried on his person might offer some legal challenges, but it wasn't anything that a good lawyer couldn't work out. If the young men had been worried about further criminal charges putting them in prison, that meant they had a criminal history of some

sort. And there was no denying the weapons they'd
brought. But Annja knew she was in grave danger.

She moved, trusting her instincts and not trying to
reason through the improbable situation. Huangfu had
killed the three young men and he was going to kill her,
as well. She dodged behind the nearest tree. A bullet tore
bark from the trunk and spewed splinters across her cheek.

She didn't break stride, plunging deeper into the
forest surrounding Volcanoville. The sun was setting to
the west, steeping the forest in darkness. She headed in
that direction, knowing the long shadows and the loss
of depth perception against the fading brightness would
make her a harder target.

More shots rang out behind her. Bullets cut through
the trees, ricocheting from thick limbs and trunks, and
cutting small branches free.

Taking brief respite in a hollow between two large
fir trees dug in tight against the hillside, Annja realized
she was still holding the items from the dig site. She
shoved the belt plaque into the leather pouch, then tied
the pouch to her belt. Metal clicked inside and she
guessed that some of the contents were coins. The cold
ate into her, but she knew the adrenaline and fear coiling
through her increased her vulnerability to it.

The forest continued to darken and the shadows
deepened.

Annja listened for footsteps but didn't hear any.
Either Huangfu wasn't moving, or—

The man suddenly appeared out of the darkness with
the pistol in his hand.

Annja made herself stay put and trust the shadows.
Any movement would make her visible.

Huangfu stopped beside a tree. His breath puffed out

in front of him. He lifted his left hand and Annja saw that he was holding a satellite phone. He pressed a number.

I'll bet that's not 911. A sinking sensation coiled through Annja's stomach. She was a long way from help.

After finishing a short conversation in which he did all the talking, Huangfu put the phone away. "Miss Creed." His call echoed in the forest.

Annja let her breath out, knowing she had to keep breathing in order to keep from hyperventilating. Her fight or flight instinct surged madly, but she kept it in check.

"Miss Creed, you should come out." Huangfu started walking again. "There's been a mistake. I'm not going to hurt you."

Annja watched the man moving carefully through the forest. He took advantage of cover and stayed within the shadows. She thought he moved like a military special forces soldier. She hadn't been around those men often in her life, but there had been occasion at some dig sites to talk to them. Many ex-soldiers had moved into security work.

"I panicked," Huangfu said. Three more steps and he vanished into the trees.

Annja didn't feel comforted by his disappearance. At least while she could still see him she knew where he was. She listened intently, but Huangfu was more silent than the wind blowing through the budding tree limbs and the fir trees.

Taking a moment, remembering the bodies of the three young men back at the dig site, Annja reached for her sword. She felt the grip against her palm, then pulled it from the otherwhere.

Annja had found the last piece of the sword while in France, but she hadn't known what it was then. Roux, who claimed to be over five hundred years old, had spent those years tracking down the pieces of Joan of Arc's sword. He'd stolen the last piece from Annja in France, but it hadn't been until she had touched all the pieces that it once again became whole.

Roux claimed that the sword brought a legacy with it, unfinished business that Joan was supposed to have been given the chance to do. Annja didn't know if she believed that, but she did know that her life had changed after the sword had come into her possession.

In the stillness of the night, she considered her options. People knew she and Huangfu had come out to Volcanoville—park rangers and a handful of Georgetown residents. But they might not think anything was amiss until morning. Perhaps not even then.

You're going to have to save yourself, she resolved. She hated the thought of leaving her backpack behind. Her notebook computer had a lot of information—pictures, as well as writing she'd done—that she hadn't yet backed up.

Nearly all of the information on Ban Zexu was on the notebook computer. All of the recent information was, as well as pictures of Huangfu. Bart had a couple, but those might not be enough to help find the man if he succeeded in killing her.

She had a satellite phone in her backpack. All she had to do was grab the backpack—at least the phone—and stay hidden in the forest long enough to call for help.

She took a quick breath, concentrating on the sure weight of the sword in her hand.

Annja moved out of her hiding spot reluctantly, then headed back up the hillside. She stayed within the brush, using every available scrap of it for cover. Her eyes swept her surroundings for Huangfu.

Thankfully, her backpack was out of the way, at the edge of the tree line. In the brush only a few feet from the backpack, she squatted to survey the ground.

Huangfu wasn't anywhere to be seen. The three dead men remained where they'd fallen.

In the failing light, Annja searched the ground for their weapons and knew at once that Huangfu had come back that way. All of the weapons were missing.

Easing forward, Annja stayed low. When she reached the tree line, she stretched and grabbed one of her backpack's straps. Suddenly, she felt someone's eyes on her. Her senses and instincts seemed to have sharpened since she found Joan's sword. Or maybe dodging killers had sharpened them.

Either way, she knew Huangfu had her in his sights.

Annja jerked sideways, getting ready to run. A bright yellow muzzle-flash broke the darkness hovering over the grave. In the next instant, Huangfu rose up from the grave and opened fire.

Bullets slapped the trees over Annja's head and tore divots from the ground in front of her. She spun and slung the backpack across her shoulders, managing to get only one arm through a strap. Running down the incline, she pushed off the trees with her free hand and blocked brush and small branches from her face.

In the distance, a horse snuffled and stamped its feet. Immediately, the horse smell lingering on the three young men came to her mind.

Shifting directions, Annja headed toward the sound of the horses. She overran her vision in her haste, catching an exposed tree root and tripping. Out of habit, she pulled the backpack to her and rolled, landing on her side and cushioning the impact.

She surged to her feet again. Four long strides later, she realized she was holding the backpack with both hands. The sword had disappeared on its own. She quickly stuffed the leather bag from the dig into a cushioned pocket of her pack.

Bullets ricocheted from a tree trunk to her left, leaving white scars behind. She turned right and vanished behind a wall of pine trees that grew closely together. More bullets hammered the trees and broke branches.

In the distance but coming closer, she heard the sound of helicopter rotors. She hoped it was park rangers, but immediately dismissed that. Park rangers didn't fly around in helicopters unless there was an emergency, and they probably couldn't get one on such short notice.

There was a small airfield in Georgetown, though. It wouldn't have been a problem to put a private craft there and have it on call. Her mind suddenly filled with nasty suspicions about Huangfu's phone call.

Only a short distance away, horses snorted again and stamped nervously.

Annja ran, weaving through trees, staying so close to them at times that she collected an assortment of abrasions and bruises from glancing contact. Her breath whistled in the back of her throat. Timing her strides, she managed to sling the backpack across her shoulders. With her hands free, she could pump her arms and lengthen her stride.

The helicopter came into view through the trees. It was a sleek corporate aircraft, black-gray against the starry sky under the pallor of the three-quarter moon. The helicopter coasted over the tops of the trees less than a hundred feet away. The trees bent under the assault from the rotorwash, and the noise drowned out all other sounds.

Two men hung out the sides of the helicopter. Both of them had assault rifles.

This isn't just about where Ban Zexu was buried, Annja thought.

Cutting around a wall of brush growing through the tangled remains of a fallen tree, Annja found three horses standing in a small clearing. All of them were saddled. The bridle reins were tied to the branches of the fir tree in front of them.

The horses flattened their ears and pulled at the reins in an effort to get free. The helicopter had them spooked.

When Annja ran up to the closest one, the horse reared up to defend itself. The front hooves kicked the air.

"Easy. Easy, boy." Annja caught hold of the bridle halter and held on to the horse's head, guiding it back down onto all fours. She knew the animal probably couldn't hear her over the noise of the helicopter, but she kept talking to it anyway.

From the corner of her eye, she saw the helicopter swing around and start a pass back in her direction. She untied the reins and prepared to pull herself onto the saddle. The horse reared again, twisting violently to the left and shying away from her.

Suddenly, bright light lanced through the darkness and stripped the shadows away. When it fell across Annja, she knew the bullets wouldn't be far behind. The horse continued pulling away from her, and that helped save her life.

Huangfu stepped from the trees with both hands on his small pistol. "I don't want to have to kill you, Miss

Creed." He shouted to be heard over the noise of the drifting helicopter. "I will, though. All I want is the—"

Annja shouted at the horse, letting slack into the reins. Muscles bunching, the animal sprinted away from the helicopter sound and straight toward Huangfu. The sharp hooves cut divots from the ground.

Sprinting alongside the horse, staying close while she gripped the pommel and the rear of the saddle, Annja lifted both feet and swung them into Huangfu as he fired at her. She felt the bullet's impact vibrate through the saddle pommel inches from her head, then her hiking boots collided with Huangfu's chest and knocked the man from his feet.

Dropping to the ground again, Annja took three strides, got her rhythm, and heaved herself atop the horse. She had to duck immediately to avoid a low-hanging limb that scraped painfully along her back.

The men aboard the helicopter opened fire. Every third round was a purple tracer. They were wide of her and behind the horse, but she knew they'd quickly correct their aim.

She kicked the horse's sides, urging it to faster speed, though she knew it was foolhardy in the darkness. But she was out of time to be careful about her escape. The horse rolled beneath her, shifting as it read the terrain and dodged trees.

Abruptly, the men in the helicopter stopped firing. The aircraft dipped. Too late, Annja realized that she was about to run out of tree cover. She tried to alter the horse's direction, but the animal was crazed with fear.

Riding braced in the stirrups, her weight balanced on her feet instead of sitting in the saddle, Annja reached for the sword again. She'd no more than thought about it, wished she was holding it, when she had it gripped in her hand.

The helicopter pilot flew in very low. Glancing over her shoulder, Annja saw the man on the right side of the helicopter swing out wide, depending on the umbilical that connected him to the aircraft as he kept his feet on the skids.

She ducked beneath him as he tried to grab her.

The helicopter cruised by like a shark. But only a short distance ahead, it swung around in a full one-eighty. The man hung farther outside the aircraft.

Annja didn't try to dodge the helicopter. Instead, at the last possible minute, Annja lifted high in the stirrups and swung the sword up and across the man's midsection.

The sharp blade cut through flesh with ease. She got a glimpse of the man's surprised face, then she was past him. Glancing over her shoulder, she saw him suddenly dangle from the line that kept him tied to the helicopter. The aircraft jerked a little as the pilot corrected for the sudden deadweight.

Annja stayed low over the saddle and the horse's neck. The animal stumbled over loose rock and almost went down.

Stay on your feet, Annja thought fiercely.

Twisting in the saddle for a moment, she saw the helicopter hovering above the treetops. The body at the end of the line jerked and flailed its limbs as someone hauled it back into the helicopter.

The horse's hooves drummed the ground in a rapid staccato. Annja adjusted herself in the saddle, keeping her weight distributed and as low to the horse as she could to help the animal better handle her weight.

She thought she was headed west, back toward

Georgetown, but she didn't want to check her compass yet. The horse was handling the terrain, but she knew that could change at any moment.

The helicopter rotorwash sounded louder again. Looking back, she saw that it was coming in her direction.

Annja willed the sword away. Steering the horse toward a thick copse of trees, she waited until the animal slowed to navigate the thick press of brush, then leapt off.

The horse kept going.

Annja hit the ground and rolled. Brush and tall grass slapped at her, leaving stinging lacerations in their wake. She protected her backpack as much as she could. Then she was up on her feet, pushing and shoving her way through the forest at a ninety-degree angle to the path the horse had taken.

Controlling the panic within her, feeling her breath hot and dry in her throat, Annja kept running even after the helicopter passed by in pursuit of the horse. When she couldn't run anymore, she dropped to her knees and laced her hands over her head to open her lungs.

As she watched the helicopter sailing above the treetops with a finger of illumination reaching down from a searchlight, Annja hoped the horse was just hitting its stride and wasn't going to stop anytime soon. Then she reached into her pack for her phone.

3

Standing in the darkness, Huangfu Cao watched the helicopter speed over the treetops. He held his phone close to his face, listening to the helicopter communications officer. The man monitored not only the cell phone connection but also the emergency band communication in the area.

"She's called the park rangers, sir," Lin said.

Anger roiled within Huangfu. He had badly underestimated the woman. But no one could have expected her to react as quickly as she had to the shifting situation.

It was true that he hadn't liked the idea of killing her. He liked her. She was competent and knowledgeable. More than that, she had come looking for his "ancestor's" body for reasons of her own, not just to do a good thing. He liked that.

But he hadn't hesitated when the time came. He'd shot as quickly and as accurately as he always did. Somehow, though, he had missed.

Not only that, she'd surprised him with the horse. His chest and abdomen still hurt from the impact.

And now she had managed to call the park rangers.

"Sir?" Lin prompted.

"Stay with her. She has what we came for." If the three young men hadn't stumbled onto them, Huangfu would have the artifact his employer had sent him for.

The helicopter dipped quickly, gliding through the treetops.

"Do the rangers have aerial support?" Huangfu stared into the night. His eyes burned with the effort.

"No. They took the phone call and sent ground forces out," Lin replied.

"How many?"

"Three rangers and some of the local emergency response people. Their number is unconfirmed."

Huangfu knew there wasn't much in the way of a police force at Georgetown. The park rangers were another matter. In this part of California, the rangers went armed not only for illegal marijuana growers but also predators. None of them would be as well trained as his people, but he'd been ordered not to leave a mess behind.

And there were already three dead bodies.

If things hadn't gotten out of hand, he'd planned on dropping those into the hole he and Annja Creed had dug. That wouldn't have been a problem. Even if the bodies had been found later, they couldn't have been tied to him. His cover was complete. Any search into his background would lead only to elaborate lies.

"Even though these initial forces don't have aerial support," Lin said, "they will get it as soon as the situation escalates."

"Let me worry about that." Huangfu watched the helicopter flying low to the ground. "Get the woman." Feeling tense, he continued watching.

In the next instant, the helicopter broke pursuit and lifted into the air.

"There's a problem." Lin's voice was calm and precise.

"What problem?" Huangfu asked.

"The woman isn't with the horse."

Huangfu cursed, knowing that Annja Creed had evaded them again. "Turn the helicopter around. Search the forest again. Now!"

Looking out over the forest, Huangfu knew the effort was going to be wasted. They'd underestimated Annja Creed again.

HOOFBEATS WOKE ANNJA. As uncomfortable and keyed up as she was, she hadn't expected to fall asleep.

For a moment she thought maybe the horse she'd freed had found her again, and perhaps even led Huangfu and his allies to her. She opened her eyes but didn't move. Motion attracted predators, and the men hunting her were definitely predators.

After she'd placed her call to the park ranger's office and asked for help, she'd climbed one of the fir trees and hidden on a thick branch twenty feet above the ground. Using leather straps she carried in her backpack, she'd fashioned a crude nest to keep her from falling out of the tree. She'd spent the night in trees in a similar manner on digs. It was never truly restful, but she'd learned to sleep.

Shifting, she peered through the darkness and gathered her feet under her on the thick branch. She felt through the otherwhere, touching the sword's hilt and drawing it to her.

Less than a hundred yards away, two riders on horse-back approached. Both of them had flashlights that strobed the woods. They also carried rifles canted on their thighs. A third horse trailed behind them.

Tense, Annja waited, trying in vain to see through the darkness. Her phone vibrated in her jacket. Cautiously, she took it from her pocket, shielded the glow of the screen from the riders inside her jacket, and saw the call was from a New York area code.

"Hello." She kept her voice low, watching as the riders veered slightly away from her.

"Annja?" The tense voice of Bart McGilley greeted her.

"Yes."

"Are you all right?"

"Yes."

"Is something wrong with this connection?"

"I can't really talk now." Annja watched the riders as they slowed. They wore tactical gear, combat harnesses festooned with equipment.

"Are you in trouble?"

"Maybe a little."

"In California?"

"Yes."

"I flagged Huangfu Cao's file after you asked me to background him. I didn't expect the Department of Natural Resources to call to check on you."

"I called them in."

"They said someone was killed."

"This is *so* not the time to talk about this, Bart."

"You're all right?"

"For the moment." The fact that Bart was worried about her made Annja feel good. She hadn't made a lot of lasting friends with her unusual lifestyle. But Bart was one of the best. "I'm going to need a favor," she whispered.

"You didn't kill anyone, did you?" Bart asked.

"Actually, I think I did." Annja thought about the sword slicing through the man hanging from the helicopter. She didn't want to kill anyone, but when it came to preserving her life or the lives of others, she'd learned to accept that sometimes there was no other way. "But I think Huangfu's men picked up the body."

"What's going on?"

The two riders milled around for a moment. They talked and moved their flashlight beams around.

"I don't know," Annja answered. "About that favor…"

"If I can."

"I'm going to need an introduction to the local police departments."

"They'll probably know you from your television show." Bart wasn't a big fan of the series.

"Not that kind of introduction. The kind more along the lines of me not being a homicidal maniac introduction."

"Why?"

"Three local guys are dead."

"Did you kill them?"

"No."

"Your buddy, Huangfu Cao, did."

Irritation flared through Annja. She didn't like making mistakes. "As it turns out, he wasn't my buddy after all."

"I told you to watch out for that guy."

I really don't need an "I told you so" while I'm up in a tree, she thought. "I *was* watching out for him. That's why I'm not dead right now."

Bart sighed. "Sorry. I just worry about you, you know?"

"I know." Annja also knew that Bart was engaged to be married. No date had been set and the engagement was relatively new. If things had been different, if she didn't want to see the world as much as she did, if she were more certain that Bart wouldn't want someone who was home every night, their friendship might have explored more of the attraction that put them in each others' lives. But they were what they were.

"Do you have this number?" Bart asked.

"Yes," Annja replied.

"Okay. Whoever you end up talking to, put him or her in touch with me. I'll vouch for you."

"Thanks, Bart." Annja's phone vibrated again. "I've got to go."

"Call me when you can. And stay safe."

Annja said she would, then picked up the incoming call. It was a local area code. "Annja Creed," she whispered.

"Miss Creed," a no-nonsense voice said, "this is Captain Andrews of the Eldorado National Park Ranger Station."

"Yes, Captain."

"I've got men out searching for you. Two of them are at the GPS coordinates you sent when you called. You're not there. If this is some kind of prank, you're going to be prosecuted in federal court—"

"I moved since that last call." Annja looked at the two men. "Have your men wave their flashlights."

"What?" The ranger captain sounded exasperated.

"The men that were looking for me have already killed three people." Annja spoke plainly. "I want to know these are your rangers."

"Wait just a minute."

An owl passed by, momentarily obscuring the moon. A feral cat cried out in the distance. Frogs in the nearby stream croaked.

The two men with flashlights waved them in the air.

Annja took her flashlight from her backpack and switched it on. "Tell your men to look north of their position. I'm in the trees." Even though she was talking to the ranger captain, she still felt nervous. One misstep or a bit of bad luck could get her killed.

"All right," Andrews growled in displeasure, "they see you. Climb out of the tree and stand with your hands over your head where they can see you."

"It'll take just a second to get my gear."

"Leave your gear where—"

Annja broke the connection and slid the phone into her pocket. It vibrated as she recovered her rope and shoved it into the backpack. By the time she was climbing down, her flashlight held by Velcro straps on her backpack, the rangers had pulled their horses to a stop under the tree.

Both of them were young. One was clean-shaven and the other had a short beard and long hair. They introduced themselves as Dobbs and Carew. Neither of them put their lever-action rifles away.

Carew, the long-haired ranger, stepped down and separated Annja from her backpack. Then he asked for identification.

Annja complied, but the whole time she was distinctly aware that Huangfu or his men could have been only a short distance away with a sniper rifle. You've been reading way too many thrillers, she told herself ruefully. But the truth of the matter was that lately she'd been living a life not far off from those fictional heroes.

"Are you okay, Miss Creed?" Carew handed her identification back. He spoke in a pleasant baritone.

"Yes."

"You're not hurt?"

Annja shook her head. She wished she was back in her loft in Brooklyn. Before she'd left she'd just got the third season of *Gilmore Girls* on DVD and was looking forward to watching it. A bath, a glass of white wine, and an episode or two of the show and she could have slept like a baby.

Instead, her mind was filled with questions. She'd explored the belt plaque by touch but she still hadn't gotten a good look at the piece.

"You said there was a helicopter?" Carew looked at her.

Annja met the ranger's gaze. "There was. It left the area about ten minutes after I called you."

Carew nodded. "You said the bodies of the three men this Huangfu fella killed were up near Volcanoville?"

"Yes." Annja dreaded the next few hours. In her experience any time she dealt with law enforcement agencies she had to tell the same story over and over and over again.

"We've got a team over there looking into that. In the meantime, let's get you out of here." Carew held the stirrup out for her to mount the extra horse.

With easy grace, Annja pulled herself into the saddle and leaned down to gather the reins. She was glad to be going, but she knew her ordeal was far from over.

4

Darkly tinted windows in the conference room blunted the sun. Ngai Kuan-Yin stood in front of the windows and gazed out over the Bund. The early afternoon tourist crowd was making its way through the stores and shops along Zhongshan Road.

The wharves and docks just beyond them were also full. Among the historic buildings, the bones of the old walled city of Shanghai—which had been the international settlement area where the English and French had lived in the eighteenth and nineteenth centuries—remained visible if someone knew where to look.

Normally such a sight would have brought peaceful thoughts to Ngai. He owned many of the shops along Zhongshan Road and had an interest in several others. Many of the fishing boats were among his holdings, as well. Ngai's family had been in Shanghai for generations.

But Ngai wasn't happy. He was in a murderous rage, though his calm demeanor didn't allow it to show.

"Mr. Ngai, what do you wish to do?" The voice was

soft and offered no threat or rebuke, though he knew the question had been offered because he hadn't responded when he'd been asked minutes ago.

Slowly, Ngai turned to face the ten men seated at the long conference table. For the past twenty years, the men at that table had helped him build an empire of his father's pharmaceutical company. He owed all of them something. They, in turn, owed him their lives. Without him, they would have been nothing.

To a man, they wore dark business suits that looked neat and professional. All of them were lean, hard men. Much like Huangfu Cao.

Ngai courted that image. His tailored black suit fit him like a glove. He was in his early forties and still followed the discipline of the sword and the warrior. Silver threaded his black hair. His face, unlined and cruel, had graced the covers of international magazines about wealth and business.

Calmly, Ngai sat at the head of the table and turned his attention to the matter at hand. "I have been informed by Huangfu Cao that he has lost the belt plaque he went to recover. The woman archaeologist, Annja Creed, has escaped with it."

"Does the woman know that we—" Hong stopped himself "—that *you* are involved?"

Hong was in his eighties and grew more frail with each passing day. When Ngai had been younger, Hong had taught him in all subjects. Whenever Ngai thought of his old teacher, he remembered him as a strong young man, clever and fearless. Times had changed as age had robbed him of his strength and confidence.

"No." Ngai barely kept himself from exploding. He

was no longer young and no longer foolish. "I have not been compromised." He glared at the old man in warning.

Hong cleared his throat, then spoke softly. "Perhaps it would be better if you were to let this go."

Ngai tried to restrain himself and couldn't. All of his life while his father had railed at him to get his education and to keep his imagination from running away with him, Ngai had thought only of the treasure that might one day be his—if he was smart enough and daring enough.

Ngai glared at the old man. "I will not give this up. The treasure is out there. That is why the government has sent in their archaeological teams."

"Those teams," Hong said, "have been sent in to discover what secrets Loulan might hold."

Ignoring the old man for the moment, Ngai switched his attention to Yuan. "You have spoken with Suen Shikai?"

"On several occasions, sir. I have made every offer to him that you suggested."

"He still refuses to sell it?"

"He does."

Ngai leaned back in his chair. "Then we will take it from him."

Silence was heavy in the room.

"Do you hear yourself?" Hong asked.

"It is the only way," Ngai stated.

"Suen Shikai was a friend of your father's."

"He's not a friend of mine."

Sorrow touched the old man's features. "He has been a friend to me also."

"Can you convince him to give me the map?" Ngai knew the old man had tried.

"You know I was not successful."

"I do. Today you will have to choose between friendships."

Hong frowned. "Is Huangfu still in California?"

Reluctantly, Ngai nodded.

"Then there may yet be another chance to get the object from the American archaeologist. If you're patient."

"If I am patient," Ngai said forcefully, "then I am only giving our government more time to discover the treasure that rightfully belongs to my family."

Hong's lips tightened in disapproval.

"Suen Shikai will be a bad enemy to make," Yuan said.

"Then I will not make him an enemy," Ngai said. "I will make him a corpse." He glared at Yuan. "See that it is done. Today."

After only the briefest hesitation, Yuan bowed his head. "It will be as you say."

"You're dismissed."

Without a word, nine of the men left the room. Only Hong remained when the conference room door closed.

"Well," Ngai said angrily, "you might as well say what's on your mind."

"This course of action you've chosen for yourself isn't good," Hong said.

"It suits me perfectly." Ngai glared at the old man. "I've always been aggressive."

"You call your actions aggressive. I say that they're impetuous."

Ngai narrowed his eyes. "And I say that you're flirting dangerously with insubordination."

"Perhaps you inherited your willful ways from me."

"My father always insisted he was to blame."

"Your father only provided your bloodline," Hong

said. "I trained your mind. In my youth, I, too, was weak."

"Do you mean the wine and women you chased after?"

"No." A faint smile twisted Hong's withered lips. "Those are follies of a young man. I pursued them with no less zeal than your father. And you."

Ngai nodded.

"I was weak because I accepted your father's offer to educate you rather than remain with the university."

"If you had remained with the university, you would have been living in the streets by now."

"Or maybe I would have been living with a son or grandson of my own who loved me." Hong's eyes were sad. "Your father's appointment afforded me a lavish living that I couldn't have gotten anywhere else. I chose to live that life alone so that I could spend it all on myself. Now I have neither sons nor grandsons."

"Having regrets?"

"Pointing out the downside of a life lived selfishly."

"I would rather live my life selfishly and have all that I might rather than give it away." Ngai smiled. "Perhaps you are responsible for this after all."

"Me?" Hong lifted his eyebrows in surprise.

"You were the one who told me all those old stories of the Three Kingdoms, of Cao Cao's treasure that was lost to the City of Thieves."

"The City of Thieves is a myth."

Ngai hated hearing the old man say such a thing. When he had been a boy, Hong had filled his head with dozens of stories of the thieves who struck along the caravan roads, including the Silk Road, and made off with incredible treasures. He'd imagined streets paved in gold and jewel-encrusted houses. As he'd grown, he scaled the visions of treasure back, but he still believed there were hidden rooms filled with gold, silver and fantastic gems.

Ngai had spent a small fortune ferreting out information about the City of Thieves. It was also sometimes referred to as the City of Assassins for the men emperors and warlords had hired to kill their enemies. For a time in the second and third century, while all the turmoil of the Yellow Turbans was taking place and the Han Dynasty was collapsing, the thieves had struck hard and fast, claiming vast treasures.

Then—they'd disappeared. And no one knew the reason why. Hong had said that the thieves had gathered enough gold to set themselves up as kings in Africa or the Middle East.

Ngai didn't believe that. He had hired historians to track the tales he'd been able to find. Although the history of those periods was spotty at best, there'd been no mention of the thieves leaving China.

"Even if the stories of the City of Thieves are true," Hong said, "have you forgotten the curse?"

"I choose not to believe in the curse." Ngai knew the story well. There had been an emperor's tax collector who had killed an old man and his wife. Before the old woman had died, she had cursed the tax collector. He and the emperor's gold had disappeared. One of the guards had survived long enough to talk about the fox spirit that had descended upon the carriage and killed all the guards.

According to legend, the emperor's greed had summoned vengeance from the celestial plane. Divine retribution for the old woman's death had come in the form of the fox spirit. The stories told that the fox spirit had grown aware of the City of Thieves and had destroyed it.

"You can't simply choose to believe whatever you wish." Hong sounded put out.

"How many fox spirits have you seen?" Ngai asked the question in a mocking tone.

"None," Hong assured him. "I have been fortunate."

Ngai made himself a drink. "Spirits don't exist. They are myth only."

"How are they any less believable than the City of Thieves?"

Ngai turned to face the old man. "In the studies that I have undertaken, and paid others to do on my behalf, I became aware of two objects that could lead me to the City of Thieves. One of them is Ban Zexu's belt plaque. The other is the map that Suen Shikai has."

"If either man knew where the City of Thieves lay, don't you think they would have gone there?"

"A man has to be strong enough to hold on to his treasure. Doubtless, these men were not. Neither were their fathers before them."

"Unless their fathers spent what little gold there was before they were born," Hong said.

"No!" Ngai spoke more sharply than he wanted to. Emotion was weakness, and he hated to let the old man know how much what he said bothered him. "They were not strong enough to get the gold. It's still there."

"And if it's not?"

Ngai didn't reply. He couldn't fathom the gold not being hidden somewhere near the archaeological dig sites around the old city of Loulan.

"If it's not there," Hong spoke softly, "then you will have killed your father's friend for no reason."

"He defied me," Ngai replied. "That's reason enough."

"SHIKAI, DO YOU HAVE ANY good fish?"

Suen Shikai pulled his small fishing boat onto the shore of the Huangpu River, then looked up at the woman standing on dry land. He was wet from the waist down from walking the boat to shore.

"I do have good fish, Mai." Suen took a handkerchief from his shirt pocket and mopped his face. The weather was particularly humid along the river.

Mai was overweight and in her forties. She had a husband and three children to care for, and that took all of the hours of her day. She lived in a tenement building not far from where he kept his fishing boat. Whenever he went fishing she came out to offer to buy fish.

Mai's efforts to buy fish amused Suen. She knew he taught music at the university, but she looked at the simple life he chose and felt certain that he wasn't making enough money to feed himself. Mai blamed his state of disrepair on Suen's generosity toward his daughter, Kelly, who had gone to school in the United States. The woman believed that Suen gave all his money to an ungrateful daughter who was ashamed of her father's poor ways.

But he also knew that Mai figured she could buy fish from him more cheaply than she could anyone else on the river or in the local markets. She had never matched market prices, and Suen had never expected it. She had a hungry family to feed.

"I would like two fish." Mai cautiously opened her worn purse and reached inside for coins.

Suen smiled at her. He liked her. In the mornings, sometimes she would bring him a cup of tea and rice cakes when she came to buy fish and they would talk for a time. She liked his stories about people he had met and of the places he'd seen. He'd been to the United States nine times.

"You're in luck. I caught four." Suen reached into the boat and brought out a stringer of fish. He loved fishing and spent hours at it when he could. While he was out on the water, he listened to the sounds of the city all around him.

Some days he read books of poetry or he would re-read some of his favorite letters from his daughter. Mostly, though, he took his guitar and practiced his music. He was currently going through what he called his Bob Dylan phase. Kelly laughed at him when they talked over the phone whenever he mentioned that.

Mai examined the fish, then frowned in disapproval. "You were unlucky. These are small."

"Not too small to eat." Suen didn't take affront at the comment. Mai was always trying to find ways to defray the cost of the fish.

"Not too small to eat, but two will no longer do. I must have three."

Suen shook his head. "I'm sorry. I can only let you have two."

"You're going to eat the other two?" Mai looked at him suspiciously.

"Yes."

Frowning again, Mai said, "You're going to get fat."

Suen didn't think there was a chance of that. He was not quite six feet tall and had always been thin. His hair and beard had gone solid gray ten years or more ago.

"I'm not going to be eating them by myself," Suen said.

Suspicion and resentment knitted Mai's eyebrows. "Oh, then you have a girlfriend?"

"No." Since his wife had died four years earlier, there hadn't been anyone that Suen had been interested in like that. He had his teaching job and he had his music. Perhaps it wouldn't have been enough for someone else, but for him it fit perfectly. "My daughter is going to join me tonight."

"Ah," Mai sniffed. "This is the one who went to live in America?"

"Yes." Suen only had one child.

"Why is she coming here?"

"To visit."

"Hmmph. She doesn't do that very often."

Suen shrugged. "She comes when she can. Her work keeps her busy."

"A good daughter would find a way to visit her father more often. There is no excuse. She should be here. To take care of you in your final years."

Suen smiled. "Truly, Mai, I hope that I am not in my final years."

"You're not getting any younger."

"I suppose not."

Mai offered to buy the two fattest fish, and Suen agreed to let her. The two smaller fish would make a fine dinner for him and his daughter.

He left his boat, knowing that no one would bother it, and walked up the embankment following the crooked steps with his guitar hanging over his shoulder. The walkways were made crooked because everyone knew that ghosts could only walk in straight lines.

Suen didn't believe in ghosts, but he appreciated the craftsmanship that went into the building. As he trudged along, carrying the fish in the basket he'd brought, he looked out over the city. He was sixty-two years old. His daughter had come to him late in life, and she'd truly been a gift from the gods. But even in his lifetime, Shanghai had changed. He loved the history of the city, the good and the bad, and he hoped that it was never truly lost.

At the top of the hill, the Bund began in earnest. Shops and merchants' pushcarts filled the thoroughfare. Voices carried an undercurrent of pleading and feigned insult, haggling and desire.

Suen lived a few blocks away. He was looking forward to his daughter's visit. It had been almost two years. The last time she'd come, he'd had to nurse her back to health. Her work had nearly gotten her killed. He had asked her then to step away from it, but she hadn't been able to.

Though he had never told her, he thought maybe her work was the result of the curse that had been put upon his family. It was the only thing that made sense to him. He had wanted to tell her about the curse, but he didn't think she would believe him. More than that, the story had been passed through generations of his family. It was time for it to die.

Since that visit, there had been several phone calls and e-mail. Neither of them mentioned her work.

Suen was lost in thought when a van screeched to a halt on Zhongshan Road. He paid no heed because he knew he was safely out of the street.

Footsteps slapped the pavement, coming close to him. Suen turned, but by then it was too late.

Two men took Suen by the arms and lifted him from his feet. He tried to escape, but they were stronger than he was. Then a third man pointed a pistol at him.

"What are you doing?" Suen demanded. "I've done nothing to—"

The man shot him. Sharp pain spread out from Suen's stomach, just below his breastbone. He looked down and spotted the small feathered dart jutting out from his body. Looking at the men, young and dressed in American clothes, Suen thought of Ngai Kuan-Yin and the document the man had wanted.

Suen tried to speak, but he was quickly sucked into a whirlpool of blackness.

5

"Why did you go up to Volcanoville, Miss Creed?"

Annja sat in the interview room at the ranger station.

"I've already told the ranger captain." Annja sat across a Formica-topped table from the sheriff. Squeeze bottle condiments on the table reminded everyone that the room was more for socializing than interrogation. Topographical maps of the area were mounted under protective plastic on the walls. A lone bookcase was filled with pamphlets and novels ranging from Louis L'Amour westerns to Jeffrey Deaver thrillers.

"Maybe you could tell me again." Sheriff Barfield was in his early forties and kept in shape. His tailored uniform was carefully pressed and the star on his chest gleamed in the light. His salt-and-pepper hair was neatly clipped. "All Captain Andrews has to do is keep the park and countryside clean. I've got to explain to three sets of parents why their kids aren't coming home ever again."

Annja nodded. She'd had a hard time resisting the impulse to open her notebook computer and research the belt plaque. But she knew if she showed an interest in it the piece would have been confiscated. She was sure she could do more toward solving the riddle it proposed than the park rangers or the sheriff's department.

"Could you answer a couple questions for me first?" Annja picked up the bottle of water she had been given and took a sip.

Sheriff Barfield sat in the straight-backed wooden chair across from her. His cologne was fragrant, Old Spice or something like it.

"Sure." Barfield nodded. "If I can."

"Have you found Huangfu?"

"No."

"What about the helicopter?"

The sheriff hesitated for a moment, as if flipping a mental coin. "We located it outside of Sacramento. It had been abandoned."

"Do you think the men left California?"

Barfield's eyes were steady. "You know more about them than I do, Miss Creed. Do you think they left California?"

"I don't know."

Taking out a small notebook, Barfield glanced through pages of notes written in a clear, concise hand. "I talked with a New York Police Department detective named McGilley. He said he looked into Huangfu Cao for you."

"He did."

"McGilley also says he told you he thought you should stay away from Huangfu because he couldn't find out much information about him."

"I'm an archaeologist, Sheriff. Sometimes I don't get to pick and choose who I deal with. Archaeologists have been dealing with grave robbers since the field of study began."

"Is that what you think Huangfu went there to do? To rob a grave?"

"I don't know. Right after we found the remains of the miners, we were held at gunpoint by those three men."

"Do you think he's a criminal?"

"Based on the skill and lack of qualms he showed in killing those men—and while trying to kill *me*—I'd have to think that, wouldn't I?"

"Are you in the habit of dealing with criminals, Miss Creed?" Barfield's voice was low and neutral.

"Not if I know they're criminals. I didn't know Huangfu was a criminal until he killed those three men. And tried to kill me."

"What did he want?"

"He wanted to find his ancestor's grave."

"To rob it?"

"He said it was so he could take the bones home to be interred in a family graveyard."

"That didn't strike you as odd?"

"Different cultures practice different beliefs, Sheriff. I've got friends in New York who believe that everyone in California is involved in some kind of environmental protection group or practice strange religion."

A faint grin tweaked Barfield's lips. "Do you help people find their lost ancestors very often?"

"No."

"But you did this time. Why?"

"Because of the story involved." That was partially the truth.

"What story?"

"Ghost towns are always interesting."

Barfield rubbed his chin. "Volcanoville isn't really known as a ghost town in the area. It's just another failed gold mining operation."

"One person's failed gold mining operation is another person's ghost town." Annja glanced pointedly at her watch. It was 2:18 a.m. With the three-hour time zone deficit, she was running on fumes.

"Did you know you were going to find Huangfu's ancestor?"

"If he was out here, I was going to try."

"What do you mean 'if'?"

Annja folded her arms and regarded the sheriff. "Stories don't always have truth in them. Huangfu had the diary of a family member that said Ban Zexu was murdered in Volcanoville."

The sheriff made notes and asked how to spell Ban Zexu's name. "Did you see the book?"

"I saw copies of the book."

"The book could have been faked."

"Why would he do that?"

"I don't know, Miss Creed. I'm still trying to figure out why three men are dead tonight."

"They're dead because they tried to kill us."

"Why would they do that?"

"Because they were high and paranoid about us stumbling across their marijuana crop."

"Is that your professional opinion?"

"That they were high?"

"Yes." Annja started to grow more irritated. She'd known she was going to face repeated and redundant questions, but this was stretching her patience beyond the breaking point.

"I've seen people under the influence of drugs before,

Sheriff. I don't need a medical degree to know what it looks like."

"Where did you get experience like that?"

"I travel frequently. Some of the cultures I've been involved with in my field of study use drugs regularly in religious ceremonies."

The sheriff flipped another couple of pages. "Do you ever do drugs yourself?"

Irritation turned to anger. "Frankly, that's none of your business, Sheriff. But the answer is no."

Annja stood. "This interview is over. I've been patient and I've been considerate, especially in light of the fact that I very nearly ended up dead myself."

"I've got three murders that I have to explain." Barfield stared hard at her. "You can't just walk out of here."

"I can unless you want to arrest me. I know my rights. I didn't have to talk to you at all. But I did. Now I'm leaving."

"And if I arrest you?"

"Then I'm going to call my attorney, arrange bail, and get out of here a little later than I intended."

Barfield sighed and stood up. "Forgive me, Miss Creed. I'm a little testy tonight. Those boys out there— and I know they're old enough to be called young men, but they weren't much more than boys—didn't deserve what happened to them."

"They were going to kill us," Annja said.

"They've never killed anyone before."

"You're right. I should have given them the benefit of the doubt," Annja said sarcastically.

"That's not what I meant. What I meant was that maybe this wouldn't have happened if you hadn't come here."

"And maybe if you look out there and find their marijuana field you'll find a missing hiker or two." Annja reached for her backpack and slung it across her shoulders. She walked to the front of the ranger station.

A handful of cars were parked out front. Most of them were sheriff's department vehicles, but there were also a couple from local news stations. Two reporters started forward at once, flanked by camcorder operators.

"You've got a fan club." Barfield stood beside Annja. "Once they found out you were involved with television, they had to come."

Terrific, Annja thought sourly.

"Let me arrange a car to take you back to Georgetown. You're staying at the bed-and-breakfast there, right?"

Annja nodded. "If you can have someone take me back to my rental car, that would be great."

Barfield spoke briefly on his radio, telling one of his deputies to meet them in back of the ranger station. He walked her back.

"I don't want you to get the wrong idea, Miss Creed," Barfield said. "I'm not a bad guy, and I don't think you're a criminal. But I do get the sense that you're not telling me everything you know."

"Sheriff, I can't tell you any more about Huangfu Cao than I already have. If I never see him again, that will be fine."

"He may not feel the same way about you. He had a helicopter standing by in Georgetown, and they hunted for you before you were able to get a call for help out."

"I know."

"If he tried to have you killed because you were a potential witness, you may not have seen the last of him." Barfield held the door open and looked at her. "But if there's something more to this, some other reason that he and his men chased you, then you may be in serious trouble."

A deputy braked to a stop in front of Annja. A news team on foot brought up the rear.

"I appreciate your concern." Annja meant it. She knew that Barfield didn't want to see her end up dead. Even if she was omitting some of the truth. He seemed like a good man just trying to do his job. That made her feel bad. Don't go there. Whatever Huangfu was looking for, it's best left to you, she told herself.

She guessed that they would have taken the belt plaque into custody, then spent weeks or months hanging on to it before calling her back to analyze it.

And there's the possibility that you'll learn nothing from the belt plaque anyway. That thought was disheartening. But even if she never learned any more about why Huangfu wanted the piece, she knew she might have an authentic Scythian piece that was museum worthy. She needed to find out some of the history on it.

Barfield walked her to the deputy's car and opened the door, holding it braced against the cold wind.

Annja sat in the front seat beside the deputy. "Thank you," she said.

Smiling, Barfield touched his hat brim. "You're welcome." He glanced at the driver. "Take her to her car. Follow her back to Georgetown to make sure she gets there safely."

"Sure thing, Sheriff."

Reaching into his shirt pocket, Barfield took out a business card and handed it to Annja. "If something comes up, give me a call."

Annja took the card and shoved it into a pocket of her backpack. "I will."

By that time, the news crew had caught up. "Miss Creed," the reporter called, "is *Chasing History's Monsters* doing a story in Volcanoville? Do the murders have anything to do with the Weeping Ghost that's said to walk through the forest in that area?"

Annja looked at the deputy. "Let's go."

ANNJA WAS A LITTLE SURPRISED to find the rented SUV still sitting in the parking lot where she'd left it. Then again, Huangfu hadn't had much time to do anything to it while making his escape.

The deputy put his hand lightly on Annja's shoulder. "Gimme a minute to have a look."

Annja nodded.

Leaning down, the deputy slid a rack out from under the seat and took out a pump-action shotgun. He racked the slide and fed another round into the gate to fill the ammo tube to capacity.

"Be right back." The deputy got out but left the car running. He took a quick look at the SUV and the parking lot, and even looked under the vehicle. He returned, looking a little relieved. "Looks good."

Annja stepped from the car. "Thanks."

"You're welcome." The deputy slid behind the wheel again. "I'll follow you into Georgetown. Make sure nothing goes wrong."

"I appreciate that." Walking to the SUV, Annja unlocked the door and got in. Everything looked fine and the deputy had checked the car out, but she was still hesitant about turning the ignition over.

"Huangfu wouldn't risk blowing up the belt plaque," she said to herself. She hoped that was true. Then she twisted the key, letting out a tense breath as the engine caught. She let it warm up just a moment then put the car in gear and started driving.

WHEN HER PHONE RANG with half the trip to George-town still ahead of her and woods on either side, Annja thought for a moment that it would be Huangfu. But it wasn't. The New York number belonged to Doug Morrell, her producer on *Chasing History's Monsters*.

"Annja, what do you think you're doing?" Doug Morrell's voice was excited and exasperated at the same time. He was twenty-two years old. Excitement and ex-asperation were two of the things he did best.

"I guess it's a slow news night if this hit CNN," Annja said.

"It didn't hit CNN, thank God. I've got a fact checker in L.A. who was on her toes and caught the story when it broke on the local stations. Hopefully the story won't go any further."

Despite everything that had happened earlier, Annja had to smile at that. *Chasing History's Monsters* didn't have fact checkers. The only pieces that carried factual history and geography were hers, and that was only because she fought for accuracy and managed to have a look at the final cut pre-air. If she hadn't delivered good stories—and looked good on television, Doug had reminded her on several occasions—she would have been cut from the show for being so strict about facts.

Annja felt certain the "fact checkers" Doug and the other producers on the syndicated show relied on were conspiracy theorists who read underground newspapers and Web sites for the weirdest stories they could find.

"I mean," Doug went on, breathing hard enough to let her know he'd strapped on his phone headset and was pacing his apartment, "you've got to remember that you're part of a big television success story at a time when television success stories are as rare as…as… well, they're pretty rare."

"Thanks, Doug. I'm fine. Really. Three people were killed in front of me, and I was nearly killed. But at least it wasn't anyone I knew personally." Annja drove through the night. She yawned so big it hurt.

"Oh. Wow. I didn't think about that. All Amy said was that the show was getting linked to three murders over there."

"*I* didn't kill them."

"I know, but some of the other stuff you've gotten involved with lately, it hasn't gone so well for the show. I mean, you have to admit some of it's been pretty weird."

"Weirder than trying to find a Wendigo in Colorado last month?"

"Hey, we were following up sightings." Doug sounded defensive.

"I think I remember hearing that Kristie wanted a skiing vacation."

Doug coughed to buy himself time. It was one of his lamest tactics. "There were stories about a Wendigo."

"There was Kristie on skis."

"Kristie skiing down the mountainside escaping an evil Wendigo," Doug exclaimed.

"That's funny. I don't remember seeing the Wendigo."

"We're not here to talk about Kristie. I don't produce her. I produce you. I have to report to people on what you do. If you get involved in something that reflects in a negative fashion on the show—"

Annja cut Doug off. "As I recall during the meeting last month, the ratings were up, advertising was up, and we had more accounts lining up to do business with us than we had spots to give."

Doug fell silent for a moment. "Yeah, well, all that's true, and I just want to keep it that way. We don't need any adverse publicity."

"In fact," Annja went on, deciding to unleash a full salvo and put an end to the debate, "I think this is the perfect time to discuss renegotiating my contract."

"You already have a contract in place." The exasperation was back in Doug's voice.

"The contract we put into place was based on numbers that have almost doubled since we inked that deal."

"You know, you sound really tired." Doug suddenly sounded nervous. "I just wanted to call and make sure you were okay."

"I'm fine, Doug." Annja decided to let him off the hook. She liked Doug and she knew how to work him to get what she needed. Maybe she didn't negotiate skiing vacations, but she often got the show to pay for international trips to places she wanted to go to do legitimate archaeological assignments.

"So we're cool?"

"We're cool."

"Are you in any kind of trouble?"

"No."

"The police don't think you killed anybody, do they? I mean, you've killed people before."

"Only when I had to." Annja didn't like talking about that.

"I know. Man, look at the time. I should really let you get some sleep. If you need anything, give me a call."

"I will." Annja broke the connection. Her eyes felt

heavy. Glancing in the rearview mirror, she saw the deputy only a short distance behind.

She took a deep breath and tried to relax, but she knew it wasn't over. Not as long as she had the belt plaque and Huangfu wanted it.

FROM THE VERY BEGINNING, Huangfu had hated Georgetown. The population consisted of a thousand citizens, more or less, and the community was tightly knit. Even though it was a tourist town, strangers stood out.

The way things had unfolded in Volcanoville, he knew he couldn't return to the room he'd taken in the bed-and-breakfast. In fact, those premises had already been invaded by the sheriff's office. But he'd been careful. Their crime scene investigators would find no fingerprints in the room, and the things he'd left behind would lead nowhere.

He'd ordered one of his men to dump the helicopter near Sacramento to lay down a false trail and lead the police to think they'd fled the area. The other four men remained with him in the hills overlooking Georgetown.

His men were, like him, well trained at hiding in plain sight. The countryside provided ample cover.

He hunkered down beside a tree and used digital binoculars capable of high magnification. He was dressed in black camouflage, complete with a Neoprene mask that left only his grease-paint covered face open.

The man next to Huangfu tapped him on the shoulder and pointed at the western road. Shifting the binoculars, Huangfu spotted Annja Creed's rented SUV entering the town.

Anticipation burned within Huangfu. The woman had made a fool of him. He felt certain that if the three interlopers hadn't come along, he would have buried her in the same grave that contained Ban Zexu.

That had been the plan. Unless the belt plaque hadn't been there. Then he would have simply arranged for Ban Zexu's body to be transported to China and disposed of.

Huangfu still didn't know how she had evaded him.

The SUV rolled through the streets and parked in the small parking lot beside the Iron Skillet Bed-and-Breakfast. A sheriff's department cruiser followed her into the parking lot.

Annja Creed got out, spoke a few words to the deputy, then went inside the two-story house. Huangfu didn't know much about American architecture, but the woman who had checked him into the bed-and-breakfast had told him the residence was over one hundred and forty years old, as if that were supposed to be something impressive. The United States was less than three hundred years old. China's history stretched back thousands of years.

The deputy sat in his cruiser. After a moment, he turned on a light and started to read a magazine. Clearly, he wasn't going anywhere.

Huangfu lowered his binoculars. He didn't mind. The plan was to see what Annja Creed did. If she left immediately, he would follow her. His crew had already hacked into the rental agency's computer and could access the SUV's GPS transponder.

This time, Huangfu vowed, the woman would not escape. It was simply a matter of time.

6

Annja loved the room at the Iron Skillet Bed-and-Breakfast. She had a lovely view through two large windows. The furniture was antique, solid oak that had to be at least as old as the building. The bed was a four-poster canopy. Black-and-white photographs of people and places decorated the flocked wallpaper. The photographs dated from the 1860s to the 1920s.

The color television inside the armoire looked out of place, a modern anachronism. Antique stained glass lamps hung on the walls beside the bed. A chandelier filled the high peaked ceiling and glowed softly against the skylight. The skylight was another anachronism, but it really set the room off.

The bathroom was at the back of the room, complete with a sunken tub and whirlpool jets. Annja couldn't wait to soak, but there was work to be done first.

She put her backpack on the bed and brought out her notebook computer and digital camera. After making sure neither was damaged, she plugged the computer into the wall outlet and brought it online.

Taking a white towel from the bathroom, Annja dumped the contents of the leather pouch she'd recovered from the grave onto it. Dirt cascaded from the pouch, mixing with the coins and the belt plaque.

A quick examination of the coins revealed that they were a hodgepodge of American and Chinese. Three of them were gold, small pieces that would bring a few hundred dollars or more from a generous collector.

The belt plaque was striking. It was carved from steatite, a soapstone that was nearly all talc. The material was also called *lapis ollaris* and potstone. A number of cultures had used it for ornamentation and seals for thousands of years because it could be squeezed into various shapes before being fired. The material was still used as insulation material for electrical components.

The belt plaque looked like it had been carved by a master craftsman, then glazed and fired. The front showed a great cat, perhaps a Bengal tiger, lashing out with one clawed paw. The piece had a dulled turquoise finish that might have been mistaken for jade, but the tiger's image was lifted out of the material through gold and black glaze that gave the image a sharp three-dimensional appearance.

It's beautiful, Annja thought as she felt the weight of it in her hand and ran her fingertips across the snarling tiger. A few nicks and scratches marred the surface, but they added character rather than detracting from the piece.

Turning the belt plaque over, she discovered Chinese characters scrolled across the back.

A message of ownership? A history?

Annja was excited. She loved mysteries.

She wiped the belt plaque clean and put it on another white towel from the bathroom. Picking up her digital camera, she took several shots of the belt plaque from all sides and angles.

When she was satisfied, she hooked the camera up to the computer and started uploading the images. While she waited for the pictures to process, she started the bathwater. After rummaging through the bath selections, she found a lavender mixture that sounded promising and poured it in.

She sank into the tub and luxuriated for a few moments, resisting the urge to turn on the water jets because they would have rendered her boneless in seconds.

After her bath she did a quick check through her e-mail, finding nothing that couldn't keep for a day or two, two or three dozen spam messages, and some obscene offers from male and female fans of *Chasing History's Monsters*.

She logged onto her favorite Usenet groups and posted a message.

I'm currently in California researching a piece for a magazine.

She knew researchers who loved the research but didn't like the idea of writing always liked helping people who wrote articles. There was always the possibility they would be credited or at least mentioned in the piece.

While I was here I found this.

Annja inserted a picture of the belt plaque. After brief consideration, she elected not to put the picture of the back in the posting. Until she had it translated by someone she trusted, she didn't want the message made public.

The article I'm writing primarily deals with Chinese immigration into the gold mining camps. There are a number of pieces in the area that owners claim are from the Chinese men and women who flooded into the area. I just want to verify that this is Chinese and maybe find out if it has any kind of history.

I think it's fairly unique. I've seen pieces like it, but never this exact presentation.

Thanks!

Annja closed the computer, and lay back on the bed. She was asleep before she knew it.

DESPITE GETTING TO BED at nearly 5:00 a.m., Annja woke at nine, somewhat surprised that the night had passed without incident or phone call.

In twenty minutes, she was at the downstairs room used as the office for the Iron Skillet Bed-and-Breakfast.

There was a note on the door that said, "I'm in the kitchen. Verna."

Remembering the tour she'd been given the previous day, Annja walked to the end of the hall and took a left into the large kitchen.

The room was filled with a stove, flat grill, three-compartment sink, two islands in the center of the room, a huge refrigerator, and pots and pans that hung over the islands. The yeasty smell of bread baking filled the kitchen, reminding Annja of lunches at the orphanage. Despite the loneliness of growing up without any family, there had been some good times. She didn't miss those times, but she was glad she'd had them.

Verna and two women were washing the breakfast dishes. A television mounted on the wall was on.

"If you ask me," one of the women said as she dried a plate, "I think that witch is guilty."

"Oh, Edith," the younger woman protested, "you think everybody's guilty."

"This one's guilty. Mark my words. Her eyes are too close together. She killed her husband. Wait till Nancy Grace gets on later and sets you straight. Nancy knows when people are guilty. She's got a sixth sense about those things, I'm telling you."

"Edith doesn't think everybody's guilty, June," Verna put in. "She thought that priest last year was innocent."

"He was a *priest*," Edith said. "Who would think a priest would murder anyone?"

"Evidently twelve other people besides you. And it didn't take them long to think it, either." June grinned in triumph, then noticed Annja standing in the doorway. "Verna. One of the guests is here."

Verna was a stout woman in her fifties. She wore her graying brown hair pulled back and had a strong face that had seen a lot. Her dress was comfortable and professional, and she had on tennis shoes.

"Good morning, Miss Creed." Verna smiled.

"Good morning," Annja replied. "I know I missed breakfast, so I thought I'd stop in and ask if there was a place you might recommend in town."

Breakfast was served promptly at eight at the bed-and-breakfast and was over by nine.

"Nonsense. I'll be happy to fix you breakfast. I thought about waking you this morning, but you got in so late I wanted to let you sleep." Verna walked over to the industrial-sized refrigerator and swung open the door. "What would you like?"

"I really don't want to be any trouble." Annja felt guilty.

"No trouble at all. The girls and I haven't eaten yet. We were just getting the dishes done before we fixed our breakfasts."

"If you're sure."

"I'm sure." Verna took out a big bowl of waffle batter and a dozen eggs. "Waffles, eggs and sausage sound good?"

"Sounds wonderful."

"Good. Coming right up."

Annja leaned a hip against one of the islands and felt awkward. Edith and June stared at her.

"Stop staring." Verna beat the waffle batter then poured it into the waiting iron. She smiled apologetically at Annja. "Would you like pecans in your waffles?"

"Please," Annja said.

"You're the television star, aren't you?" Edith asked.

"I wouldn't call myself a star. I'm more of a host," Annja said.

"She's the one that's the archaeologist," June said.

"Is that the one that wears the sexy clothes?" Edith asked.

June frowned at the other woman. "The archaeologist doesn't take her shirt off," June explained.

"Oh. Well, if I was young and built like her and taking my shirt off would get me on TV, I'd do it." Edith laughed. "I'd do it now if I thought it'd do any good. In fact, I've been thinking about trying to get on *Survivor.* Those girls go around naked half the time and get all the attention. I could do that."

"TMI," June said, holding up a hand in surrender. "That's just too much information."

"Don't mind Edith. She likes stirring up trouble and saying things just to shock people," Verna said as she poured eggs into a skillet. "Would you like your eggs scrambled or in an omelet?"

"If I have my choice, I'd rather have an omelet," Annja said.

"Are you a vegan?"

"No."

"Good. An omelet's supposed to have meat in it." Verna reached into the refrigerator for diced ham and vegetables. "What would you like to drink? We've got coffee, tea, orange juice, and milk."

Annja asked for milk, then took the tall glass the woman poured for her.

"I heard you were there when those three boys were killed last night," Edith said.

"Edith Clamp!" Verna exploded.

"Well, somebody was going to ask," Edith replied indignantly. "I don't see why it couldn't be me."

"You always ask awkward questions. You shouldn't do that to people."

Annja sighed. "I was there."

"Do you want to talk about it?" Edith asked hopefully.

"Not really."

"Well, we do," June said.

Verna rolled her eyes.

Annja debated leaving. She still had a favor to ask of Verna, and the waffles smelled fantastic.

"I knew those boys were going to come to a bad end," Edith said. "I told Neville's mom that, but she just said she couldn't do anything with him." She shook her head sadly, then fixed on Verna accusingly. "Don't you look at me that way, Verna. I wasn't the one that rented a room to their murderer." She flicked her eyes back to Annja. "That Chinese fella murdered those boys, right?"

"He did, but I don't know anything more than what the television news has reported," Annja said.

"That's too bad, because there are a lot of people in town who want to know the whole story. Some folks are saying that the Chinese fella was a hitman who came in to kill Neville and those other two."

Wow, Annja thought. "That isn't what happened. Huangfu came here to find his ancestor's body."

"Did he?"

"If he really was kin to the man we dug up last night, then yes, he did."

Edith looked stunned. "You dug up a body? The news didn't mention anything about that."

"Yes it did," June argued. "You just weren't listening."

Breakfast, Annja decided, wasn't going to be over soon enough.

WHEN THE MEAL WAS FINISHED, Annja helped clear the table. While Edith and June went back to the kitchen, she asked Verna for a moment of her time.

"Do you have a safe on the premises?" Annja asked.

The woman hesitated only for a moment. "I do."

"Will you keep something there for me?"

"Is it anything illegal? Because I run a good place here and I really don't need any trouble. I don't want any trouble."

"This isn't illegal." Annja took the belt plaque from her jacket pocket. "I need you to hold on to this for me."

"Why?"

"In case someone comes here looking for it."

"Who would look for it?"

"The man I came here with yesterday."

"He wants that?"

"I think so."

Verna looked at the object. "What is it?"

"If I'm lucky, it's a very interesting museum piece. If I'm not, then it's worthless and I've asked you to do something for no reason."

Hesitantly, Verna took the belt plaque. "I can keep it for you, but if the police come here looking for it, I'm not going to lie about it."

"I wouldn't ask you to. I just want to know it's safe while I'm gone."

"You're leaving?"

Annja nodded. "Just for a little while. Do you know anyone in town who reads Chinese? Who might have some knowledge of Chinese immigrants in the area or Chinese history?"

"There's Mr. Kim. Harry Kim. He owns a small antique shop next to the convenience store. His family has lived around this area since the Gold Rush."

Annja thanked her and got directions.

FAR EAST ANTIQUES WAS located between the convenience store and a used book store that Harry Kim also owned. His daughter managed the book store.

"People on vacation come here for all kinds of reasons," Mr. Kim told Annja. "Some of them want a keepsake to take back with them. Others are here to sightsee and relax. I do a good business selling tourists antiques and used thrillers."

Annja liked Kim. He had mild ways about him and

was knowledgeable. In his early sixties, he was balding and the rest of his hair had turned iron-gray and was neatly clipped. His eyes were tiny and crinkled easily when he smiled, which was often. He wore gray slacks and a sleeveless navy sweater over a light blue shirt. His name tag read Harry Kim, Proprietor.

The selection inside the shop was nice, offering tourist items, as well as genuine articles. None of them were overpriced. They were also a curious mix of Chinese pieces, as well as gold pans and other mining equipment.

"Do you know Verna? At the Iron Skillet Bed-and-Breakfast?"

Kim nodded. "Very nice lady. I helped her decorate her Prospector's room."

"I didn't see that one."

"It's a nice room. But how can I help you, Miss Creed?"

"You know my name. You've seen the news stories."

Kim inclined his head and smiled. "I have, but I knew you from the television show before that. My daughter is a big fan of yours. If it's not too much of an imposition, I'd like you to meet her."

"I'd be happy to. But you're sure she's not a fan of Kristie Chatham?"

"Her son is. He's fifteen and is very impressionable. My daughter got her degree in history. She says you do your research very well."

"Then I'll have to meet her." Annja grinned. "I've got a favor to ask, if I may."

"You may."

Annja removed an eight-by-ten picture of the belt plaque from her backpack. She'd blown up the picture and printed it on photograph paper on the portable printer she'd brought with her. Enlarging pictures and having copies to pass out or leave with people had come in handy many times.

"I'm trying to identify this."

Kim took the picture. "This looks very old. The artwork is Scythian."

Impressed, Annja nodded. "I thought so, but I also thought the work might possibly be Chinese."

"Why?" he asked, surprised.

"I took it from a Chinese man."

Kim regarded her carefully. "Up in Volcanoville?" he asked.

Annja decided to be as honest as she could. Kim's personality inspired that, and she'd learned to trust her instincts about people. She nodded in answer to the old man's question.

"The man you were with—the one who killed those young men—he was the one who wanted this belt plaque?"

"Yes," Annja said.

"But you still have it?"

Annja nodded.

Kim studied the photograph intently for a moment. Then he looked straight at Annja. "This is a very dangerous thing to possess, Miss Creed. This belt plaque carries a terrible curse."

7

"Curse?" For a moment Annja didn't think she'd heard correctly.

"Yes. According to legend, that belt plaque is cursed with bad luck. I wrote about this particular piece in a book I wrote on local legend and lore." Harry Kim stepped from behind the counter and walked to the door to the adjoining used book store. "Follow me, please."

Annja trailed behind the man. Their footsteps sounded loud on the wooden floor. Kim opened the door and ushered her through.

The bookshop was small and neat. Shelves filled the walls and stood upright in the center of the floor. A few posters and pictures advertised past author signings.

The woman at the counter was in her thirties and looked a lot like her father. She was small-boned and frail, her black hair tied back. Her black skirt and white blouse gave her a professional appearance, but she looked relaxed, more like she was entertaining than selling.

Kim made the introductions. "Miss Creed, I'd like

to present my daughter Michelle. Michelle, Miss Annja Creed."

Annja shook hands with the other woman. "It's a pleasure to meet you," Annja said.

Michelle's smile was broad and generous. "I'm a big fan of your television show, Miss Creed."

"Please, call me Annja."

Michelle inclined her head. "Annja." She looked at her father with mild rebuke. "If I'd known Miss Creed was coming, I could have ordered rolls and coffee."

"Thanks," Annja replied, "but I just had breakfast before I got here. And your father didn't know I was coming. I surprised him."

"I see." Michelle looked at her. "Is there anything we can do for you?"

"We need one of my books." Harry Kim stood by the counter but unconsciously arranged a stack of novels, tidying them.

Michelle turned to the shelves behind the counter and took down a hardcover book. "Don't tell me my father is punishing you with one of his books. He's shameless."

"My daughter went to the University of Southern California to study fine art," Harry Kim said, "and even with her degree, she doesn't appreciate talent as much as she should."

"So you say." Michelle put the coffee-table-sized book on the counter between them.

"I do say." Harry Kim leafed through the book. "Miss Creed has brought an interesting picture this morning." He put the photo on the countertop.

"What's this?" Michelle picked it up and examined it. "Wait. Is this that cursed belt plaque you wrote about?"

In answer, Harry Kim triumphantly turned the book around for Annja's inspection. The book lay open to a page that showed a black-and-white photograph of five Chinese men wearing dungarees, suspenders, boots, and ragged shirts in front of a hole in the earth that had a wooden sign over it. The wooden sign had Chinese characters on it and the outline of a striking tiger that looked similar to the one on the belt plaque.

"This is Ban Zexu." Kim tapped a finger on the second man from the left.

Annja placed her backpack on the floor and took out a jeweler's loupe to examine the photograph. Upon better observation, she determined that the tiger image was remarkably similar to the one she'd found.

Ban Zexu looked very young. His face was grim and hard, like there'd been little in his life to smile about.

Annja read the text beside the picture and found Ban Zexu's name listed there. "What do you know about Ban Zexu?"

Mr. Kim shrugged. "There's not much to tell. He came from a small town outside of Shanghai in the 1870s and came to Gold Mountain. That's what they called California."

"How do you know about him?"

"He's not the only one whose history I'm familiar with." Kim tapped other faces in the photograph. "I know the histories of these three men, as well." He pointed to the youngest of the five. "This man's name is Kim Chonghuan. He was my great-grandfather. He traveled to America from Hong Kong, which was—at that time—occupied by a number of British merchants and soldiers. In Hong Kong he learned to speak and write English while working for a newspaperman. Back in those days, journalists wrote long and involved stories, not like the small pieces these days."

"That was the only medium they had at that time to reach audiences," Annja said.

"I know." Kim gestured toward a wall filled with audiobooks and DVDs. "So much of today's culture is preserved on digital medium."

"It is the twenty-first century," Michelle said.

Kim waved his daughter's comment away. "Too many people trust that medium too much. I've read books about bombs that may potentially be used in the next world war. Or even used in limited engagements. Electomagnetic pulse bombs. They supposedly won't harm humans, but they will destroy computer and car engines and other things electrical in nature. Do you realize how much might be lost that we've entrusted to the care of digital media?"

It was a terrible thought. As much as Annja loved emerging technology, she loved books more. There was something about the heft of them, the smell and solidness of them, that lent authority and permanence. She'd seen manuscripts that were hundreds of years old, handwritten books on paper that remained white and pristine.

"Anyway, enough gloom and doom." Kim smiled. "Let's talk about curses."

MICHELLE INSISTED ON going around the corner to the pastry shop and getting some coffee and rolls after her father's discussion pushed past the book he'd written to the books his great-grandfather had written. Harry Kim had left the shop for a time himself to get other books. He returned carrying a box filled with journals and letters.

"When he learned the English language, my great-grandfather chose to practice every chance he got. After all, the United States was going to be his adoptive country." Kim leafed through an old hardbound journal covered in neat handwriting with occasional illustrations. "He also learned the craft of reporting from the English journalist."

Annja turned the pages of the book. "This is amazing. Has anyone else seen these books?"

"Everybody," Michelle assured her, "who has eyes has seen the books. Dad has taken them to university professors and to reporters."

"Several of my ancestor's writings have been published in various journals and periodicals," Kim said. "Bits and pieces about local history or customs that people have found interesting." He shrugged. "I don't think Kim Chonghuan would believed his work would be published like this, but I also choose to believe he would have been proud."

"I think you're right." Annja stopped at a photo of ships in a harbor. Several of the vessels listed at their anchorages, but a few others had been hauled on shore and bore hand-lettered signs advertising lodging or food. A careful notation beneath the illustration read San Francisco, 1851.

"You've heard about the ships, haven't you?" Kim asked. "How they were abandoned in the harbor when the crews ran off to the gold fields?"

"Yes."

"Entrepreneurs pulled some of those ships onto the shore and turned them into hotels and restaurants. Kim Chonghuan was fascinated by that. It was the first thing he saw upon his arrival. Two of the books he wrote are about those days in San Francisco. One before he left for the gold fields and one after."

"Ban Zexu was killed in a fire." Annja took a bite of cinnamon roll.

"I know." Kim searched through the box of books and took out a burgundy covered one. "Kim Chonghuan was there. He himself almost died. That incident, when the white miners killed Ban Zexu and the others, made my great-grandfather return to San Francisco. He became a cobbler and an investor in other businesses. For a while, he lived quite well."

Kim laid the burgundy book on the table he'd appropriated in the back of the book store. He flipped through the pages carefully.

Annja had her own hardbound journal out and was taking notes. Most of them didn't have anything to do with the Scythian belt plaque, but they were interesting tidbits she intended to follow up.

"Ah." Kim trailed a finger lightly down the page. "This is where Kim Chonghuan first met Ban Zexu." He turned the book around so that Annja could read the section for herself.

February 25, 1872

While at market this morning, I met a man new to America. My heart went out to him, because I hadn't seen a more bedraggled specimen in years. He wore homespun cotton pants and shirt that I knew had come from China. He carried a cloth bag that I was certain—and later found out—held all his personal belongings. He didn't have much. From the timid way he comported himself, I knew that he had no friends and no English.

Times had been hard in San Francisco. The

American people were never kind or giving to the Chinese as a general rule. One of the most distressing things I found, though, was that my own people had turned hard-hearted toward the newcomers, as well. If a new arrival didn't have family or friends in California, things went very hard for him. They would lie to new immigrants and steal from them, as well.

Even though my own situation was distressing, I couldn't leave such a sad fellow to his own devices. I went to him and talked to him. He seemed at once very relieved and thankful.

When he told me he had no prospects and had come to California to get wealthy digging for gold, I wanted to laugh at him and hug him at the same time. I've seen so many, American and Chinese alike, who come to this place thinking exactly that. Most are easily discouraged, but many—as I sensed in Ban Zexu, for that was his name—were truly desperate.

The entry continued, relating the events that Kim Chonghuan and his new charge took part in the rest of the day.

"Did Ban have the belt plaque with him then?" Annja asked.

Kim nodded and turned the pages of the journal. He pointed to another section.

March 3, 1872

My new partner, Ban Zexu, has had a hard time adjusting to life in San Francisco. Things move too quickly here for him. Twice, I have saved him from being run down in the muddy streets by stevedores whipping their horses unmercifully. Sometimes he doesn't even seem to see the things that are in front of him because he is concentrating so much on looking back over his shoulder. He has the air of a hunted man, but I know of several who barely escaped the wrath of the British, French, and Americans in Shanghai. I have heard their stories, and after a while they all begin to sound the same. San Francisco is rife with men who were outlaws one day and gold miners the next but this is a far better place than China these days. I only regret that my children will not be born in the country of my own birth, for I have decided not to go back.

Today, after too much liquor—which seems to be a weakness of his—Ban Zexu revealed to me a thing of beauty he claims has been in his family for hundreds of years. It is a belt plaque, like one of those worn by the emperor's guards. I believe it is a merit of honor. Ban Zexu tells me that one of his ancestors once did a courageous act for Emperor Ling of the Han Dynasty. When I ask him what this courageous act was, he refuses to tell me. I know Ban Zexu has sometime stretched the truth, but I don't know if that is the case now or if he is for some reason embarrassed.

I have sketched to the best of my ability the belt plaque Ban Zexu protects. Regrettably, because of the confidence I have extended to my new friend, I have been unable to pursue this matter among my colleagues who might know more of its origins.

Annja studied the drawing on the opposite page. Kim Chonghuan had been meticulous and faithful in his rendering.

"I would say that the sketch there is a good match for the photograph you showed me," Harry Kim said.

"So would I." Annja took another bite of her roll.

A bookshop customer entered and Michelle tended to her, pointing out some new acquisitions. She was an elderly woman. From the way Michelle took care of her, Annja assumed the woman was a regular patron.

"Kim Chonghuan was much intrigued by the belt plaque," Harry Kim said.

Aren't we all? Annja thought.

"He uncovered part of the story from another man who also saw the belt plaque." Harry Kim turned to another journal entry.

July 5, 1872

Last night I got a glimpse of the secret that Ban Zexu carries with him, though I am ashamed because I have broken—at least in part—the promise I made to him. Ma Bian, one of the old men who aided me when I first came to this country, was speaking with me this evening.

We often talk in the cool of the night about things we have seen and heard about. I have found my friend to be very knowledgeable about many matters.

We also drank, which was why I was more talkative and less mindful of promises that I had made than I normally would have been. In this talk

I brought up the belt plaque design. Worse yet, I sketched it out for him on a piece of paper.

Ma Bian didn't recognize the design, but he recognized the kind of artwork. He said the Chinese didn't invent it, that it was first used by people he called the Scythians. Ma Bian said those people traded with our ancestors and they made the style part of our culture. I didn't disagree with my good friend because he knows a great deal about such matters, for he invests in artwork and jewelry. But I doubted that someone else had invented that look because it has been part of the China I have always known.

The part that troubles me is the small insignia in the upper left corner of the belt plaque. Ma Bian said that the upside down fish signifies—

Breaking away from the journal entry, Annja studied the drawing that Kim Chonghuan had sketched. After a moment, she spotted the hourglass shape of the fish she hadn't noticed. It was upside down.

Anticipating her next move, Harry Kim slid the photograph over to her.

Annja took her jeweler's loupe from her backpack and studied the picture. It took her a moment to find the engraving. Dirt filled in some of the lines.

"The fish?" Harry Kim asked.

"Yes." Annja removed the loupe, wishing she had the belt plaque in front of her. She groaned mentally. She'd been so intent on confirming that the piece was of Scythian design that she hadn't noticed the fish. To be fair, though, the lines were dim and almost invisible.

Maybe they'd almost faded from the time Kim Chon-ghuan had seen the belt plaque.

"In China, fish are believed to bring good luck," Kim said.

"I know." Annja compared her photograph and the drawing in the journal.

"But placed as that one is, upside down in a state of death, I would believe it does not," Kim continued.

"I agree." Annja turned her attention back to the journal.

—a curse. He said that what I had drawn had a curse put on it.

I asked him who would put a curse on such an object. Ma Bian had no answer for me. He said he would have to know more about the object, but that he believed it was the work of a thieves' guild. I didn't ask him how he came by such knowledge, only accepted that Ma Bian would be the one most likely to know such things.

I have to ask myself why Ban Zexu would choose to carry around a cursed belt plaque. I don't know if I will ever get the answer.

Annja finished reading the journal entry and closed the book. "Your great-grandfather never found out anything more about the belt plaque?"

Harry Kim shook his head. "No, and it has always puzzled me since I first read these books. I've tried to research that drawing, but without luck. I've researched the upside down fish, but not been able to substantiate where it might have come from."

"The fish could have been added at a later date."

Annja surveyed the photograph. "The engraving looks different."

"It *is* different. A different artist made the fish. I know enough about such things to know that." Harry Kim sipped his hot tea. "There are a few other mentions of the piece throughout my great-grandfather's journals, and more information about Ban Zexu. My ancestor believed it was the curse on the belt plaque that killed his friend."

"If it was cursed, why didn't Ban Zexu simply get rid of it?" Annja didn't believe in curses. But, since she'd had the sword she'd found she was less certain to simply discount mystical things.

"Perhaps he tried," Harry Kim suggested. "Perhaps part of the curse was that if he did get rid of the belt plaque, his bad luck would be worse." He shrugged. "I don't know. I know in those journals, my great-grandfather mentioned that there were times when Ban Zexu was in debt from gambling and took beatings rather than give up the belt plaque. In fact, one of them had men who took the belt plaque from Ban Zexu only to return it the following day."

Annja thought about that, finding herself even more curious about the history of the piece. "There was writing on the back of the belt plaque."

Harry Kim shook his head. "I did not know about that."

Annja reached into her backpack and brought out a photo she'd printed of the back of the belt plaque. "I have a picture of it."

Excitement shone in Harry Kim's eyes.

Annja understood the old man's emotion.

"May I?" Harry Kim held out a hand for the photograph.

8

Before she had legally changed her name to Kelly Swan then buried that under a number of aliases, she had first been Kelly Suen. Her father had given her an English name at her mother's request, and he had sent her off to be educated at American schools because her mother had believed that was where her daughter would thrive.

Kelly had blossomed in the United States, becoming much more than she would have if she'd remained in Shanghai. Her mother had lived to see her graduate college, but not to see that she hadn't chosen to become a teacher as her mother had hoped. Kelly's life, as the old Chinese curse went, had been *interesting*, to say the least.

She had graduated six years earlier. Her life had changed several times during those intervening years.

But this morning she'd returned to Shanghai on a red-eye flight into Pudong International Airport. The rental car was an extravagance. She knew when her father saw the car he would roll his eyes and complain about the needless expenditure of money when she could have taken the bus into the Bund and a taxi from there.

It didn't matter that she had the money. Only that she had spent it foolishly. He prided himself on his own thriftiness, and any time she told him he was being too tight-fisted, he only pointed out that it was his thriftiness that had allowed her to go to college in a foreign country. He always conveniently forgot about the grants she'd qualified for and the work she'd undertaken on her own behalf to make ends meet.

Still, she longed to see her father. It had been three years since she'd last seen him. The time had slipped away. As she got closer, the guilt seemed overwhelming.

KELLY HAD TO MAKE one stop before driving to her father's house. The stop was downtown, only a few blocks off Nanjing Road. During business hours, the shops burgeoned with tourists and buyers, and the sidewalks were filled with a constant stream of pedestrians.

She left the car in a parking lot and went to a fourth-floor walkup. The building housed small businesses and criminal enterprises. She was more familiar with criminals than she'd ever have believed possible. In her line of work, they were known as *assets*. She'd gotten the name of this particular asset from one of the few contacts she still trusted.

Kelly knocked on the door as she'd been told—three times, then twice, then four. The effort seemed simple and ridiculous to someone used to working with cutting-edge technology, but it was effective in circles where buyer and seller never met before an arrangement was made. The man she was meeting ran a strict cash-and-carry business.

A young man in American-style gangbanger clothes opened the door. His baseball cap was pointed to the side. He wore a cocky grin, and Kelly knew that was because he didn't feel threatened.

"Are you lost?" the man asked.

Kelly didn't react well to the insolence in the man's tone. For three days, she'd dodged men who had dogged her trail from Brazil to the Cayman Islands. Less than thirty hours ago, she'd surprised them on the boat they'd rented to follow her, then dropped their bodies into the Caribbean Sea. It had been the last bit of bad business, and one of the reasons she'd wanted to return to her father's house. She didn't know what kind of fallout she was going to face. It was possible she wouldn't live another week. She wouldn't have come home at all if she'd believed that her father would be safe from her enemies.

At five feet seven inches tall and slender, Kelly knew she didn't look imposing. She'd learned to make that work for her. Furthermore, the man probably expected her to be docile and slightly cowed simply because he was male.

Reacting to him with anger, Kelly snap-kicked the man in the crotch and shoved him back into the room. Outraged, trying desperately to not drop to his knees or be sick, the young man reached under the windbreaker he wore.

Kelly blocked his right hand with her left, then reached inside his jacket with her right and pulled the Sig-Sauer P220 from his shoulder holster. The pistol was double-action, so it would fire as soon as she pulled the trigger. She doubted that the chamber under the hammer was empty.

The man flailed, trying for the pistol. She kicked him again, harder this time. The man would have fallen, but Kelly grabbed his shirt at the throat and shoved him backward. He fell, sprawling and cringing in pain.

Three other men were in the room. Two of them played video games in the corner. The other man sat barefoot on a couch with a cell phone to his ear. He was the one Kelly had come to see. She recognized his voice from when they had spoken over the phone.

The two men playing the video game reached for machine pistols lying on the floor.

"No." Kelly kept her voice sharp. She pointed the Sig-Sauer at the men to underscore the command.

Unhappily, the men drew back from their weapons.

"Hands on your heads." Kelly reached back and closed the door behind her.

The men complied.

"Keep them there or I will kill you," Kelly said. She managed to find two of the locks by feel and locked them. She wasn't sure if there would be other guards. If she'd set up the operation, there would have been.

The man on the phone looked at her. Calmly, he closed the phone and put it away, but continued to sit on the couch as if he didn't have care in the world.

"You are Guo Teng?" Kelly kept her voice firm but even, as if she did this every day.

"Yes." The man was barely into his twenties, a handful of years younger than Kelly. His platinum hair jarred against his skin tone. Hoop earrings dangled from both ears. He wore jeans and a T-shirt featuring a band Kelly had never heard of. "Who are you?" he asked.

"Your six-thirty appointment," Kelly replied.

Guo Teng grinned. "I knew you would be interesting. You speak very good English."

Kelly didn't respond.

"I wasn't expecting a Chinese woman," Guo said. "Are you still going to pay in American money?"

"Yes."

Guo started to get up, then caught himself. "May I get up to get your merchandise?"

"Yes. But move slowly. If your door greeter had better manners, perhaps I wouldn't be so wary."

"Oh," Guo said, smiling, "I don't think you know any other way."

The man crossed the room to two large suitcases sitting on the table. He used a key to open the locks of one. When he lifted the lid, an assortment of hand guns and machine pistols were revealed.

"Step away, please," Kelly directed. She'd learned that politeness never hurt. When it was extended, people sometimes accepted it and responded in kind. Other times, when she'd calmly executed someone after being polite, the survivors had been shocked—and even impressed. "Don't touch anything," she said.

Grinning, Guo stepped back. "You aren't going to rob me, are you?"

"No. And you're not going to rob me." Kelly stepped toward the suitcase and looked inside. She found two Smith & Wesson .40-caliber pistols in a double shoulder holster. Reaching inside her jacket, she took out a white business envelope thick with cash. "The money we agreed on."

Guo took the envelope and quickly rifled through the bills. He nodded and put the envelope into his pants pocket. "The hundred rounds of ammunition are in the bottom of the suitcase."

Kelly got the boxes and sat them beside the pistols.

Pulling up a chair, she put the Sig-Sauer on the table then ejected the magazines from the new weapons.

The two men sitting in front of the video game started to inch slowly toward their weapons.

"In case you're wondering," Kelly said, never pausing in loading the magazines, "I can pick up that pistol and shoot you between the eyes before you get those machine pistols off the ground."

The men hesitated but didn't pull back.

"I won't stop at killing one of you," Kelly promised. "If one of you behaves foolishly, you're sitting far too close together. I'll kill you both."

The two men leaned back.

"Cowards," the doorman snarled. "If I still had my pistol, I'd—"

"Be dead," Guo Teng said. "Shut up and lie there. I'll kill you myself if you do anything stupid."

The fallen man scowled but did as he was told.

When she had the first magazine filled, Kelly shoved it into the first pistol, worked the slide to strip and chamber the first round, then popped the magazine out and replaced the cartridge that had been taken. She repeated her efforts with the second pistol.

Standing, she took a moment to shrug into the double shoulder holsters. She slid one of the pistols into the holster and pulled her jacket on, leaving her other pistol and the one she'd captured on the table. Working quickly, she unloaded the 9 mm and field-stripped it, leaving it in pieces on the table. Taking her other pistol in hand, she walked to the door.

"If you need anything else," Guo said, "give me a call."

"Of course." Kelly let herself out the door and was

almost running to the stairs. She moved quickly, knowing bruised egos would tempt the men to follow her.

Seconds later, she was in her car and easing into traffic. No one had managed to tail her.

KELLY LOOKED AT the familiar little house near the Huangpu River. Some of the tension she'd been feeling for the last few weeks—no, months, maybe years— melted away. She was home.

She walked to her father's door, thinking that it looked smaller than it had when she'd been a little girl. Taking a quick breath to steel her nerves, she knocked on the door and waited.

A minute ticked by, then another. There was no sound from inside the house. She checked her watch. It was after seven a.m. Her father always got up at four-thirty to go fishing.

It's possible he's still out fishing, she told herself. Maybe he forgot I was coming today.

Troubled, Kelly banged on the door again, louder this time. When there was still no answer, she went around to the back of the house. If things were still as they were when she was a small girl, she knew there were neighbors who were watching her. It didn't matter. No one would call the police unless something happened. Her father would allay any suspicions among his neighbors.

At the back door, she knocked again and waited. Feeling uneasy, she walked to her father's stone garden and sifted through the raked pebbles. The extra key turned up near the right corner of the garden. Returning to the door, Kelly opened the lock and stepped inside.

The house was small and neat. Her father had kept

the curtains her mother had made, and the furniture looked the same.

From the hallway, she looked through the door to the tiny kitchen where she had learned how to cook, then into the small dining room where they had sat on cushions and shared meals.

The living room was immaculate. Her father's collection of vinyl records stood in the corner. He'd never had television in his home, but there had always been music.

She was beginning to think that her father had gone out, perhaps to breakfast. Then she saw the blood.

Kelly's heart hammered, but she steeled herself quickly. Panicking wouldn't do any good.

She drew one of the pistols and held her position, taking the time to calm herself and to listen for breathing. Only street noises and far-off voices from outside reached her ears. Girding herself, guessing what she was going to find, Kelly slid the bedroom door aside and entered the room.

The bedroom was small and neat. Her mother's vanity, her one luxury, occupied a corner of the room. The bed took up most of the space. Her father lay on the bed with a pained expression on his still face. Blood covered his body and the twisted sheets.

Sharp emotions collided within Kelly. She sipped her breath through her mouth, unwilling to take in the scent of her father's death. Walling off the pain and confusion, she relied on her training and experience.

Crossing the room to her father's side, taking care to stand away from the windows even though they were covered, she touched her father's face.

He was cold.

Looking at his neck, Kelly saw that the blood had

started to settle. No longer pumping through his heart, the blood pooled and created a definite stripe, separating the pale blood-drained area from the blood-gorged area.

She sensed movement in the other bedroom. She sank back against the wall and raised her weapon just as a shadow moved in the hallway.

Then a hand snaked out from under the bed and yanked her feet from under her. She fell backward, slamming her head against the wall, and sliding down as she fought the encroaching blackness.

9

"This is a very old language." Harry Kim studied the photograph through thick-lensed reading glasses.

"The fact that the surface is scratched up and worn smooth doesn't help." Annja sipped her coffee and picked up another breakfast roll.

"No." Mr. Kim ran a finger under a line. "This is a Cantonese language, not Classical Chinese." He looked up at her. "Do you know Classical Chinese?"

"Not the language. But I know what it is. The Qin Dynasty established the written language that's become known as Classical Chinese so that Emperor Qin Shi Huang and his advisors could keep track of the various provinces they subjugated. The Qin Dynasty didn't remain in power too long."

"No, they did not," Harry Kim smiled. "You might know more about China's history than I do, Miss Creed."

Annja smiled back. "But I don't know the language."

Turning his attention back to the photograph, Harry

Kim shrugged. "I do. A little. The problem with language is that it changes over the years."

"I know. Slang. References to people, places, and events. New technology. New philosophical or social thinking. All of those things get introduced into a culture and come out as new words or terms somewhere," Annja said.

Kim nodded. "Your parents must be very proud of you."

Normally Annja would have ducked such a statement, but Harry Kim was so honest she couldn't just ignore his generosity.

"I don't have any parents," she said. "I was raised in an orphanage."

Kim looked embarrassed. "I'm sorry. I didn't mean—"

"It's okay."

"Family is important," he said. "One should not go through this world without it."

"I agree." Annja walled away that old familiar pang. She'd watched Harry Kim talking to his daughter and saw their easy relationship. Having someone like that must be nice, she thought.

Incredibly, Roux and Garin, the two men who had searched for the pieces of the sword for over five hundred years came to her mind. Actually, only Roux had looked for it. Garin had hoped it was never found. Neither man was family to her, but they shared ties that had come from the sword's reforging. Annja didn't know how deeply those ties ran, but they were deeper than anything else she'd ever had.

"In Chinese culture, family is one of the most important aspects." Harry Kim pointed at the photograph. "That is the meaning of this belt plaque."

"It's a family history?"

"Partly. But it's larger than that." Harry Kim sighed. "I can't understand everything here. Cantonese is largely dependent on common usage. There are references here that I don't understand."

Annja woke her PDA and took out the stylus. "Let's work on what you can understand. If we can't fill in the blanks, we can at least define them."

LONG MINUTES LATER, ANNJA glared at the sparse information Harry Kim had gleaned from the photograph. She hated being stymied.

"Have you ever heard of a place called the City of the Sands?"

"No. No place by that name. Not until this photograph," Kim said.

"What about in legend or myth?"

Harry Kim shook his head. "I'd not even heard of Loulan City before today, Miss Creed. You were the one with the knowledge of that place."

Annja sighed.

"You said Loulan City was near the desert," Kim said. "Perhaps *it* was known as the City of the Sands."

Annja stood and stretched. That possibility just didn't *feel* right to her. She had no other explanation for it than that. So much of archaeology remained based on conjecture and educated guesswork. The absence of facts could be very frustrating.

"Loulan City was at the northeastern edge of the Taklamakan Desert," Michelle suddenly spoke up from where she stood at the computer. Several Web pages were open on the screen. She'd obviously been following the discussion.

"I know." Annja glared at the photograph of the belt plaque that refused to give up its secrets. "Sven Hedin found the ruins of the city in 1899 while he was working on an exploration of the Silk Road. That area has been explored on a regular basis."

"A Chinese archaeological team is working a dig in that area right now." Michelle clicked on another screen, bringing it to the top.

Annja recognized the Web site as one of the pages she often visited.

"According to this, Dr. Michael Hu has returned to the dig site to follow up on the Chinese mummy that was found in—" Michelle trailed her finger along the screen.

"1980," Annja said.

Michelle looked at her. "You already knew that?"

"I did a lot of research before I came out here. Not just on the California Gold Rush and Chinese immigration, but on things that were currently going on over there. Dr. Hu's work caught my eye."

"You remembered that detail?"

"I've got a really good memory. In my line of work, you have to have one."

Michelle raised an eyebrow as she contemplated a picture on the computer screen. "Dr. Hu appears to be a good-looking man."

Annja refused to take the bait. "He's also published a number of papers and a few books on the history of the Silk Road. He seems very knowledgeable. From what I gathered, Dr. Hu is there looking for more evidence of the Mesolithic culture that was settled there before the city sprang up."

"Would that tie into this?" Harry Kim asked.

"I don't see how." Annja looked at her notes again. "The belt plaque didn't come from the Mesolithic era. I think the belt plaque might be a thousand years old or more, but the Mesolithic time is generally assumed to have started 10,000 years ago, then ended when humans started developing agriculture to supply food. Those periods ended at different times for different cultures, but first began in the Fertile Crescent area in the Middle East."

"This belt plaque also mentions the curse." Harry Kim was still studying the photograph. "Not only was the bearer of the belt plaque cursed, but so were all his progeny."

Annja waited, feeling excitement stirring within her. "What was the curse? And why was that person cursed?"

"If the reason is written here, I can't fathom it," Kim said. "Some of what is written here mentions a fox spirit. Are you familiar with those legends?"

"Yes. The fox spirit was supposed to be a fairy that lived on the life-force stolen from men." Annja had learned that a variation of the legend was common to most Asian cultures. "A fox spirit was supposed to be made up of yin, the female force. She sought out yang, the male force, and fed on it."

"Fox spirits are not always evil," Michelle said. "They can be good. Have you heard the legend of Daji?"

Annja thought for a moment. "I can't call it to mind."

"Daji was a character in a novel written during the time of the Ming Dynasty. The book was called *Fengshen Yanyi.*"

"My daughter the scholar." Harry Kim leaned back and folded his arms over his thin chest. His words carried a hint of sarcasm, but Annja saw only pride on his face. "I sent her to college to learn stories she could have learned at her grandmother's feet."

Michelle rolled her eyes at her father's comments. "In the story, Daji was forced to marry Zhou Xin, who was quite villainous. During her suffering, a fox spirit entered her body and forced out the real Daji. The fox spirit was just as villainous as Zhou Xin, and together they taxed the populace unbearably and invented new tortures that had never before been seen. In time, Zhou Xin's generals rose up against him and one of them founded a new dynasty. After the generals beat Zhou Xin, the fox spirit was driven from Daji."

"What happened to Daji?" Annja asked.

"I don't remember. I'm sure it wasn't a happy ending."

"Fox spirits sound pretty evil to me," Annja said.

"But they're just as often romanticized." Michelle pulled up a picture on her screen of a lovely, near-naked woman. "Pu Songling, a writer in the early Qing Dynasty, authored hundreds of stories that usually featured supernatural elements. Many of them had fox spirits as characters, and several of those were love stories between men and ghosts and spirits. The thing to remember is that a fox spirit is not one thing or the other. It depends on what a fox spirit is here to do." Michelle looked at her father.

Harry Kim nodded. Then he smiled and shrugged. "If you believe in such things. These are enlightened times, Miss Creed. No one believes in fox spirits any more."

Annja thought of the sword she carried and how she could summon it when she needed to. "I'm sure there are still believers."

Harry Kim eyed her speculatively. "Perhaps you are right. I've seen things in my lifetime that I haven't been able to explain."

"Does it say why the original bearer of the belt plaque was cursed?" Annja asked.

Tapping the photograph, Harry Kim pursed his lips and paused. "Not exactly. There is some mention of some great wrong." He shrugged. "I can only translate that it had to do with the demise of the 'City of the Sands.' I suppose it could mean the city itself, but I would think it would be more in keeping if the person who delivered the curse were an emperor or a warlord or a leader of some kind."

"Who did the transcription?"

Surprise tightened Harry Kim's features. "That's a good question. Not everyone would have known how to read or write when the belt plaque was made."

Annja nodded. "The person who made the belt plaque either knew how to read or write, or told someone who could."

"Or the person who placed the curse upon the man inscribed the back of the belt plaque," Kim said.

"Did Ban Zexu know the belt plaque was cursed?"

"It's not the belt plaque that was cursed. It was the original ancestor. And all those who came after him." Harry Kim looked at Annja. "The whole lineage was cursed."

Annja considered that. Familial curses, both given and received, figured into a lot of myths and legends.

"Why would Ban Zexu carry the belt plaque?" Annja looked at the photograph again. "Why would he want a constant reminder that his family had been cursed?"

Harry Kim sighed. "I have no idea. He would not have wanted to be reminded. Nor would any of his ancestors before him."

"Someone should have gotten rid of it along the way," Annja said.

"Or at least been careless and lost it. I lose things from time to time. Even things that I want to hang on to," Kim said.

"The belt plaque would have been worth something to a collector," Michelle pointed out.

"Perhaps, Ban Zexu or his family were not the original owners of the belt plaque. He could have purchased it or stolen it. Perhaps the man—Huangfu Cao—who contacted you and brought you here had discovered the belt plaque had been taken from his family. Perhaps Ban Zexu only found it after the cursed family member died. It could have been a keepsake," Kim said.

"Who would want a cursed heirloom, Dad?"

"Someone who didn't know what it was." Kim considered the photograph. "Or someone who believed that getting rid of the belt plaque would have brought forth even worse luck."

"There's no family name on the belt plaque?" Annja asked.

Harry Kim shook his head. "No."

Dead end, Annja thought morosely.

"If you ever find out the truth of the belt plaque," Harry Kim said, "I would very much like to know." He tapped the book of local legend that lay on the table. "For my book."

"Of course." Annja smiled at him. "I hope that one day I can tell you that story." That means I'll know it myself, she thought.

10

Pain flared through Kelly Swan's left ankle as her attacker continued pulling on it. The hard calluses that edged the man's grip bit into her flesh. More pain exploded in her lower back as she registered the impact of landing on her back after having her feet yanked out from under her. But she felt the comfortable weight of the pistol in her hand. Still, he was strong enough to pull her toward him, away from the wall.

The man was young and looked vicious. He wore street clothes—khaki pants and a green pullover—and held a nickel-plated pistol in his other hand.

He snarled an order at her in Mandarin. "Give up!"

Footsteps sounded in the other room, coming fast.

Her attacker tried again, pulling her toward him and crawling on top of her legs.

Shoving the pistol only inches from her would-be captor's face, Kelly squeezed the trigger and put a round through the young man's head. He died with a look of surprise that froze on his cruel features.

Kicking free of the dead man's hand, Kelly lay on her side and extended her gun arm. From the sound of the footsteps, she judged that more than one other man was in the house. She couldn't get the image of her father's corpse from her mind. Silently, she stilled herself, taking control of her breathing the way she had been trained.

A man appeared in the doorway. He had his weapon pointed before him. He was aiming too high and by the time he realized his mistake and tried to adjust, Kelly had fired twice, punching bullets through his heart.

She scrambled to her feet as the man fell. With her pistol tucked in close to her body at almost shoulder height, she remembered how awkward she'd thought the stance was when she'd first been trained to use it. She went forward with her profile turned to the door to make a smaller target. She wished she had a Kevlar vest.

A third man stood at the far end of the hallway. He held a machine pistol in his hands and opened fire as soon as he spotted her.

Recognizing the threat, Kelly dove back into her father's bedroom. Bullets chopped at the door frame, then slapped into the dead man lying half in and half out of the door.

Kelly threw herself prone on the sanded wooden floor. The thin walls weren't going to offer any resistance to the hail of bullets. Instead of waiting for the man to realize that, she took deliberate aim with the pistol, guessing at the man's location.

The bedroom filled with noise. The pistol's deliberate reports stood out against the deadly chatter of the machine pistol.

Abruptly, the machine pistol stopped firing. Kelly took a moment to feed a fresh magazine into her weapon. She knew she had two rounds left. Even in the heat of battle, she kept count the way she'd been trained to. She also knew to optimize her ammunition and have a full magazine at the ready whenever she could.

Looking at the dead men, seeing the forearms of the first man and the exposed back of the second where his shirt had ridden up, Kelly spotted the multicolored tattoos that covered their skin.

Gangsters. The possibility rattled inside Kelly's head and she immediately denied it. Her father wouldn't have anything to do with Triad members. As far as she knew, her father had never dealt with the Chinese organized crime syndicates.

But the tattoos marked the men as such.

She heard the sound of a window opening in the other room.

Kelly rose and ran forward. She reached the doorway, her gun before her, just in time to see the gunman getting to his feet outside. He sprinted toward the backyard.

Instead of following through the window, Kelly raced to the back door. Pausing, she held the pistol beside her head and peered out across the yard. The gunman vaulted over the low wooden fence in the back and raced north along the narrow alley.

Kelly plunged through the doorway and crossed the yard. She threw a leg forward and vaulted like a hurdler. Landing on the other side, she dropped into a three-point crouch and spotted the gunman ahead of her.

He saw her, too. He whirled and brought up the machine pistol. The barrel spat flame. A handful of bullets peppered the low fence and tore chunks from the earth as Kelly rolled to cover behind a wall of brush across the backyard of the neighboring house.

The man was out of bullets. Angrily, he threw the pistol down and ran full-tilt toward the alley mouth.

Kelly gave only brief consideration to killing the man. She had her sights over his back. It would be an easy matter, a simple squeeze of the trigger.

Instead, she pushed herself to her feet and gave chase. She had questions. She couldn't ask them of dead men. Driving her legs into the thin asphalt that barely covered most of the alley floor, she closed the distance on her quarry.

He reached the street first and stood looking wildly for a moment. Traffic passed in front of him. Then he headed to his left.

Kelly reached the corner, feeling her breath tight in her lungs. She dropped the pistol to her side. Neighbors peered out from the windows and doors of their homes. She pushed herself into motion, but before she had gone three steps a small sedan cut across traffic and bumped up over the curb.

The running man caught hold of the door as the car passed. He reversed direction but was still jerked like a puppet on a string. In the next instant, he had the door open and was inside. Horn blaring as the driver leaned on it, the car roared away, cutting through the slower moving traffic.

Unable to pursue, Kelly memorized the tag number out of habit. Here in Shanghai, she didn't have the connections she needed to trace a vehicle. Furthermore, she felt certain it had been stolen for the murder of her father.

That was, after all, what she would have done.

BACK IN HER FATHER'S HOUSE, barely able to control her grief, anger and sense of helplessness, Kelly looked at her father. He'd been tortured. She saw that from the cuts and burns on his body, the bruised and battered features. Ligature marks showed on his wrists and ankles where he had been bound.

Her father hadn't died easily.

Wiping the tears from her face with her sleeve, Kelly turned from him and surveyed the two men she'd killed. The police would arrive soon. She needed to be gone by that time.

Taking a pillowcase from the bed, Kelly went through the dead men's clothes. She emptied their pockets of wallets, money, keys and weapons. She dropped everything inside the pillowcase. She didn't have anyone locally who would do things for her, but men could be bought.

By the time the first strident double *whoops* of the police sirens reached her ears, she was finished. She took a last look at her father, then raced out the front door to the rental car.

A few of the more curious and less cautious neighbors had left their houses and stood in their yards. As soon as she appeared, they scuttled back inside their dwellings.

Kelly dropped into the seat, keyed the ignition, and pulled away as the first police car roared around the corner ahead of her. She didn't hesitate as she drove past. A quick glance at the rearview mirror revealed that the police car had stopped in front of her father's house. Two uniformed men got out with weapons drawn and cautiously advanced.

Kelly wiped her tears away and focused on her next moves. She had to stay alive at least long enough to avenge her father's death. Anything past that, with the enemies she had pursuing her, was too much to ask.

LITTLE MORE THAN TWENTY minutes later, after being mired in the crush of morning traffic, Kelly pulled the rental car to a halt at the public docks and got out. She carried the pillowcase to the edge of the Huangpu River.

Human voices, the screech of seagulls, and the popping of gasoline and diesel engines created a familiar cacophony. Acrid smoke burned her nose, but the odor was mixed with the stench of fish. Families that included several generations who'd lived all their lives out on the water, fished and worked at hobbies that helped support their meager ways of life.

Kelly knelt on the dock and wasn't too out of place among the tourists, shoppers and fishermen. Quickly, she went through the contents of the pillowcase. The papers gave her names, but she guessed they were probably fake.

She left the weapons inside, though she did take ammunition she could use, and she took the money. Working in the shadows as she did, money was both a weapon to reach her enemies and a defense to block them.

When she was satisfied she could learn nothing more, she dropped the pillowcase into the water beneath the wooden pier and walked away. The men had been Triad. Someone would know who owned them. Once she found that person, she could discover who had ordered her father's death. She only wanted to live long enough to kill that man.

AS SHE APPROACHED THE PIER on the south side of Huangpu Park, Kelly spotted the boat she was looking for. The tall, concrete Monument to the People's Heroes stood only a short distance away at the confluence of the Huangpu and Suzhou Rivers. The structure looked like three bayonets leaning edge-first into each other for support. She'd never before seen the monument in that light. A lot of the local people hated it.

The boat she was looking for was a ramshackle affair that had never seemed seaworthy, but it had been home to generations of family. It was much larger than the traditional *sampans* most river dwellers lived on.

Thirty feet long and nearly half that wide, covered by sun-faded cloth draped over a bamboo skeleton, the boat offered luxurious accommodations when compared to the other craft around it. Rubber tires lashed to the sides stood as a buffer. The Chinese flag, five yellow stars on a field of brilliant red, flew proudly on the stern. An array of antennae protruded at the ship's stern, as well. She was named *Fragrant Moon Lotus,* after Tse Chu-yu's beloved wife.

Seeing the boat made Kelly feel a little safer. Tse Chu-yu had been a good friend of her father's all of her life. He was one of the few men she'd known when she was young who hadn't looked down on her simply for being female.

Do you really want to bring your troubles to an old man's home? Guilt assailed Kelly as soon the thought entered her mind, but the anger and confusion she felt over her father's murder won out.

She walked forward.

11

After telling Harry Kim and his daughter how much she appreciated their help, Annja drove her rented SUV back to the bed-and-breakfast. Her mind was so consumed with questions over the belt plaque and the curse that she barely noticed a new sheriff's deputy sat in a cruiser beside the building.

On the other side of the sun-kissed windshield, the deputy sat listening to a combination of the scanner and some jazz music. The tourist traffic had picked up slightly, trickling through the shops and market areas.

Annja parked her vehicle and walked over to the deputy.

He was a middle-aged man with thick hair and a sculpted mustache. His uniform was crisp and showed knife-edge creases. His hat occupied the passenger seat and pump-action shotgun leaned forward over it.

The window rolled down and the cool of the air conditioner rushed out. The deputy looked at Annja.

"Hi," Annja greeted.

"Miss Creed." The deputy smiled a little.

"Who are you?"

"Deputy Connelly."

"I see Sheriff Barfield hasn't lost his paranoia over me." Annja tried to keep the irritation out of her voice but wasn't sure she was successful.

The deputy's smile widened. "I wouldn't get my feelings hurt over it if I was you," he said.

"But you're not."

"No, I guess not." Connelly shrugged. "Sheriff Barfield doesn't have big trust for anyone involved with media. He's gotten his interviews twisted around before, and had stories that weren't anything at all suddenly balloon into major events when they were actually nothing at all."

"What's that got to do with me?"

"The sheriff has looked into your record, Miss Creed. Seems you're a trouble magnet. He's just going to be happy to see you leave town."

"That isn't exactly hospitable," Annja said.

"No, ma'am. I don't think the sheriff was trying to be."

I guess I can't blame him, Annja thought. She offered Connelly the rolls Michelle Kim had sent with her, in case she needed a snack.

Connelly thanked her for the food.

Hefting her backpack over her shoulder, Annja walked away.

INSIDE HER ROOM, Annja set to work. She was online and cruising through the sites where she'd posted pictures of the belt plaque.

Twenty-three responses awaited her. Most of them only wanted her personal details or to make suggestive comments.

But there were some interesting contacts.

What you've found looks like Scythian art, but it could be Chinese. Those two cultures intermingled a lot along the Silk Road.

Annja already knew that, but she kept reading.

The weird thing is it looks a lot like a photograph posted by someone else looking for a belt plaque like that. The guy claims it's some kind of inheritance and was lost during the big migration of Chinese to the United States during the Gold Rush.

I checked and the posting's still up at www.treasureslostandalmostforgotten.net.

Curious, Annja clicked on the link the poster had provided. Another window opened up. Immediately, the page filled the screen.

The belt plaque lay in a man's hand and the photograph was cropped so close—that only the hand and the object were visible. The photograph was black-and-white.

Something about the image jarred Annja's memory. She took the book Harry Kim had given her from her backpack and flipped it open to the pages marked with yellow Post-it Notes.

One of the photographs in the book showed Ban Zexu holding the belt plaque in his open hand. Evidently the photographer had gotten Ban Zexu to pose with his keepsake.

Moving the book close to the computer screen, Annja quickly decided that the Web posting had been cut from the image in Harry Kim's book. Someone had cleaned up the image a little, but the pose was the same. The scars on Ban Zexu's left hand were visible. The picture came from the book.

Switching over to a search engine, Annja entered the title of the book and Harry Kim's name and discovered the book was also offered as an electronic download with searchable text.

Okay, so Huangfu Cao didn't have to come here to find out about the belt plaque, Annja realized.

She returned to the posting.

If the piece is genuine Scythian art, it could be quite a find. Could be worth a few bucks to a museum or a private buyer.

And there's always the guy at the Lost Treasures Web site.

The thing I found most interesting, though, is the image. I've got a Masters in Fine Art with an interest in anthropology, so I'm kind of big in art history (which is how I could tell you it might be Scythian art). I found a link that might involve that object you found.

According to a local legend out of the Taklamakan desert area, death—and I mean the embodiment of death—came to live along the Silk Road. He, she or it set up residence there and went into business. From what I've been told, death made deals with merchants. For enough money, merchants could pass along the way without being killed. They had to have belt plaques much like the image you've posted here.

A tariff imposed by Death. The thought intrigued Annja. Several rulers of port cities or along heavily traveled trade thoroughfares often claimed a cut of

profits. Taxation was a key contributor to the American
Revolution. Citizens, including some historians, often
forgot that the U.S. was founded on the precept that
taxation wasn't going to be allowed.

I'm still researching this, so maybe I'll have more
later. I'm digging into the Chinese mythology, one
of my favorite loves. Where else can you get such
cool dragons?

Annja typed a quick reply, thanking the sender for the
posting, and letting the person know she would be on
and off the Internet over the next day or so. With no
clues left to explore in Georgetown, Annja suspected she
was going to have to return to Brooklyn.

It was possible that the story would simply die out
and she might never know the end of the tale. She hoped
that didn't happen, but there were a lot of archaeological and historical mysteries that were hundreds and
thousands and millions of years old. Being educated
didn't mean that she got to know everything.

Except that I've got the belt plaque. There was a
certain satisfaction in that.

Opening her phone, Annja placed a call to a guy she
sometimes employed to track down e-mail messages.
After a brief discussion and a little flirting—which
probably cut down the fee somewhat—he agreed to try
to find out who had posted the photo and query about the
belt plaque.

Then she dedicated herself to some cyber sleuthing
of her own. The clue about Death and the belt plaque
being used as a pass card of sorts intrigued her.

In minutes, Annja lost herself in the eternal library
of the World Wide Web.

TIRED OF WAITING, FRUSTRATED at every turn and
feeling the grim certainty of a gun at his head—something that would happen if he failed at his assigned
task—Huangfu Cao strode toward the deputy sheriff's
car. Huangfu had spent the night in the forest beyond
Georgetown's city limits. He'd slept intermittently.
After the long flight from China to rendezvous with
Annja Creed, he was bone weary.

He wore jeans and a lightweight corduroy jacket,
like a lot of other tourists around town. But he carried
a pistol filled with tranquilizer fletchettes wrapped
inside a newspaper.

The deputy noticed his approach at once and sat up
straight.

Huangfu smiled innocuously, like he was happy to see
a man in uniform. He spoke in English. "Good morning."

"Good morning." The deputy nodded and regarded
him through dark lenses.

"I appear to be lost." Huangfu affected an English
accent. He'd worked in Hong Kong and could mimic the
speech pattern perfectly.

"Sure." The deputy maintained his distance. His right
hand was out of sight and Huangfu knew that it would
be on his service weapon. He hoped the weapon was in
its holster, not lying on the seat beside the deputy. That
could cause a problem.

Moving quickly, Huangfu fired three times in rapid
succession. All three fletchettes pierced the deputy's
neck, jutting out from the flesh below his ear down to
the hollow of his throat. The deputy tried to pull his
weapon into play, struggling against the effects of the
drug already overtaking his system.

The deputy almost managed to free his weapon.

Huangfu leaned through the open window and trapped the deputy against the seat while shoving the man's gun arm down with his left. The deputy fought, but his efforts only forced the drugs through his system even more quickly. In the space of a drawn breath, the deputy went limp.

Reaching across the unconscious man, Huangfu picked up the cowboy hat on the passenger seat and placed it over the deputy's head. The man looked like he was asleep.

Huangfu ripped the radio's wires loose, leaving them dangling beneath the dashboard. Satisfied that the deputy was out of play, Huangfu turned away from him and strode toward the bed-and-breakfast. He gazed up at Annja Creed's room. He knew where it was—he'd made the reservations himself.

This time she would not escape.

12

Tse Chu-yu stood in the prow of the boat as Kelly approached. The old man was short and wizened, bent by the decades he had struggled through. Life had never been easy for him.

He had barely been a young man when the Japanese had invaded Nanking during World War II, and he had fought them in the streets with knives and swords. In the years since, there had been other battles, against thieves, pirates, drug smugglers, and corrupt policemen who would have taken his boat and home from him.

He wore khaki pants and a long-sleeved gray cotton shirt that he had rolled up to his elbows. Sweat dappled the shirt. Paint smears and bleach marks from harsh chemicals stained the material. The sluggish wind pulled at the smoke from the unfiltered cigarette between his lips.

Tse Chu-yu recognized her. Kelly knew that from the way the old man's head stopped moving for just a moment. Years ago, she had been impressed by the way he seemed to know everything that went on along the river. She hadn't known it was a skill that anyone might learn.

Later, she'd discovered that Tse Chu-yu knew far more about espionage than he did about fishing. He had worked for the Americans, the Russians and the British, but he favored the Americans because they paid him best, and he'd learned they would even pay him to lie if it confirmed a story and gave them an excuse to act.

The other espionage agencies probably did, too, Kelly had to admit, but she felt particularly rancorous against the United States at the moment. They were the reason she was living so dangerously.

Tse Chu-yu nodded. Just once. It was enough to let Kelly know that it was safe for her. She didn't know what she would have done if it hadn't been.

By the time she reached the end of the dock two young men ran out a gangplank. Her hand was already inside her tote bag.

Five young men occupied mats on the deck. One of the young men held out his hand for the tote bag. "Let me have that."

Kelly stopped on the gangplank just out of reach.

The other young men stood. All of them were armed. Tse Chu-yu's life was constantly at risk.

The first man looked at her, clearly angry. "You may not board."

Kelly didn't speak.

"Step away." Tse Chu-yu's voice was a ragged whisper, but there was no denying the power that it held. "This is my niece you see before you. Treat her with respect."

The men stepped back but remained wary. Despite Tse Chu-yu's confidence, they were responsible for his safety.

Smiling warmly, Tse Chu-yu gestured to the boat. "You are welcome here."

Kelly took her hand from the tote bag and stepped onto the boat.

Tse Chu-yu flipped the stub of his cigarette into the water and let out a last lungful of smoke. "We can talk in my quarters."

THE QUARTERS CONSISTED of two small rooms. Kelly was familiar with them from her many visits with her father. Sometimes her father had fished with Tse Chu-yu, sometimes they had reminisced, and sometimes they got together to feel sad over the loss of their wives and to drink.

The outer room was elegantly appointed with simple things, pictures from happier times. There were a few books and a computer on a small desk. Despite the availability of e-mail, the old man commonly dispatched handwritten letters that were delivered by one of the young men on the boat. Sickly sweet incense hung heavily in the air.

They sat on folded knees on the floor. A low table separated them. Before Kelly could speak, one of the young men brought in a teapot and two cups. He placed them on the table without a word.

"Do you still drink tea?" Tse Chu-yu regarded her. "You have been gone such a long time that I don't know."

"I do. May I pour?"

The old man nodded.

With more calm than she knew she had any right to have, Kelly steeped the leaves from a small cloth bag and poured the tea. There was something about the ritual that was calming.

No matter what else goes on, there is always tea, she

thought. Her father had said that, and during her life Kelly had come to understand what the ritual really allowed.

She served Tse Chu-yu with both hands, turning the cup to present it properly to him. Sometimes, when the fast-paced world she lived in got to be too much, she retreated to the old ways.

"You still remember how to present tea." The old man took the cup from her hands with both of his.

"My father trained me well." Kelly's voice broke as she remembered her father lying dead in his bed, but she kept herself strong. *I will not lose control here.* "I will never forget."

Tse Chu-yu waited until she'd served herself tea. "I was sorry to hear about your father," he said quietly.

"Thank you." Kelly's hands trembled slightly. He had been murdered only hours ago, and they were already talking about him as if he'd been gone for months or years. She sipped the green tea, finding it gentle but aromatic.

"Why did you come to me?"

Kelly put the teacup down. "Because I want to kill the man responsible for my father's death. I think that you'll know who they are."

"Killing them will not be an easy thing."

"But it is necessary."

Tse Chu-yu was silent for a moment. "Your father said you live a rather unconventional life these days."

Kelly chose not to be delicate. "I am a trained assassin."

"I do not recall that ever being one of the occupations you wished to do when you were growing up."

"My perceptions were changed." Memories crowded in at Kelly. "I finished my journalism degree at the University of Southern California. I wanted to work in the entertainment field." She knew her mother would not have been pleased. Her mother had intended her for greater things than following Hollywood gossip. "I was in Kosovo doing a piece on the political unrest there."

"A very dangerous place."

"Yes." Memories of artillery rounds whistling through the air and detonating echoed in Kelly's thoughts. Tank treads cracked pavement as the American cavalry units crashed through houses looking for insurgents. "My news team was taken captive by one of the terrorist groups. A woman, a fellow intern on the news team, was executed in front of us." That horror had haunted her for years until she'd finally seen things—and done things—that were even worse. "I believed they were going to do the same thing to the rest of us. Until I saw her killed, I believed the American military was going to save us."

"They didn't." Tse Chu-yu didn't sound surprised.

"No. *I* saved us. By the time they would have acted, it would have been too late." Kelly took in a slow breath and let it out. "It was already too late. I killed one of the guards—" She still wasn't sure how she'd managed it. "I took his weapon, and killed another man while I freed the prisoners."

"That sounds very heroic."

Kelly looked at him. "You've killed people, Uncle." She called him that out of respect.

He didn't refute her statement. Everyone who lived on the Huangpu River knew that Tse Chu-yu had blood on his hands.

"You know that killing someone is never heroic." Kelly sipped her tea. "It's done as a necessity. Or as a pleasure."

"Not out of vengeance?"

"Vengeance is one of the most basic pleasures."

"Is it so easy for you?"

In a flash of insight, Kelly knew that Tse Chu-yu *was* surprised by her plain talk and obvious comfort level with it. Father didn't tell you everything, did he? "This will be."

"You have killed others. In your service as an assassin?" the old man asked.

"Several."

"I see."

"A few months after Kosovo, I was approached by a man who claimed to be with the Central Intelligence Agency."

"Claimed?"

"I still don't know for certain. The training I received was secret, and it was conducted by men who were once in the military and espionage trade."

"You see assassination as a trade?"

"Some would call it an art." Kelly felt some of the tight knots of pain unraveling within her as she spoke. It had always been that way with Tse Chu-yu. The old man listened and asked questions and listened again. He never passed judgment or offered an opinion without being invited. "The fact of the matter is that anyone can be trained to kill anyone else," Kelly said.

The old man nodded.

"This man came to me and told me he could have me trained. He told me I could make a difference. Like I had in Kosovo. I believed him." Kelly drew a breath and wondered if she had been home if her father would still be dead. "More than that, I wanted to make a difference. I'd been a journalism intern long enough to know that I wouldn't make much of a difference there."

"While you were an intern, your mother died." Tse Chu-yu's voice was calm and gentle.

Okay, maybe I had some anger issues to work out, as well, Kelly thought. She didn't say anything. She felt like the old man could see right through her to her secret self.

"You became a good assassin?"

"I'm still alive."

"In that line of work, it's just as important to escape unknown as it is to kill the target you've been assigned."

"I know." Kelly regarded him intently, wondering how much he knew. "I want to talk about the men who killed my father."

"Of course."

"Do you know who killed him?"

Tse Chu-yu hesitated. It was a weakness she seldom saw in the old man, and she was trained enough now to see it and to exploit it. She would know if he tried to lie to her.

"I do know them. They are very dangerous men."

"Who do they work for?"

"Ngai Kuan-Yin. Do you know of him?"

Kelly nodded. "Ngai Enterprises."

"Yes."

"Why did he order my father's death?"

"You didn't come here just to learn the names of your father's murderers, did you?"

"My father trusted you with everything he had. Those men at my father's house were searching for something." She paused, not wanting to ask.

"He left something with me. I will get it." Despite his age, Tse Chu-yu stood easily and walked to his private quarters.

Kelly remained on her knees and stared after him. All

she could think of was her father lying helplessly on his deathbed. She feared she would be sick.

Tse Chu-yu returned only moments later. He carried a burgundy cloth bag that Kelly could remember seeing at her father's house.

Tse Chu-yu handed the bag to Kelly. The weight was negligible. Pieces moved inside it. Through the thick cloth, they felt like sticks but they had odd shapes.

She looked up as the old man sat across from her. "What is this?"

"One of your father's projects."

Kelly thought about that. Her father was the most curious man she'd ever known. Music consumed his soul and brought his passion to life, but she felt certain he never went through a day without thinking of at least a thousand questions.

"Do you know what it is?" Kelly asked.

Tse Chu-yu nodded. "It is a puzzle."

Not satisfied with the answer, Kelly opened the bag and poured the contents onto the low table. Pieces spread out in a growing pool. At first she thought they were sticks, then she saw the porous and pitted surfaces and thought they might be soapstone used by the carvers to sell good luck charms to fishermen and tourists.

She picked up one of the pieces, surprised by its lightness. The piece seemed fragile, but when she tested it between her fingers, she found it was rigid and strong.

"Have you seen this before?" Tse Chu-yu watched her intently.

"No. I've seen the bag before, but not what was in it." Kelly ran her fingers through the odd pieces. "Do you think this is why my father was murdered?"

"In all the years that I knew your father, this is the only thing he ever asked me to keep for him."

"He trusted you."

Tse Chu-yu nodded. "He honored me with his trust."

"Did he tell you what this was?"

"Only that it was a very important secret that he wanted you to have."

Kelly looked at the old man. "Did you try to find out what it was?"

Tse Chu-yu smiled. "Of course I did. Your father asked only for my caretaking. Not for my disinterest. He knew me well enough to know that he could never have that."

"Did you find out what these are?"

"I did not find out the secret of those pieces, but I did learn that they were made of bone."

Kelly looked at the pieces. Her stomach spasmed. "Bone?"

"Finger bones, to be exact. Human finger bones. They are hundreds of years old. Perhaps thousands."

Kelly looked at the ivory-yellow pieces scattered across the table's surface. She couldn't believe her father would have such things. Or that they were anything someone would kill her father to get, or that he would give his life to protect them. It didn't make any sense.

She checked the burgundy bag again. This time she found the note.

13

"What are you doing here?" The middle-aged woman stood drying her hands on her apron in the hallway.

Huangfu Cao lifted the tranquilizer gun and fired at her from pointblank range. She yelped and turned to run, but by then it was too late. Two fletchettes stood out from her chest and stomach. She managed two steps, then collapsed without a sound.

By the time Huangfu reached the stairway leading to the second floor, one of his men had stepped out at the other end of the hallway. He held Verna Thompson prisoner, one arm bent behind her back and a pistol pressed against her throat.

"Mrs. Thompson." Huangfu chose to be polite. It didn't help when prisoners were too frightened to think coherently enough to be cooperative. "Can you understand me?"

The woman nodded.

"I do not wish to hurt you."

Verna's eyes cut to the woman lying motionless on the floor.

"She's only been drugged. She will recover. Look at her. There is no blood. Do you understand?"

After a choked sob, Verna nodded.

"Good." Huangfu smiled reassuringly. "Do you have a safe on the premises?"

Verna nodded again.

Huangfu had felt certain the woman had. "Do you have anything of Miss Creed's in the safe?"

At first, Verna didn't answer. Then her captor pulled up on her arm hard.

"He will break your arm if you don't answer me."

Tears ran down the woman's face. "Yes." Her voice was a choked whisper.

"Take my associate to the safe. Give him what Miss Creed gave you and you will not be harmed."

Huangfu went up the stairs. He stayed to the outside of the tread so no loose boards would creak and give his approach away.

Two of his men joined him, letting him know the downstairs rooms were secure. They followed, silent as shadows.

Annja Creed's door was locked.

Huangfu debated only a moment between picking the lock or breaking the door down. Stepping into the hallway, he set himself and drew back a leg. Then he kicked, putting his weight behind the effort.

The door frame splintered. Wood facing snapped like kindling and screws screeched as they pulled loose from their moorings.

With the tranquilizer pistol raised before him, Huangfu rushed into the room, arms braced in a defensive square, the pistol close to his body. Even then he was almost caught flatfooted when the woman turned on him with amazing speed.

She had her backpack over her shoulder, but Huangfu wasn't clear on whether she'd heard them coming or had been ready to leave. She drew her right hand back like she was going to throw something in a sidearm motion, but her hand was empty.

Only it wasn't empty after all.

Huangfu didn't know how he'd missed the sword she was swinging. The long blade whistled through the air, barely missing the wall, and arced straight for his throat. He stumbled back and lifted the tranquilizer gun to defend himself.

Metal grated harshly, hurting Huangfu's ears and making his teeth ache. The impact tore the pistol from his hands and left most of his fingers numb. He crashed back against the two men behind him, all of them going down.

Annja Creed turned from them, fleeing toward the bathroom. As she ran, the sword vanished like it had never been there.

Although Huangfu had never been a believer in the old legends of monsters and magic, the hair at the back of his neck stood. *Something* had touched him and left his hand numb. Blood on his wrist leaked from a shallow cut that had grazed his skin. *Something* had touched him that was suddenly no longer there, disappearing as quickly as it had appeared.

Cursing, Huangfu drew his pistol from his shoulder holster and took aim as he scrambled to his feet. He fired, knowing he was rushing the shot.

IN FULL FLIGHT, ANNJA ran through the open bathroom door, put a foot on the edge of the tall tub, and launched herself at the translucent glass. She ducked her head and threw an arm in front of her just before she hit.

She fully expected to rebound from the glass like a sparrow hitting a storm door. It was possible that Verna had installed impact-resistant glass. But there was no other way out.

The glass shattered when she hit it and she hoped she didn't get cut to pieces as she went through and out onto the slanted roof. The brightness slammed into her with almost the same physical intensity as the window.

Her heart thumped wildly. She was surprised that Huangfu and his men had invaded the bed-and-breakfast. She couldn't believe they'd taken that kind of chance. But that only meant they knew more about the belt plaque than she did.

She didn't have time to be surprised or curious or even scared, because she was sliding for the edge of the roof, riding a wave of cascading glass shards.

Huangfu shoved his pistol through the broken window and fired at her. Bullets ripped across the shingles near Annja's head. Two of the shingles slid free and skidded over the roof's edge. Annja pushed herself forward, knowing she had no choice. She leapt from the roof, controlling her descent and throwing herself forward so she wouldn't land in the rosebushes behind the bed-and-breakfast.

Her boots hit the soft earth and she dropped to her knees, catching herself on her hands. Nothing's broken. Get up and run, she told herself. She pushed herself up, noticing the shadow growing on top of the house. She veered to her right just as more gunshots rang out.

Doubling back close to the bed-and-breakfast Annja streaked for the parking area. The deputy was there. Her car was there. She only hoped Huangfu hadn't left a guard there.

She paused at the corner of the building for just a moment. Behind her, caught in the corner of her eye, Huangfu hung over the roof's edge and pointed his pistol at her again.

Annja went forward as bullets chipped the corner of the building above her head. She ran for the deputy's cruiser, not sure the man was still in his vehicle.

Peering through the windshield, Annja saw the deputy sprawled across the seat. She didn't know if he was alive or dead. She kept running.

Using the electronic key fob, Annja popped the locks on her rental SUV, clawed the door open, and slid inside. She started the engine, then dropped the transmission into gear. Rubber shrieked as she stomped on the accelerator and roared toward the street.

One of Huangfu's men stepped in front of the SUV and took aim with his pistol. The windshield spiderwebbed.

Annja never slowed. The man tried to dodge away at the last moment, but the SUV caught him from the side in a glancing blow and spun him away.

Pulling hard on the wheel, Annja powered out onto the street in a controlled slide. She fought the wheel just for a moment as the SUV fishtailed. Dodging cars, she headed for the highway as quickly as she could.

She didn't even think about going back for the belt plaque. Annja knew she was better off leaving that mystery unsolved. She sped out of town, wondering if Huangfu and his men would pursue her or if they'd be content with their prize.

"Is VERNA OKAY?" Annja held her phone close as she spoke. She'd driven the SUV down a dirt side road only ten miles out of Georgetown. She assumed Sheriff Barfield would have put an APB out on her and the vehicle. She couldn't crawl out of her own skin, but she could ditch the rental.

"Where are you, Miss Creed?" Barfield sounded more than a little irritated.

"Safe. For the moment." Annja looked around at the sheltering trees and wondered how long it would be before she would feel safe.

"You need to come back to town and let's get this thing sorted out." Barfield sounded adamant.

"Huangfu Cao tried to kill me." Annja knew some of her own raw anger sounded in her words. *"Again."*

"I want to know why."

"Believe me, Sheriff, so do I." The only thing Annja could come up with was the fact that Huangfu knew she took pictures of him and possibly the belt plaque. "In fact, you might want to put Harry Kim and his daughter under protective custody for a few days."

"Why would I want to do that?" the sheriff asked.

Annja paced as she talked, then finally decided that she wasn't leaving in the SUV anyway and she might as well put some miles between herself and the vehicle. She headed back toward the highway three miles distant.

"Because I showed them something."

Barfield covered the mouthpiece with a hand, but Annja could still hear his gruff voice. When he returned to the conversation with her, he sounded even more put out. "What did you show them?"

"A belt plaque I recovered from the grave last night."

"Why didn't you mention that last night?" Barfield shouted.

"I wanted to know what it was," Annja said.

"If this guy Huangfu wanted to kill you for it—"

"I don't know if that's why he tried to kill me last night."

Barfield's tone took on a decidedly sarcastic note. "Maybe it was the reason he tried to kill you today."

"I think he tried to kill me today because he believes I took pictures of the belt plaque."

"Did you?"

"Of course."

"I'd like to see those pictures."

Annja gave him the Web site posting.

"That's not what I meant. I want to see those pictures *and* you."

"Do you have an arrest warrant out on me? For trying to escape an execution?" Annja tried to dump as much *I-can't-believe-you're-serious* into her voice as she could.

"We can protect you, Miss Creed."

"Is your deputy still alive?"

Barfield took a breath and it rasped over the phone. "They drugged him."

"You'll understand if I'm not exactly wowed by your offer of protection."

"At this point, Miss Creed, you're considered a person of interest. But I can get an arrest warrant for you."

"Did you catch Huangfu?"

Barfield hesitated.

"I gather the answer is no. In that case, I'm not coming back there just because you want to talk to me. I've told you everything I know. Having me there isn't going to do anything but endanger my life. I just wanted to know that Verna and the other guests at the bed-and-breakfast were all right."

"They're fine. No one was hurt."

Annja relaxed a little. "Good. I'm glad. You have my phone number if you want to reach me, but I'm not coming back. And I'm not going to answer your call again until I talk to a lawyer."

Annja ended the call and tucked the phone into her backpack. She retrieved a bottle of water from one of the side pockets. She sipped water as she continued walking, and she thought about the belt plaque, wondering what secrets it actually held.

No one would go to the lengths Huangfu had without something important being involved. Annja just couldn't imagine what it might be. But she knew she was going to try to find out.

14

The note was dated only a few days earlier, and Kelly recognized it as being written by her father. She looked at Tse Chu-yu. "Have you read this?"

"Your father did not ask me not to."

Kelly turned her attention back to the note.

Dearest Daughter,
I wish things had ended differently. If you're getting this letter, it means I didn't get to see you. I regret that, and I hope that you don't think too badly of me.

Hot tears burned Kelly's cheeks. Her vision blurred and she had to blink them away to keep reading.

This has all been a surprise to me. This bag that Tse Chu-yu has given you is a legacy given to me by my father's grandfather.
He was a very old man, and very wise, when I

knew him as a child. Many in the village where he lived thought him insane. Those were unkind thoughts from people who knew no better.

Your great-great-grandfather was not a learned man. Just one who knew his way in the world. He hung on to legends and myths more than anyone else I ever knew. And he knew magic. At least, to me as a boy, I felt certain it was magic.

Kelly held on to her emotions with an iron grip. Across from her, Tse Chu-yu sat quietly.

The bag before you offers a puzzle. I'm not certain of its true origins, but I will give you the story my great-grandfather gave me all those years ago.

When I was twelve, not yet a man in my father's eyes, I saw my great-grandfather a final time before he died. He was very sick and I knew that his time in this world was at an end. As he lay there, taken by fever, he pressed this bag of bones into my hands and told me that he was going to tell me a story that he had never told anyone.

As I listened to him, I thought him sick with the fever that was slowly taking his life. His stories were wild and improbable. He said that one of our ancestors belonged to a group of assassins thousands of years ago, during the time of the Emperor Ling.

These assassins were of great value to the emperor and other men of power. They were specialists in silent death. They had their own poisons. I found the stories quite fascinating.

For hours, in his weak and failing voice, he told me how feared the assassins were throughout

Asia and Eastern Europe. He also said that they were hunted. Though they did the emperor's work, and took on tasks from the warlords, everyone they did business with feared them, as well. After all, the assassins could just as easily turn on those who had hired them only the day before.

The city of assassins lay somewhere along the Silk Road. They charged trade caravans for safe passage along sections of the road.

For years they lived in such a manner, and the collection of wealth grew larger. They lived in a cave, somewhere underground in the shifting sands of the desert.

And it was there that they died. I do not know how. Our ancestor died there, too. At least, it is believed that he did. Before he did, though, he gave that bag of bones to his wife and bade her keep hold of it. If he did not return, she was to give the bag of bones to their oldest son and tell him that the bones would show him the way to the treasure.

That child became a man, and the man searched for his father to no avail. It was as if the desert had swallowed him.

And so it has been for generations. There have always been sons in our family to pass this bag on to.

Now I have you.

I've searched for the answer to the bag of bones, though I have not let myself be consumed by it. Until lately, I thought perhaps the story was only that—a story. But now a man has found out about this bag of bones. A very wealthy and powerful man who is accustomed to getting his way.

It was this man's zeal to find this bag of bones

that I'd never told anyone about that convinced me the tales of the treasure might be true.

I still don't know how this man discovered that I had this bag. But he has, and it could end my life.

I know you are grieving for me, Kelly.

For a moment Kelly couldn't continue. She breathed out and fought to keep the overwhelming emotions at bay. She blinked, wiped her face, and began to read again.

Keep the bag of bones safe. See if you can ferret out the truth behind them.

I have always loved you, and I love you still. I will be with you always.

Your Devoted Father

Kelly read the letter through twice more, hoping to find some indication of who the wealthy and powerful man might be. Frustrated, she looked at Tse Chu-yu.

"Ngai killed my father for this?" She pointed at the bag of bones. "Something out of a child's fairy tale?"

"No." The old man spoke softly. "Ngai killed your father because he *believed* in the bones."

"That's stupid."

"Perhaps. But your father believed also. That's why he refused to sell them to Ngai."

Kelly closed her eyes as her senses whirled. Images of her father kept spinning inside her mind. *It was stupid to die for them, too, Father.* She felt guilty the instant she thought that.

Trembling, Kelly worked on her breathing. She had been trained to handle this. She didn't have to be overcome by her emotions.

But she had existed for months, almost a year, since her betrayal. She'd lived in shadows and watched everyone around her. That had been no way to live, but it had been the only way she could survive. She had lived in small rooms and taken on bloody, dangerous work that had bordered on outlaw behavior. If she'd had a choice, she wouldn't have ever done most of the things she'd done.

"Your father was a brave man." Tse Chu-yu's words drew Kelly back to the present.

"No." Kelly's voice was hollow. "He was a foolish man."

"He thought he was giving you a future."

"He threw away his life."

Tse Chu-yu frowned at her. "My friend didn't act just for you, niece." The old man only addressed her by that borrowed relationship when he was irritated with her and intended rebuke. "He also acted for the honor of his ancestors, for all those who had died protecting the secret he gave you."

Kelly returned the old man's steel-hard stare. "Do you believe this story?"

"If your father did, then, yes. I choose to believe it, too."

"What if it turns out to be false?"

Tse Chu-yu considered for a moment. "For every tale that is told, there is always a kernel of truth. If you wish to know the truth of this, then you must seek it out."

Kelly was quiet for a moment. "When you read this letter, were you tempted?"

The old man paused, then nodded. "Yes. I still am."

"Then either you respected and loved my father more than the thought of an immense treasure, or you don't believe in the story much."

"You've become very cynical."

"It's a cynical world."

"Perhaps you are more my niece than you are your father's daughter."

Kelly felt like she'd been slapped. She had never known what had drawn the two men together, especially when she'd gotten older and figured out what it was that Tse Chu-yu actually did.

"Do not dishonor your father's memory. He loved your mother, you, and his music. In that order. I will not allow you to so casually dismiss his feelings in this matter." The old man's face was stern. "If you will not try to find out the secret of those bones, then give them to me and I will." He held out his hand.

Angry, hurting, Kelly grabbed the bag and almost thrust it out to him. Tse Chu-yu knew it, too. His eyes glinted, but she didn't know if it was in anticipation or disappointment.

Finally, Kelly put the bag of bones into her jacket pocket. She took another breath and centered herself, getting focused. "The men I killed in my father's house had tattoos. I think they were Triad men."

Tse Chu-yu nodded. "Ngai Kuan-Yin has men like that who work for him."

So did most Chinese corporations, Kelly knew. The Triad served not only in illegal matters, but as security and labor enforcement, as well.

"Both men had distinctive tattoos on their right forearms." Kelly touched her arm to show where. "They were of a great winged dragon holding koi in its claws."

"I know those men. They belong to the Razor Claws."

"Do you know where I can find them?"

15

Annja headed southwest toward Sacramento. She had no intention of going back to Georgetown. Returning there meant lawyers and delays, and she hadn't done anything wrong. She hadn't left any bodies behind that needed explaining. She's simply escaped.

The day warmed, but the season was still cool and the altitude kept some of the heat at bay.

She stayed within the forested area that lined the highway. Twice, she'd seen vehicles marked with the sheriff's department logos pass by. She'd been out of sight both times.

Sheriff Barfield, or someone in his office, continued to call on a regular basis. Annja ignored the attempts to contact her. She didn't have anything further to say until she found out exactly where she stood.

DOUG MORRELL CALLED in the afternoon. Bored and wanting to hear a friendly voice, Annja took the call.

"Hello, Doug."

"Ah, my favorite fugitive."

In spite of the situation, Annja grinned. Maybe being on the run wasn't exactly conducive to continued good health, but there was a part of her that enjoyed it. Was that part always there? Or did it come with the sword? she wondered.

"Did it take you long to think that up?" Annja asked.

"Actually, it wasn't me. It was my boss. He called me and asked me if I knew my favorite fugitive was on the run again."

"I take it you're in trouble." Annja felt bad, but only marginally so. Doug was a nice guy and she enjoyed their friendship. However, he'd chosen the volatile field he was in. In media, yesterday's heroes were today's tragedies.

"Nope. We're getting a lot of free advertising as a result. For some reason CNN and Fox News have picked up the story of your evasion of local law enforcement."

Annja was perturbed. Being a nationally recognized fugitive was going to make her attempt to purchase a plane ticket back to New York difficult.

"My boss thinks it would be better if you turned yourself in. Eventually," Doug said.

"Eventually?"

Doug sighed. "Right now my boss is happy with all the free advertising *Chasing History's Monsters* is getting."

"Then why are you calling?" Annja asked.

"Just, you know, checking on you. Trying to make sure you were okay."

Annja detected a note of dishonesty in Doug's words. Suspicion honed her paranoia to a sharp edge. "You called because you cared?"

"Well, yeah. Where are you?"

"On the highway headed to Sacramento."

"Okay." Doug was quiet just long enough to make his next question sound awkward. "Can you see a mile marker?"

"A mile marker?"

"Yeah. You know. One of those sticks that tell you how far you are from somewhere?"

Annja counted to ten. "Are you planning to tell the sheriff's office where I am?"

"No!" Doug's answer was immediate and too vehement to be believable. "I wouldn't do something like that, Annja!"

"When I get back to New York, we're going to talk about this." Annja shut the phone, wondering if the show had a way of tracking her phone.

ANNJA GLANCED OVER her shoulder when she heard a diesel engine bearing down on her position.

A bright blue fully-dressed eighteen-wheeler roared along the highway.

Annja sprinted toward the road, hanging on to the backpack's strap with one hand. She threw her other hand out with her fingers curled and her thumb extended. She barely resisted the impulse to yell at the driver to stop.

Air brakes whistled and thudded. The eighteen-wheeler put on its emergency flashers and pulled over to the side of the road.

Jogging, the backpack thudding against her spine, Annja caught up with the truck just as the passenger door popped open and swung wide. She hauled herself up the first couple of rungs.

"You all right, missy?" A grizzled truck driver sat behind the wheel. He wore a baseball cap, a cowboy shirt with snaps, and had a full beard that was a mix of black and gray.

"I'm fine. Can I catch a lift?"

The driver looked back in his rearview mirrors. "Where'd you lose your car?"

"A dirt side road a few miles back."

Nodding, the driver waved her into the truck. "Come on ahead."

Annja climbed up into the seat and stowed her backpack between her feet. "Thanks."

"You know that hitchhikin' ain't exactly the safest thing a young woman can do in this day an' age."

"Yeah. I didn't exactly plan for it today." The strong odor of dog tickled Annja's nose. She held back a sneeze.

The driver grinned. "I reckon not. Where you goin'?"

"As far as Sacramento if you're going that way."

Both hands on the wheel as he eased back onto the highway, the driver nodded again. "I am. You thirsty? Hungry?" He jerked a thumb over his shoulder. "I got a refrigerator in the back with water and soda. Got a couple ham sandwiches in there, too."

"You don't mind?" Breakfast and the rolls she'd had afterward were long gone.

"Not at all. Help yourself. While you're back there, I'll take a sandwich, too, if you don't mind."

Annja turned and found herself face-to-face with an English bulldog. The dog's heavy jowls quivered as he barked and snapped. She froze.

The driver glanced in the mirror. "Almost, you be quiet now. She's a guest."

Almost whined a little, then retreated to the far side of the bed in the back of the cab. It was almost as big as an efficiency apartment and stocked with the refrigerator, a television set and stereo components, and a closet area.

The driver smiled. "You can't mind Almost. He's just protectin' the truck. Me an' him been together a lot of years."

"I just wasn't expecting him there." Annja swung the refrigerator open, then took out two sandwiches wrapped in wax paper and two bottles of water.

Turning around in the passenger seat, she handed one of the sandwiches and a bottle of water to the driver. She opened her own sandwich and bit in. She was rewarded with unexpected flavor. "The bread is great."

Grinning, the driver nodded. "My wife bakes it fresh. Makes it easier for me to pass by these greasy spoons I see on the road." He looked in the driver's side mirror with interest. "I sure hope you left your car a ways back there."

Glancing out the side mirror, Annja spotted a sheriff's cruiser closing in fast. For a moment she thought she was caught, that Doug had turned her in and she was going to spend the next few hours or days being interviewed. It wasn't a pleasing proposition.

Abruptly, the cruiser pulled into the other lane and sped by the truck.

The driver shrugged. "I guess you hid your car pretty good."

Annja took another bite of her sandwich. "You know that picking up fleeing fugitives isn't the safest thing a truck driver can do these days," she said.

"Yes, ma'am. But I gotta keep up my outlaw ways. We'll get you to Sacramento all right, but after that you're going to be on your own."

ABOUT TWENTY MINUTES from Sacramento, Annja got another call. She didn't recognize the number, but she recognized the exchange. Paris, France.

Roux. Annja felt an unexplained surge of excitement at talking to the old man. More than a month had passed since their last communication. She was never quite sure where she stood with him because sometimes he acted like he didn't care if she lived or died, but the sword linked him to her. And to Garin Braden.

The sword made them family, of sorts, and she didn't know if she liked the idea or should feel frightened by it. But maybe it made sense that her feelings were in both camps. That was what she had gathered most people's families were like.

She answered her phone.

16

"Annja." Roux's voice was boisterous. "You are well, I trust."

Instantly wary, Annja decided to buy herself some time to get the lay of the land. "I am. How are you?"

"Mystified, actually."

"Why?"

"I've been perusing your archaeological postings."

"I didn't know you did that," Annja said, surprised.

Roux's voice was dry and didn't offer any clues as to why he'd called. "Sometimes. When I get bored."

That hurt, just a bit, and she felt certain he'd intended the comment to. *A warning shot to keep my distance?* She didn't know. She turned cool, masking her feelings the way she'd learned to do in the orphanage.

"I thought you were off playing poker."

"I am back," Roux said.

"What posting are you referring to?"

"The new one of course."

Annja smiled a little at that. Even though he'd lived

for centuries, Roux wasn't all-knowing. Annja posted nearly every day on various Web sites, constantly asking for help in pinning down facts or offering it.

"Oh, you mean about the Grecian urn." Annja couldn't help twisting the knife just a little. Roux had pompous and arrogant down to a science. "I found out it was a fake after all. It had been cast at least a hundred years later than the museum thought. But it was interesting. Did you know that Grecian urns have been around since the twelfth century B.C.? And that it wasn't until the eighth century B.C. that Greek potters began painting the figures black to contrast them against the red clay material they made the urns from?"

Roux sighed irritably. "I did."

"Did you ever throw a Grecian urn on a potter's wheel?"

Roux made a disgusted noise that sounded like a lion coughing. "I didn't call to talk about Grecian urns. I called to talk about the Scythian belt plaque."

That stopped Annja dead in her tracks. There was no way he could know for a fact that the belt plaque was Scythian. *She* couldn't tell that, and she'd handled the piece, not referenced it from a Web posting. "I haven't ascertained that it's Scythian," she said.

"It is."

"You can't tell that from a photograph." Despite her enthusiasm at bedeviling Roux, Annja was starting to feel irritated herself. Roux had a familiarity with things, but he wasn't trained as an archaeologist as she was.

Still, he knew an awful lot about history from hands-on experience. From the conversations she'd had with Roux, Annja believed he'd traveled most of the known world.

"I can identify *that* artifact from the photograph."
Roux sounded adamant.

"Why?"

"Because I've seen it before."

"How old is it?"

"Two thousand years, more or less."

Annja wondered how much Roux was letting slip.

"I saw it in Shanghai. Four hundred, five hundred
years ago. I can't remember exactly. I could look it up."

"Look it up where?"

"I'm writing my memoirs."

Annja was stunned. Memoirs? From a man she
knew to be at least five hundred years old? "I didn't
know you were—"

"Of course I am." Roux's voice was brusque. "I
was trained to document my travels, observations,
and ruminations."

By whom? Annja's mind danced around the possibilities.

"Sometimes I forget things, or I need to remember
them better. I use the memoir to remind myself."

"Would it be possible for me to—"

"No. Not in your lifetime. Only when I reach the end
of mine. The world isn't ready for the things that I know."

A woman's soft, entreating voice spoke somewhere
in the distance, calling out Roux's name. He growled
an impatient noise at the interruption. "Where is the
belt plaque?"

"Why do you want to know?" Annja liked having the
upper hand. She often didn't in her dealings with Roux.

Roux sighed. "You lost it, didn't you?"

So much for that, Annja thought. "Not exactly."
There was the possibility that her computer expert friend

could track Huangfu Cao. Or that she could find the man's trail herself.

"Of course you did. If you still had the belt plaque and wanted to pique me, as you witlessly tried to do just now, your response would have been that of course you had it. Possession would have given you total control during this discussion."

Annja let out a tired breath. I'm really going to have to step up my subterfuge game to play against him, she told herself. "Okay. I lost it."

"How did you manage that?"

"Guys with guns. Guys with helicopters. More guys with guns. It gets repetitive."

Roux gave a displeased grumble. "There are some things, girl, that are not meant to be lost."

Frustration chafed at Annja. It often did when she had to answer to Roux. Since she'd left the orphanage, since she'd graduated college, she hadn't had to answer to anyone the way she felt compelled to when working with—or was that for—Roux.

"It was in a grave for a hundred and thirty years before I found it last night. I'd say that was pretty lost."

"Misplaced. Now, with the belt plaque in the hands of someone else, it's lost. Do you intend to try to get it back?"

Annja recalled the cold way Huangfu Cao had executed the three young men at the gravesite. Crossing his path again was going to be risky. Even more so when it was on his home turf. She hoped there was a way around that.

"No," she said.

The irritation in Roux's voice grew stronger. "Why not?"

"The men who took it were very determined to kill me."

"Upon occasion, I'd find that understandable, but not acceptable. Do you know who took it?"

"I'm working on that."

"Do you mean to say that you not only lost that belt plaque, but you don't know who took it, either?"

"He lied to me about his name. Actually, there was a lot he lied to me about."

"And you bought into his lies?"

"Everybody, it seems, lies to me." Annja leaned back in the seat. The driver, Joe, listened to her every word. They'd been sharing a pleasant conversation, trading stories, up until Roux called.

"I seem to recall a few you've told me," she said.

"I'm better at it than most."

Annja bit her tongue.

"What are you going to do when you find this man and the people he works for?" Roux asked.

"I don't know." The answer was honest. Annja lacked the funds to travel whenever and wherever she wished. *Chasing History's Monsters* didn't pay *that* well, and with China involved, visas would have to be arranged.

"It sounds to me that you've rather botched this," Roux stated.

"Thanks for the post-game summary." Annja knew she sounded angry but didn't care. "I didn't know you had a vested interest in this."

"I don't."

"Now *that* is a lie."

Roux cursed and Annja knew she should have been offended, but she actually felt like laughing. "And the game's not over," she said.

Roux was silent for a moment. "What do you mean?"

"I've got digital images of the inscription on the back

of the belt plaque. I intend to find out what's written there." Annja hung up but held on to the phone.

Joe glanced over at her. "Talkin' to your dad?"

Annja thought about that, realizing that the whole story couldn't be told and the relationship she had to Roux was all but impossible to explain. "He's my grandfather."

"Sounds like a tough old bird."

"He is."

"But it sounds like he cares about you."

Annja didn't know where Joe had gotten that idea. The phone rang again. Checking to make sure it was a Paris exchange again, she answered.

"You hung up."

"You were being rude."

Roux took a deep breath and let it out. "We should meet."

"Why?"

"Because there is something that I—" Roux paused. "Because there is something that I want to find that is connected with that belt plaque."

"Something of yours?"

"I don't want to go into it."

Annja hung up again. A sign beside the highway announced that they were entering Sacramento's city limits. She knew she didn't have much time.

Joe made a lane change, then turned to her. "Where do you want me to take you?"

That was the question. If she went anyplace public there was a chance she'd be recognized and the police would be called.

"Give me a minute."

Joe smiled. "Waitin' on your grandpa to call back?"

Annja smiled back. "He will." She was starting to doubt herself, though, when the phone finally rang. "Yes."

"That is getting really annoying," Roux said.

"I'm tired of not knowing what I'm dealing with here." Annja stared at the tall buildings in the state's capital. At the moment they were far away, but they were closing in fast. "So far that lack of knowledge got three people killed last night."

Roux's voice was more contrite. "I wasn't aware of that."

"You didn't ask."

"No. I should have. But we need to talk about this. I need to see that inscription."

"Why?" Annja asked.

"Can we talk about this somewhere else? This isn't something that should be gone into over the phone. Not with Homeland Security possibly listening in."

Annja didn't know if the paranoia over Homeland Security was warranted, but she needed help. Roux's desire to talk later and elsewhere provided her with leverage.

"In Brooklyn. At my loft."

Roux agreed without hesitation. "I'm in Paris. I'll book the first flight out."

"I may not be able to make it."

"Why?" Sharp suspicion edged Roux's words.

"I'm in California at the moment. I'm also wanted by the police."

"Don't tell me you killed someone." Roux sounded exasperated.

"I think so, but that's not why I'm wanted by the police."

"Then why?"

"I'm a person of interest."

"A suspect?"

"They're not calling it that."

Roux cursed again, but it was gentler and not directed at her. "You want to leave California without being apprehended."

"Unless you want to talk to me in jail where I'm being held as a material witness to crimes I can't explain."

"Where are you?" he asked.

Annja hesitated just a moment, thinking about Doug and how he might have been about to turn her in to the police. You don't have a choice at this point, she thought. "In Sacramento."

"Find a public place to be for the next few hours. A mall or something like that. I'll have someone meet you who can get you back to Brooklyn."

"Okay."

"I'll meet you there. If something comes up, let me know."

Annja said she would, and she felt grateful but knew she wasn't going to mention it and he wasn't going to expect her to. That was just how things worked between them, and she thought it was because both of them were used to being solitary people. Garin Braden wasn't like that. He was more social. But so were predators that preyed on their own kind.

"He's gonna help you?"

Annja glanced over at Joe. "Yes. He has a friend who's going to get me out of Sacramento."

Joe grinned. "Sounds like you know a lot of outlaws."

Annja laughed. "I guess maybe I do."

"He must care an awful lot about you to do something like that."

He just wants to see the inscription. That realization hurt Annja a little before she could get it walled away quickly enough. Whatever her relationship was with Roux, it was based on information and skill, not affection.

She'd learned as a child that she couldn't allow herself to be vulnerable. She had the distinct impression that Roux had learned the same lessons.

But where? And how long ago?

"MISS CREED?"

Startled, Annja looked up at the man addressing her. She sat on a bench with her notebook computer across her knees.

The man was in his late thirties or early forties, a squared-off, compact man of average height. He wore jeans, a golf shirt, dark sunglasses, and a lightweight jacket.

After Joe had dropped her at a truck stop and wished her well, Annja had thanked him and caught a cab to the closest mall. She'd welcomed the air-conditioning, and the book store had taken her mind off things for a bit.

"You don't know me, Miss Creed. Mr. Roux sent me."

Hearing Roux's name that way sounded alien to Annja's ear.

"I'm supposed to escort you back to New York." The man looked at Annja through his dark lenses, but the way he held his head told her that he also watched the mall traffic. "If you're ready."

"I am." Annja closed down the files she'd been reading, put the computer away, then slung the backpack over one shoulder and stood.

The man stepped back and nodded. "This way,

please. I've got a car and driver outside. We'll go through the Macy's exit."

"Sure." Annja started walking. The man fell into step just behind her and to her right. "Do you have a name?"

"Call me Ishmael," he said with a straight face.

Annja shot him a look. "Your idea or Roux's?"

The man's lips twitched a little. "I'm known for my humor."

"I'll just bet you are. How long have you known Roux?"

"Not to be rude, Miss Creed, but that topic isn't open to discussion."

Somehow Annja had known it wouldn't be.

17

"Hey, lady."

Stepping out of the car Tse Chu-yu arranged for her, Kelly looked over at the three adolescent boys sitting in the alley where she'd parked. They looked scruffy and ill-kept, but that was the neighborhood.

She was near the junction of Julu Lu and Changshu Lu, both streets that offered a tour of the wilder side of Shanghai. Girly bars lined the streets, their neon signs bright and harsh against the dark night. It was a place her father had never allowed her to go, but she had occasionally gone with girlfriends wanting to meet the gangster boys.

"That's not a safe place to park your car." The oldest of the three sat on an empty crate and smoked a cigarette. His gaze looked dead and cold, far older than his years. "This alley is private property."

"Is it?" Kelly acted like she hadn't known. But she knew exactly what was going on. A lot of the neighborhood boys rented out "protection" to civilian vehicles.

"If I could find the property owner, maybe we could come to some arrangement," Kelly suggested.

The boy's brow wrinkled. "What do you mean?"

"I could rent this space for a couple hours."

Features brightening, the boy nodded. "Sure. You could do that. You could pay us to watch your car while you're gone."

"How much?" Kelly haggled over the price for only a moment. The money didn't matter, but if she didn't haggle the boys might think she was trying to protect something valuable inside the car. They agreed on the price in short order and she paid it. "Where can I find the Revolver Club?" she asked.

The tallest of the boys counted the money, made the split, and nodded to the right. "Take a right. Five doors down. You can't miss it. It has a picture of a big gun."

THE REVOLVER CLUB did feature a large pistol as part of its neon plumage. The image was engraved in electric blue and glowing black tubes. Bullet tips showed in the cylinders.

This part of Shanghai had held a Western flavor as long as Kelly could remember, but she thought it had changed during the time she'd been gone. The English, French, and Americans had maintained an influence in the city since the early 1800s, and the youth—and the criminal element—had always reached out to emulate them.

A doorman stood guard at the club's entrance in the foyer. He grinned at Kelly, revealing betel-nut stained teeth.

She'd dressed like a party girl, bright red wig that was clearly artificial, cream-colored Capris and a revealing top. She didn't carry a pistol. If she needed one, she figured there would be plenty inside.

After she paid the entrance fee, she walked inside. The club was longer than it was wide. A dance platform supported two exotic dancers who looked enough alike to have been twins or at least sisters. They were dressed like high school cheerleaders, complete with pom-poms, then disrobed in record time to the grinding beat of industrial metal music.

A long bar filled the back of the club. Tables and chairs filled the empty space between the bar and the stage. Even though the club featured exotic dancers, almost as many women were in the bar as men.

According to Tse Chu-yu, the Razor Claws hung out at the Revolver Club. Kelly didn't know if the man who'd escaped her father's house was there, but she had to go. The bag of bones her father had left her had offered no clues, and Ngai Kuan-Yin was too well protected.

Kelly went to the bar and ordered a drink. The music was so loud she barely heard the bartender. Swaying to the music, she kept watch over the crowd in the long mirror behind the bar.

In less than two minutes, a guy hit on her.

"Let me buy you a drink." The man was young, in his early twenties, with slicked back hair. He wore slacks and a good shirt.

"I have a drink." Kelly held hers up to show him.

"I'll buy you the next one. Maybe we can talk a little."

Kelly looked at his hands, noting the tattoos that showed across his knuckles. "I'm not looking for talk. I just stopped in for a drink."

The guy made an exaggerated production of

snapping a cigarette from a pack and lighting it. Smoke wreathed his head and he squinted.

"You didn't dress like someone who came in here just for a drink."

Kelly turned to him and smiled. "Maybe you're right. Is there a place we can be alone?"

Grinning, the man nodded. "My gang runs this bar." He took her by the hand.

Controlling her immediate reaction to free herself and possibly break his arm or dislocate his shoulder, Kelly allowed him to lead her away from the bar to a small stockroom in the back. The man became aggressive at once, reaching for her like an animal.

Kelly hit the guy in the throat with the Y between her thumb and forefinger, just hard enough to paralyze his throat for a moment, but not to kill. Sliding behind him, she wrapped an arm around his neck and shut off blood flow. His brain shut down in seconds and he collapsed into a loose-limbed heap.

As she searched him, Kelly watched the slow, rhythmic rise and fall of his chest that reassured her he was unconscious, not dead.

Her search turned up a 9 mm pistol with a full magazine. She made certain a round was under the hammer and that the weapon was double-action. She crossed to the door and locked it.

Looking around, she found an electrical cord sitting on one of the metal shelves. Working quickly, she tied her captive's hands behind his back, then tied his feet together.

A quick search of the shelves turned up a bottle of astringent pine-scented cleaner. She shoved her finger into the bottle and wet it with the cleaner, then traced a line under the unconscious man's nose.

He woke, jerking his head and cursing.

Kelly rapped him between the eyes with the pistol just hard enough to claim his attention. He focused on her, then lay still.

She squatted beside him. "I'm looking for someone."

He cursed at her.

Calmly, Kelly shoved the pistol's barrel into his ear. The man shut his mouth and glared at her.

"The man I'm looking for killed an old man over in the Bund this morning." Kelly remained calm and dispassionate. "The murder was arranged by Ngai Kuan-Yin."

He started to speak.

She silenced him by laying the pistol against his lips. "If you tell me you don't know who this man is, I'll kill you instead of him."

The man stared at her for a moment, then nodded slowly.

"Tell me his name."

"Meng. His name is Meng."

"Is he here?" Tse Chu-yu had told Kelly that the Razor Claws kept back rooms in the bar.

"No."

"Where can I find him?"

"In the Birdcage. It's a bar. Two blocks north. You can't miss it."

Taking a bar towel from a stack on the shelf, Kelly shoved it into the man's mouth and tied it in place with the electrical cord. She took an apron from the shelves, too, and folded the pistol in the material. Then she left the room and locked the door behind her. None of the club's patrons paid any attention.

LESS THAN TEN MINUTES LATER, Kelly walked toward the front door of the Birdcage. With the pistol tucked into the apron and vengeance burning through her, she approached the entrance.

The doorman stepped in front of her. "Where are you going?"

"I have to cover a shift." Kelly hoped she sounded tired and frustrated enough. Adrenaline slammed through her.

The man didn't move.

"I can go home." Kelly turned and started to go.

"Wait." The man stepped away. "You're new?"

Kelly nodded.

"Tell them to send me a drink."

"Okay." Kelly went inside. She knew the clock was working against her. At any moment someone could discover the man she'd left tied up at the Revolver Club.

The Birdcage actually had two ornate six-foot bird-cages hanging from the low ceiling. Women in garish costumes gyrated in the birdcages. Black light strobed the walls, illuminating dragons, tigers, and other mythical creatures from legend.

Kelly swept the bar with her gaze and recognized Meng immediately. He was sitting at a circular back table. He had two young women seated on either side of him. All of them were laughing, but only Meng was talking.

Keeping the pistol covered in the apron, Kelly made her way around the dance floor to Meng's table. He was young and thin. His black hair hung to his shoulders. He wore slacks and a nice turtleneck under a red leather jacket. The young women fawned on him, both of them barely clad.

Kelly sat across the table from Meng. She kept her hands below the table and held the pistol in her right hand. She had no intention of letting Meng live, not after the hard way her father had died.

Her father's memory had haunted her the whole afternoon she'd spent at Tse Chu-yu's boat. The old man had tried to get her to calm down and sleep, but Kelly hadn't been able to. There were a number of ghosts in her past—some she had killed and some she had been unable to save, and with her father's murder only hours old, she hadn't been able to escape any of them. They had haunted her, bringing confusion and despair. She'd clung to thoughts of vengeance.

Gradually, despite the feminine distraction, Meng's attention turned to Kelly. He frowned, and his eyes were bleary from intoxication.

"Do I know you?"

The two women turned scathing glances on Kelly, resenting her presence.

"You killed my father this morning."

Meng tried to get to his feet. Kelly planted a foot in the middle of his groin and kicked him back against the seat. He groaned in pain. The women drew back.

Kelly revealed the 9 mm she'd taken, showing the muzzle just above the table's edge. "If you go for a weapon, I'm going to kill you. Keep your hands on the table where I can see them."

The man did as he was told.

Kelly didn't look at the women. "Leave us," she ordered.

Gathering their things, the women left. Kelly knew there was no guarantee that they wouldn't run straight to the club's security or other Triad members.

"Who sent you to kill my father?"

"You're in way over your head," Meng replied.

"I'm not the one about to die at this table if he doesn't start talking."

Meng grimaced and cursed.

"You don't have much time." Kelly tracked the progress of the young women as they made their way across the club. "Once they stop to talk to someone, if you haven't answered my questions, I'm going to kill you."

"Ngai sent us." Meng spoke rapidly. Sweat rolled down his face from the alcohol and the fear inside him. His hands trembled on the table.

"To kill my father?"

"No. We were supposed to find something. The old man—" Meng stopped himself. "Your father wouldn't cooperate. But I wasn't the one who tortured him or killed him."

"What were you supposed to find?"

The young women still hurried through the dance crowd, glancing back frequently.

"Some kind of bag. It was supposed to have bones or something in it."

"How did Ngai know about the bag?"

"I don't know. We're not told everything."

Kelly believed him. He was too afraid of her to lie. "What were you supposed to do with the bag?"

"Give it to Ngai."

The young women stopped by the door and hesitated. Kelly knew they were deciding between fleeing for their own lives or trying to help Meng. If he was just business for them it would have been in their best interests to flee. They didn't. Instead, they headed toward the bar, evidently spotting someone they knew.

"Don't kill me." Meng's voice cracked. "I can tell you something else."

"Quickly." Kelly knew there was a back way out of the club.

"Ngai is also interested in work being done out at Loulan City."

Kelly wasn't aware of the place, but something twitched in her memory. "What work?"

"The government has an archaeological team out there. Some guy named Hu is in charge. They're looking for something Ngai is interested in."

"What?"

"I don't know."

The young women talked to three men at the bar and pointed wildly in Kelly's direction.

For just a moment, Kelly was undecided about whether or not to kill Meng. She kept remembering how her father's body had looked, speaking volumes about the torture he'd undergone in the final minutes of his life.

Killing Meng would have been easy. She'd learned to kill strangers without hesitation. She had personal reasons to execute Meng.

Instead, she chose not to. She'd come to China to get away from the killing. She'd already killed two men that morning, and threatened others.

And you already have enough people who want to kill you.

Without a word, Kelly stood, concealed the 9 mm in the folds of the apron again, and left the table. The three men from the bar muscled their way across the dance floor. Their hands slid beneath their jackets for weapons they carried.

The loud techno music reverberated across the room, filling the club with sound. The women in the birdcages whirled and danced. Then the crowd on the dance floor suddenly parted before the three advancing men.

Meng stood, looking wild-eyed and afraid. Kelly knew he was torn between acting to reclaim his sense of honor in front of his fellow gangsters or self-preservation. He went for the pistol at the back of his pants.

Still on the move, Kelly pointed her pistol at him as he brought his own weapon up. He fired twice, hurrying both shots, and struck people on either side of Kelly. She paused, took deliberate aim, and shot Meng between the eyes.

The Triad member's head snapped back, splaying his long hair, and he collapsed, overturning the table on his way down.

The crowd dropped to the floor, screaming and wrapping their heads in their arms.

Kelly ran, vaulting over patrons as she made for the club's back door. She hit the panic bar and crashed through, emerging into the dark alley. She got her bearings, looking at both ends of the alley and the streets beyond, then ran.

The Triad gunmen didn't reach the alley until Kelly was already turning the corner. They fired at her, the bullets going wide and striking a passing car and the buildings across the street. The car veered into another and created an immediate traffic snarl.

Kelly kept running, putting more distance between herself and her pursuers. She had a direction now, though she didn't know what connection the archaeological dig at Loulan City had to Ngai. She intended to find out.

18

Annja woke in darkness and knew at once she was on a plane by the constant hum around her and the sensation she was falling.

Falling!

There was no doubt about it. Her stomach whirled in protest. She sat up and made a frantic grab for her computer as it threatened to tumble from her lap. Almost at the same moment the falling sensation abated.

"It's all right, Miss Creed." The man who had picked her up at the mall sat on the other side of the private jet Roux had arranged for her. "Just a minor bit of turbulence."

"We lost altitude."

Ishmael nodded. He was reading a copy of *Scientific American*. "I'd guess about a thousand feet or so. We hit a major storm system a few minutes ago."

The jet bucked and twisted violently.

Lifting the window cover, Annja peered out at the

night. White-hot lightning blazed through the violet sky, then everything went black.

"The pilot's getting clearance to get us up out of this." Ishmael sounded totally calm.

"I didn't figure you for the *Scientific American* type. No offense."

Ishmael smiled. "None taken. Are you hungry? There's a small galley aboard. Surely we can find something."

Annja discovered she was very hungry. "How long have I been asleep?"

"A few hours. We've got a couple more hours till we reach New York." Ishmael closed his magazine and unbuckled his seat belt. "I'm going to eat. Would you like anything?"

"Sure." Annja freed herself and stood.

Then, almost like flicking a switch, the jet smoothed out. Her stomach muscles unclenched a little. She enjoyed flying, but the thought of crashing in a plane scared her. It was the lack of control, the inability to act to save herself, that caused that fear and she knew it.

"So what do you read about in *Scientific American?*"

Ishmael took out a bottle of white wine and showed it to her. "Emerging technology."

Annja nodded at the wine. "What field interests you?"

Ishmael poured the wine into a glass. The liquid carried a faint ruby tint. "Anything to do with information systems and covert security."

"Spy toys," Annja said.

Smiling, Ishmael took a bottled beer for himself. "You could call it that."

"You're a bodyguard?"

"Sometimes."

"And when you're not?"

"I'm something else."

"All for Roux?"

"Mr. Roux employs me upon occasion. So do others. I've reached a point in my life that I work pretty much for who I want to work with."

They returned to the main cabin and ate.

A FEW MINUTES LATER, ISHMAEL took out his cell phone and took a call. When he was finished he looked at Annja, who was looking over her notes about the belt plaque.

"That was Mr. Roux."

"He didn't want to speak to me?" Annja was surprised.

"He wanted you to know he is going to arrive a couple hours after we get you home. He suggested you wait for him there."

"Suggested? That doesn't sound like Roux. He's more the type to tell people what to do," Annja said.

Ishmael shrugged and smiled a little. "Perhaps I'm more diplomatic than he is."

"Did Roux tell you to keep me there?" Annja asked.

"No."

"Why not?"

"Because that's not something he can pay me to do."

"And he knows that?"

"Yes."

Annja looked at the man. During the whole time she'd been around him, she hadn't picked up anything on him other than he was courteous, professional, and dangerous. She'd seen examples of the first two, but the third was an educated guess made from the way he moved and the way he watched everything.

"Can I get you another beer?" Annja reached for his empty bottle.

"That would be great." Ishmael took time to wipe the bottle free of fingerprints with his napkin, then handed it to her.

Annja grimaced. She'd intended to hide the bottle and smuggle it off the plane in her backpack. Bart McGilley could have run the prints for her.

"Mr. Roux mentioned that you were tricky. He told me about some coin you'd lifted his fingerprints from when you met in France."

Annja shrugged. Then she went to get more wine and another beer for Ishmael.

Giving up learning anything useful from Ishmael, she turned to her computer. She discovered another post from her contact.

I've been searching all over for more information about that legend associated with the belt plaque you posted. Haven't been able to find much more, so don't be disappointed. I'm still looking.

Annja read over the posting a second time and was disappointed. She'd been hoping for a new lead to chase. She was wondering what to do next when an instant message box suddenly popped up on the computer screen. It was from the Web site poster.

Are you online?

Annja responded immediately. Yes.

I was about to post, saw you online and thought I'd IM instead. Okay?

It's okay. I appreciate everything you're doing. This thing has been hard to research, Annja typed.

That's probably because you're going through regular history and archaeological sites to try to find answers.

Annja knew that was true. I am.

I'm not. I've been noodling around in conspiracy sites, myths, and lore. Not exactly factual material.

It was precisely the kind of research *Chasing History's Monsters* did. Annja sighed in displeasure. No matter how much she hated it, when a researcher went back far enough, there wasn't much that separated fact from fiction. Lore was an odd combination of "accepted as fact" truths and things half-remembered. Sorting through that kind of material was challenging.

I didn't go there, she responded.

I thought not. It's not everybody's cup of tea. Do you know who the Penglai are?

Annja thought for a moment, coming up with only wisps of a clue. I think it's a city.

There is a city, but the city took its name from a myth about Penglai Mountain. That's where the Eight Immortals were supposed to live. They were thought to be based on eight wise men and wise women. All of them were supposed to be forces of good.

Penglai Mountain has existed as a myth since the Qin Dynasty.

That puts us at two hundred and fifty years B.C. Annja thought. But Annja knew the time frame also tied in to the Scythian art.

Emperor Qin Shi Huang sent several explorers looking for Penglai Mountain. The land was supposed to be totally white. Palaces were supposed to be made of platinum and gold. Jewels were supposed to grow on trees. And, of course, there was supposed to be the elixir of life that prevented anyone from growing old.

I can understand how Emperor Qin could have been motivated, Annja typed.

So can I. But you can find that information nearly anywhere. The thing that interested me was the theory of the Ninth Immortal.

I'm intrigued, but I don't know how it ties in with the belt plaque.

Supposedly while Emperor Qin's warriors were out searching, they sailed through a treacherous storm and ended up on a beach of white sand. After exploring for a time, they discovered they were on an uncharted island.

Or they could have been mixed up and simply been lost, Annja thought, her natural cynicism kicking in.
Any palaces of gold or platinum? she typed.

No, but they did find what some people believe was the Ninth Immortal. The other Eight Immortals are viewed as forces of good.

Heroes, Annja responded.

Exactly. This one wasn't a hero. Everybody wanted to forget about him. This one was a villain.
This one was Death.

19

A chill ghosted through Annja and lightning flickered in the dark mass of clouds just below the jet. For a moment the computer screen was too bright to see. The message continued.

The legend was that the survivor was Death. The warriors found him in a shipwreck just off the coast. They rescued him and took him back with them. When he regained consciousness, he claimed to have been the only survivor of the ship, and that he was a merchant.

Was he the only survivor? Annja asked.

No one else was found. Anyway, Emperor Qin's warriors took this guy back to the mainland and took him to the emperor's court. This guy called himself Sha Wu Ying, which means Dancing Shadow of Death.

Meaning what? Annja asked.

Meaning he was an assassin. Maybe the best ever. He offered his services to Qin and proved his worth by killing two of the emperor's enemies. I've only found a few stories about this guy, but they all agree that he was dangerous.

What happened?

Gradually, his fame grew. He decided to take on other clients, or maybe he had a love affair going on with one of the emperor's wives. I've found stories that suggest both. Emperor Qin tried to have him killed.

That didn't work out?

No. Have you read how Qin died?

Annja pulled up another folder and reviewed her notes. Reading through them, she was surprised. He died from taking mercury.

Right. Qin was obsessed with death. He kept sending people out looking for the elixir of life. Supposedly his court physician was giving him "immortality" pills. Historians figured they were mercury. But what if Sha Wu Ying arranged for the court physician to give Qin mercury knowing it would kill him?

It's a fact that Emperor Qin was the target of several assassins.

There was a guy named Zhang Liang who became the most dedicated assassin after Qin.

Zhang had to flee the emperor's wrath. While he was running he met an old man who gave him a book. Supposedly, Zhang used the techniques in the book while he served as military advisor to Liu Bang and helped establish the Han Dynasty.

But what does that have to do with my Scythian belt plaque? Annja asked.

Suppose instead of an old man giving the book to Zhang, it was actually Sha Wu Ying?

Is there anything to indicate that's true?

Nothing factual. But look at the evidence. Sha Wu Ying was a trained assassin. Probably means he had military experience, too. Zhang got that book on military strategy from someone. Someone who had reason not to want Qin in power.

Doesn't mean it was Sha Wu Ying, Annja wrote.

I know. Forgive me. My head's just buzzing with this stuff. I love it.

Annja knew the feeling, but she was frustrated that her initial mystery seemed to be growing exponentially.

From what I've been able to read between the lines, Sha Wu Ying became the head of a criminal cabal

located on the Silk Road. His name became synony-
mous with death.

And he founded an assassin's cult that hired out
to warlords and lords of the court. Their symbol was
the tiger carved on that belt plaque.

Can you send me your research? Annja asked.

Sure. I'd be happy to. Maybe you can do more with
it than I can. At this point, I'm stuck. If something else
breaks, I'll let you know.

Annja logged off the page and opened her e-mail
server to wait for the arrival of the documents at the
address she'd given the anonymous poster. Her mind
buzzed with everything she'd discovered.

Why would Huangfu Cao want a belt plaque that might
be connected to an assassins' cult? Was it a valuable
artifact in its own right? Did the mysterious inscription
on the back hold something more than just the curse?

She set the computer aside while she returned to the
galley for a bottle of water. One thing was certain—she
hadn't yet found out everything she needed.

"WE'RE ON THE GROUND NOW."

Annja looked up from the computer screen. She'd
been going over the notes the poster had sent her. There
weren't any real facts in the papers, just conjecture and
supposition.

Ishmael stood in the aisle and looked at her.

Blinking, realizing only then what the man had said,
Annja looked out at the tarmac. Bright sunlight beat

down on the hangars and runways. They weren't at La Guardia. She didn't know where they had landed.

I don't even know if I'm in New York. The realization exploded inside her. She'd been accepting everything Ishmael had told her.

"Are you feeling all right, Miss Creed?" Ishmael looked at her with concern.

"Where are we?" Annja shut down the computer and stowed it in her backpack. Fatigue ate into her bones. She wanted a shower and at least six hours in a real bed.

"Long Island. A private airstrip."

"Why did we land here?"

"In case anyone was looking for you at La Guardia."

"Is anyone looking?" Annja asked.

"I've been tracking the story coming out of California. Sheriff Barfield would still like to talk to you, but the story has died down. I don't think anyone here will be looking for you."

Annja followed Ishmael to the door, then down the steps.

"Mr. Roux arranged a driver to take you back to Brooklyn, Miss Creed." On the tarmac, Ishmael guided her toward the car. "He's also offered accommodations at any hotel you'd care to stay at if you don't feel safe returning home."

"That's fine. I'd rather be home." Her work often kept her from home. She liked being there when she could be.

Ishmael opened the rear door of the waiting limousine and put her inside. "Good luck, Miss Creed."

"You're not coming?"

Ishmael hesitated. "Would you like for me to?"

"No. I mean, I'm fine. I appreciate you taking care of me."

"Mr. Roux told me you were independent."

"I am. I actually figured I'd have to fight with you to get any privacy."

Ishmael smiled and shook his head. "Not this time. It's been interesting meeting you."

"Likewise."

Ishmael closed the door, then spoke briefly with the driver and told him Annja's address in Brooklyn. He stood and waved as the limousine slid into motion.

20

Annja sat in one of the chairs at the dining table and watched Roux. The old man stood at the stove and worked in his shirtsleeves with a confident air. His jacket hung from one of the dining room chairs.

The aroma of food filled the loft and whetted Annja's appetite. As he worked, Annja related the story Sha Wu Ying.

"Do you believe this person actually existed?" Roux asked.

"The belt plaque is real."

"The story about the City of the Sands could just be a fable."

"Maybe. But you seem to be very interested in it," Annja said.

Roux covered the skillet full of meatballs and turned his attention to the sauce simmering in another pan.

Knowing he wasn't going to respond, Annja plunged ahead. "I was told that the carving on the belt plaque might tie in with a group of assassins that lived along the Silk Road. Warriors that Sha Wu Ying trained."

Roux snorted. "Sha Wu Ying's 'warriors' were more thieves than assassins."

"You seem to know a lot about them."

"I do." Roux picked up his wine glass and gave the skillet a shake.

"How long did you know Sha Wu Ying?" Annja thought the question was worth a try.

"I never met him." Roux looked troubled. "But I've heard of him." Going to the refrigerator, he took out the bag of salad and poured it into a bowl. He started to set the table.

Annja got up and took over, placing plates and silverware on the table. "What do you know that I don't?" she asked.

Roux hesitated. "Sha Wu Ying built a city in the desert around Loulan City. I'd heard it was called City of the Sands, and it was reportedly filled with thieves."

"Have you been there?"

"No. It was lost. The desert reclaimed many things men had built out there. Civilizations were swallowed whole."

"But the City of the Sands did exist?"

"Yes. And several others besides. Most of them have had their bones picked clean by those who struggled to stay there and survive, but some are still there. Somewhere. Buried under tons of sand."

"And the stories about Sha Wu Ying are true?"

Roux shook the skillet again to roll the meatballs, then dropped spaghetti into boiling water. "Some of them are true."

"What about the one that says Sha Wu Ying was immortal?"

"I've never met a man who was immortal."

Annja shot him a glance filled with doubt. "Oh, *really.*"

"I'm not immortal," Roux stated firmly, indicating the subject was closed.

"What happened to Sha Wu Ying?" Annja asked.

Roux shrugged. "I don't know. I'd heard he was killed."

"By whom?"

"Do you know what a fox spirit is?"

Annja nodded.

"By one of those."

"Oh." Annja filed that away for reference. She needed to take a look at the fox spirit myth again to see if there was anything she'd missed.

"Are you sure the City of the Sands was near Loulan?" Roux asked.

"Yes. I've studied what little he's written about the area."

"Then why hasn't more been written?"

"Are you familiar with Chinese history?"

Roux nodded.

"Then you know the Qin Dynasty preceded the Han Dynasty."

"Yes."

"Emperor Qin was an ambitious man. He came to power when he was thirteen years old, then he set out to conquer the rest of China. At the time there were seven states that constantly warred and fought for trade. Qin created a massive army and led them into battle. Under the rules of warfare at the time, enemy prisoners were supposed to be taken care of. After one of the battles, Qin's army had ten thousand warriors to care for. He knew that would only slow them down while they raced across the countryside. He executed one of the prisoners himself, telling his men there would be no more prisoners. They killed their enemy to a man after that."

"He changed the face of warfare in China," Roux said.

Annja nodded.

"Being totally ruthless is, sometimes, the only way to win."

"If you want to destroy something, yes."

"You always want to destroy your enemy if there's a chance he'll rise up and put a dagger into your back."

Then why haven't you killed Garin? The question came to Annja's mind but she didn't ask it. She knew she wouldn't get an answer. Despite the enmity that existed between the two men, she'd sensed there still remained some shadow of the mentor/student relationship that had been there first.

"After Qin died in 210 B.C., he was succeeded by his second son."

"The first son died?" Roux asked.

"Fusu, the eldest son, was ordered by his father's will to commit suicide to make way for the second son, Huhai."

"Why did Qin want his second son to rule?"

"He didn't. The Imperial Secretariat, Li Si, conspired with the chief eunuch Zhao Gao to alter the emperor's will. They wanted Huhai to take control of the country because they could manipulate him. They stripped command from the army leader and had his family killed. They continued alienating the country until uprisings started."

"Sounds like a recipe for failure," Roux said. "So the peasants revolted against Huhai."

Annja nodded. "Zhao Gao forced Huhai to commit suicide—"

"I guess if you've got a winning strategy, you stay with it."

"It didn't help. He had Ziying, Fusu's oldest son, named as emperor and tried to win the people over. But it was too late. And Ziying had other plans. He killed Zhao Gao and surrendered the throne to Liu Bang, the general who had risen up to command the army against the emperor. But there was another general who wanted to be king."

Roux scowled. "There always is. Unless you kill everybody that's got any kind of ambition."

"This general's name was Xiang Yu. After Ziying surrendered to Liu Bang, Liu Bang was going to appoint Ziying as prime minister because he was strong, had killed Zhao Gao, and was liked by many people. Xiang killed Ziying, then burned the Qin palace to the ground. That included the royal library where—presumably—several royal histories were kept."

Roux gestured to the food he'd prepared and served while Annja told her story. "Eat. Before it gets cold."

Annja did even though she was brimming with questions. She knew from experience that it wouldn't have done any good to ask them. Roux wouldn't answer until he was ready to. And even then she might not get the truth.

21

"Professor Hu. Do you have a minute?"

Grateful for the interruption, Professor Michael Hu put down the small shovel he was using and glanced up from the sweltering heat of the pit. His back ached from sustained, meticulous effort.

He was thirty-five years old, dressed in sweat-drenched khakis caked in dust and dirt. He was lean and muscular. He knelt on the loose planks he and the other workers in the pit used as a platform to keep them above the ground where they labored.

Buckets held the meager finds they'd discovered. Most of it was junk, not at all what they were looking for, but it would still require cataloguing and might provide some information.

Song Xin, the young graduate student in charge of the computers and files, peered down at him. Xin was slightly built and looked clean beside the rest of the people in the pit with Hu.

"What is the matter?" Hu took his glasses off and cleaned them with a handkerchief.

"I have something you should see." Song offered a hand up.

Hu hesitated. He'd been so hopeful at the start of the dig. Now, he was beginning to believe that Loulan City's bones had been picked almost clean.

Leaning against the dirt embankment, Hu caught Song's hand, then scrambled up the side as the younger man pulled. Out of the hole, the heat seemed greater. The desert sun burned down on them ferociously, and the wind sucked the moisture from his body. In seconds he felt like he was baking.

Canvas tents were set up beyond the dig site. The ancient city of Loulan had existed on the western banks of Lop Nur, the cluster of seasonal salt lakes and marshland located between the Taklamakan and Kuruktag Deserts. It was the remnants of the mighty postglacial Tarim Lake that had once been there.

In its day, the lake had covered over ten thousand square kilometers. But all that remained of the lake was scars in the form of a helix that was large enough to be seen from space.

A few jeeps and motorcycles shared space with the camels the archaeological team had ridden into the site. With the heat of the desert, as well as other problems, Hu hadn't wanted to depend solely on one means of transportation. Men left out in this unforgiving desert would die in a matter of hours.

Hu followed Song to the tent that housed the crew's communications. Hu had cut deals with several international television agencies to produce shows on things he took from the earth at the dig.

Song sat in front of a computer and pointed at the monitor. "I've been cruising through Web sites like you suggested, looking for any information on Loulan that we might have missed. And talk that might have arisen once people found out we were here."

Shocked at what he was seeing, Hu studied the pictures. "Could you enlarge them a little?"

Song did with a few clicks of the mouse. "This is the image we were looking for, isn't it? The tiger?"

Excitement gripped Hu as he recognized the carving for what it was. "Yes. Where did you get this?"

"One of the archeological Web sites."

"Can you contact the person who posted this?"

Song nodded.

"Do so. I want to speak to them as soon as possible."

Hesitant, Song turned to face him. "You know that Ngai Kuan-Yin is also searching for that tiger."

Hu did.

"The person who posted this may already be working for Ngai."

"If so, we'll soon find out," Hu said.

A moment later, Song turned to him. "It's done."

"Good. Let me know if you get a response." Hu put his hat back on and stepped from the relative coolness of the tent back out into the fetid heat of the desert.

Vultures circled in the sky in the distance, riding the wind.

A chill shook Hu. Something had died out there.

ASTRIDE THE CAMEL, WHICH WAS better suited to the tall sand dunes than the jeeps or the motorcycles, Hu lurched uncomfortably in the saddle. Song rode beside him on another camel.

Two other men, locals Hu had hired to help with the dig, rode camels on either side of them. The locals carried assault rifles. Hu had tried to talk them out of holding the weapons in plain sight, but they had ignored him.

Finally, after a long climb up a shifting sand dune where they had to traverse back and forth across it, Hu reached the ridgeline. He took out a pair of binoculars and gazed at the dark speck lying on the sand.

There was no question the man was dead. He lay in a fetal position, but the carrion birds worked at his corpse with their sharp beaks.

Song stood in his stirrups and shaded his eyes with a hand. "Is it a man?"

"It is." Hu put the binoculars away. "There's no need to hurry." But he wanted to all the same. He knew how quickly the vultures could work.

HU COMMANDED THE CAMEL to kneel. He rocked in the saddle as the big animal lowered itself.

Their arrival had scared away the vultures, but the big, ungainly birds continued to circle in the air above. The dead man was covered in blood, along with a light frosting of dust and dirt.

Yao, the oldest of the two locals, looked ill at ease. He propped his rifle on his saddle horn. "You should not be out here, Professor. You should ignore this."

"I can't just leave someone out here at the mercy of those birds. That's inhuman," Hu protested.

The local looked passive. "Yet you root through the graves of others."

"That's not the same thing."

"If this man were to remain out here for a thousand years, some other archaeologist might find him interesting."

Hu ignored the callousness of the man's words. The local people lived by their fingernails in the desert. Jobs were not plentiful, and the desert was unforgiving. The professor supposed men could learn not to care.

Swinging a leg over the saddle pommel, Hu dropped to the ground. The camel remained still on its folded legs. The smell of death was sharp and pungent. Hu pulled his shirt over his nose but it didn't help. Sickness jumped and jerked in his stomach. Looking at freshly dead men was not the same as looking at skeletons a hundred or a thousand years old.

Hu knelt by the dead man and inspected him the same way he would a find on a dig.

The thing that stood out immediately was that a large section of the back of his head was missing. When Hu studied the man's face, he spotted what looked like a bullet hole above his right eye. Hu only knew about bullet holes because some of the sites he'd worked had been in war-torn lands where dead men had fallen as recently as thirty and forty years ago.

The man had been murdered. Or he'd fought for his life against a foe.

The man wore loose, lightweight clothing. He was clean-shaven, and the nails of the hand that hadn't been savaged by the carrion feeders were clean and smooth. He hadn't been a common laborer. Tattoos showed beneath the sleeve of one arm.

Hu slid the sleeve back, trying to avoid the blood

spatters. The tattoos continued up the man's arms. All of them were interwoven, a tapestry of myths and legends.

"He was a Triad member." Song joined Hu on the ground but didn't come close to the dead man. "Usually if there's one, you'll always find another. They don't work alone."

Hu didn't ask how the younger man knew that. The criminal organization was a temptation to all the teenagers at some point in their lives.

"Let's spread out." Hu walked back to the camel. "Maybe there's someone else out here that needs help."

Hu ordered the others to ride out around the dead man in ever-widening circles. Thirty minutes later, he accepted the fact that if another man had come with the dead man they weren't going to find him.

"Professor."

Tracking the voice, Hu saw Song standing at the mouth of a cave.

Song waved. "I found their camp."

"HOW MANY MEN DO YOU THINK?" Hu crouched as the older local surveyed the base camp.

The camp was simple and stripped down. There were sleeping bags, a couple weeks' worth of supplies, and about the same amount of water. There was no sign of transportation. But there were weapons and a telescope. There was even a radio that had been set to the archaeology base camp's frequency.

"Two men stayed here." Yao surveyed the ground noting the shoe treads. "But someone else brought them here."

"You know that from the shoe treads?"

Yao glanced over his shoulder at Hu. "I know that

because there is too much water here for two men to pack in alone." He nodded at the large plastic containers against the wall.

Song found a flashlight among the supplies and switched it on. The batteries worked. He walked into the back of the cave.

Hu tried to wrap his mind around everything. He kept coming up with the same answer—Ngai Kuan-Yin. The man had sent these men in to spy on him.

But who had killed them? And why?

"Hey!" Song turned around and waved his flashlight. "I've found another guy! He's still breathing!"

Hu went quickly, but Yao slipped his rifle's safety off and took up a position to cover the cave's entrance.

The second man looked like he was in his twenties. He'd been shot in the abdomen and had nearly bled out, judging from the pallor of his features.

"Get the medical kit and some water." Hu knelt beside the man as Song ran for the needed items.

Even from the quick examination he gave the man, Hu didn't hold out much hope for the man's survival. If the wound had been treated early enough, if gangrene hadn't set in, if he hadn't lost so much blood, maybe he could have been saved.

When Song returned with the water, Hu wet a cloth and pressed it against the wounded man's lips. He didn't want to risk having the man aspirate the water and drown.

Abruptly, the man's eyes opened. "You...must... stop...her." He gripped Hu's shirt in his bloody hand.

"You need to relax." Hu tried to free himself from the man's hand but it was fastened like a claw. "We're going to get you to a hospital. Conserve your strength."

"No!" The man turned his head and glanced around wildly. "She's still *here!*"

Concerned that there was yet a third person they hadn't found, Hu leaned close to the man. "Who's still here?"

"The fox spirit." The man shuddered. "The fox spirit did this."

22

Once dinner was finished, Annja did the dishes and put them away. Then she poured them both another glass of wine.

"What do you want from me?" Annja asked.

Roux was quiet for a time, and Annja had begun to think that he wasn't going to answer.

"I need your help in recovering an object," he said quietly.

Annja's heart beat a little faster. Roux had searched for Joan's sword for five hundred years. What else can you be responsible for finding? she wondered. "Why should I help you?"

"Because you want to."

"No, I don't." I want to know what you know, but that isn't the same as wanting to help you. Annja was very clear about that in her own mind.

Roux grimaced. "It's a shame to ruin the digestion of such a good meal."

"My digestion isn't going to be affected." Annja kept her eyes on him.

"Without my help, you can't go to China."

"Who said I wanted to go to China?"

"You did. The instant you set foot on that plane in California."

Annja knew, there was no way to win that argument. "Maybe I can't go right away, but I'm working on getting the show to pay for the trip."

"Oh, really?" Roux looked smug. "Is that why you've been dodging your producer's calls for the last few days?"

Annja knew Roux wouldn't tell her how he knew about that.

"Look, we're both over a barrel here. Otherwise you wouldn't have come to me. Furthermore, I don't even know why I should want to go to China," she said, bluffing.

"To Loulan, more specifically. And you want to go there because the answers are there."

"I don't even know what the questions are."

Roux smiled. "The man who accompanied you to the grave in Volcanoville was hired by a man named Ngai Kuan-Yin. Does that name mean anything to you?"

"No."

"He's a very wealthy businessman. He's well connected in China, England and Canada. He's starting to make some inroads in the United States."

"Ngai wanted the belt plaque?"

Roux nodded.

"Why?"

"Because he believes in the legends of the City of the Sands."

"He thinks there's some kind of treasure there?"

"Oh, I'd be very surprised if there wasn't a treasure there," Roux said.

"Is that why you're interested?"

"No. Getting treasure of any size out of China in this day and age would be problematic. I'm not after treasure. I already have great fortunes that grow more every day."

"Then what are you after?" Annja asked.

"Something that was lost."

"What something?"

"I can't go into that, I'm afraid."

Annja blew out an angry breath. "I'm supposed to drop everything I'm doing and go with you to China?"

"Otherwise I'll go without you."

"Why do you need me?"

Roux was silent for a time. "Because you're an archaeologist, Annja. This is what you do. Your curiosity about the past pushes you forward through your own life."

"You've lived through a lot of those years."

"I have, but that's the problem, you see. I've *lived* through those years. I've not studied them. And I only lived in certain areas. Villages, towns, cities. I know those places, and I was fortunate to meet a few important people over the years. But I don't know history the way you know history."

"You could have learned."

Roux smiled. "My dear girl, I'm far too old to be learning new tricks, and those aren't tricks I'm interested in. I've always been more caught up in my own pursuits and diversions than I have been in the world around me."

"You've been more self-involved, you mean," Annja said.

Roux spread his hands. "Most people are. But you see, that's something that sets you apart from a great deal of other people. That's another reason you and the sword were reunited." He nodded at her glass as he stood. "Can I get you some more wine?"

"No. Thank you." Annja didn't want her wits slowed down by the wine. "There's bottled water in the refrigerator."

Roux replenished his own wine.

Annja accepted the chilled water when Roux handed it to her. She screwed the top off and drank, thinking of ways to get around the old man's reticence to tell her what he was truly after. "It might help if I knew what you're looking for."

"If you find the City of the Sands it will be there or it won't."

"If it exists the city was buried over two thousand years ago."

"I know," Roux said.

"Why didn't you go get it before now?"

"Loulan City died out in the fifth century. Do you know why?"

"No one does."

"Really?" Roux frowned. "Pity. That might have answered some questions I had. Oh, well. The point I was making was that everyone thought that if Loulan had died, so had the City of the Sands."

"Because Sha Wu Ying died?" Annja asked.

"I certainly hope he's dead. While he was alive, he was a lot of trouble."

"What kind of trouble?"

"He interfered with things, and he tried to harness powers that he had no right to." Roux looked at her for a moment, then seemed to waver. "As you know, there are items of incredible power in this world."

Annja found herself almost hypnotized by his words. She knew he was speaking the truth, but she didn't know how she knew.

"Joan's sword—*your* sword now—is one of those tools." Roux peered at her with his blue eyes, and Annja saw a softness in them that wasn't often there. "There were others. It was up to the individual who possessed them to do what he or she wanted to with them. Most have been lost to this world, but a few have been lost *in* it."

"Is that what Sha Wu Ying stole?"

"One such object, yes."

"What is it?" Annja asked.

"It was an object of the greatest evil, Annja." Roux's voice was soft. "More than that, I cannot—dare not—say."

Annja's imagination ran wild for a moment. Throughout all of history, mankind had dreamed of— or remembered—weapons and objects of great power. Excalibur, the philosopher's stone, the Holy Grail and hundreds more.

"Let's just say that I can help you find the City of the Sands. If I do, what are you prepared to do with your mysterious object if it's still there?"

Roux was silent for a moment. "I don't know yet. But I know we have to find it."

"Why?"

"Because Garin is looking for it, too."

23

Kelly Swan sat in the shade of the main tent where the workers came to eat, rest, and replenish their water. She was covered in sand and dirt, and it chafed at her. She wanted a bath and a comfortable bed instead of the thin pallet she'd been assigned.

But she knew that wasn't going to happen for some time.

She also felt naked without a weapon. Especially in the middle of the desert.

Getting into the camp had been easy. After she'd gotten directions in Dunhuang, she'd purchased an Enduro motorcycle and driven to within five miles of the dig. She'd left the motorcycle buried under a tarp that might preserve it if she needed it. She'd buried her weapons just outside of the camp after she'd used them to eliminate Ngai's spies. It would serve as a warning of sorts. She hoped it might even draw Ngai himself.

Then she'd walked into camp and joined the other new

arrivals to the dig. She'd worked all day, learning the backbreaking labor involved with searching for relics.

One thing she had discovered was that no one questioned the labor pool as long as they worked. She worked hard both days she'd been in camp, soaking up information every chance she got while carrying buckets of sand away from the open pits where Professor Hu and his handpicked crew worked.

"Miss Lin."

It took Kelly a moment to remember the name she'd borrowed while in the camp. She looked up at Po, the old man who served as chief among the local population that had been brought in from Dunhuang.

"Yes."

"Do you feel well?" Po was thin and heavily wrinkled from the sun. He wore ill-fitting wraparound sunglasses and a Yankees baseball cap that was at least a size too large for him.

"I'm fine," Kelly said.

Po squatted beside her and clapped a bony hand to her forehead.

Kelly kept from breaking his arm through a sheer effort of will.

"You are very warm." Po removed his hand. "Very warm."

"It's very warm outside."

Po grunted, then handed her another bottle of water. "You keep drinking water. It's a long way to hospital if you get sunstroke."

Kelly uncapped the bottle and drank.

The old man smiled at her, then moved on to check the rest of his troops. He had a position on the dig site more as morale booster than as a laborer. He managed people and made sure the things Professor Hu wanted done were done on time.

A young man ran into the tent. "Professor Hu's coming back. He's bringing a body with him."

Instantly, everyone in the tent rushed out to see. Kelly joined them, knowing what to expect. She'd noticed the vultures gathering that morning.

She shaded her eyes with her hand and watched as the camels plodded toward the camp. Professor Hu was in the lead. A body was slung over the saddle pommel.

"THE PROFESSOR FOUND two men up in the mountains. One of them is still alive."

Worry gnawed at Kelly's stomach. She'd been certain of the kills two nights ago. She didn't see how one of them could have survived. But there had been something in the cave, some kind of vapor that had made her feel woozy. And she'd been running on so little sleep for so long that she was all but exhausted.

Cautiously, she made her way to the front of the line, staying just behind Po.

Professor Hu, his face running with sweat, commanded his camel to kneel. As the large creature did, he held on to the man in front of him. Blood covered the man's midsection.

"Help me." The professor held on to the man.

Men ran forward to ease his burden.

"Gently. He's still alive. I want to keep him that way." Hu lowered the man to a waiting blanket, then ordered the men to help him lift it. They used the blanket to carry the wounded man into the main tent out of the sun.

Kelly stayed outside while the rest of the group went

inside to watch the drama unfold there. She walked to the camel that carried the other man.

There was no doubt of the man's state. The scars left by the vultures marked his fate clearly. Half of his face and one eye had been eaten away. Three fingers of one hand were gone. Huge strips of flesh were missing from his back and legs.

"Do you know him?"

Turning, Kelly was surprised to see that Song, the second in command of the dig, stood beside her. She shook her head. "No. I don't know him."

"Are you sure?" Song stepped closer. "Because for a minute there it looked like you did."

"I've seen dead men before. That's all." Kelly shook her head and tried to look scared. "It's never seemed right."

"I know." Song looked like he might be sick. "Someone murdered this man and tried to kill the other."

"Who?" Kelly knew she had to ask that question. Any normal person would have.

Song sighed. "I don't know." He looked out toward the mountains. "Someone out there. Bandits, maybe."

Professor Hu called for Song from inside the tent. Song looked at her. "It's better not to dwell on something like that."

"I know." Kelly watched him as he turned and went back into the tent. She wondered how long it would be until Ngai discovered his men were dead.

And what he would do.

IN THE BACK SEAT OF THE LUXURY limousine, Ngai Kuan-Yin studied the belt plaque in his hands. He was fascinated and frustrated by his possession of it. As soon as he'd seen its picture online he'd known what it was and pursued it.

But it didn't tell him as much as he'd hoped. The inscription on the back had only confused him. It contained a lament by the original maker that the owner of the belt plaque was cursed. There was also a prayer that was supposed to offset the evils that would plague each generation.

The limo slowed.

Glancing through the tinted window, Ngai saw that he was at the Old Bank of China. Most of his legitimate business was done in those offices.

The two bodyguards seated in front of him moved into position as the luxury car eased to a stop at the curb. Ji Zi, the head of Ngai's security detail, spoke quickly and quietly over his radio. When he was assured everything was ready, he opened the door and stepped out.

Ngai moved out with his bodyguards. As always, he was aware of the vulnerability of being out in the open. If he had been a different way, he might have been resentful of the lifestyle he maintained.

But he wasn't. He loved what he had. He just wanted more. Especially the fortune his ancestor had bought with his treachery, and ultimately his life.

Ngai's bodyguards swept him by the abbreviated landscaped lawn and into the building. Across the foyer, Ji used the specially coded electronic pass key to open one of the private elevators used by the bank officials.

Just as the doors began to close, a large scarred hand slid between them and held them back. The man who owned the hand was over six feet tall. He was broad and fierce looking, with shoulder-length black hair and magnetic black eyes. His goatee was carefully trimmed.

"Mr. Ngai, I mean you no harm." The man spoke flawless Mandarin.

Ji whipped his pistol from under his jacket and pointed it at the tall man's face.

If the man was afraid, he didn't show it. His black eyes held Ngai's. "I know the secret of the belt plaque."

Ngai made his decision in a heartbeat. With such an announcement, there could be only one response. "Do not shoot him."

Ji never moved his pistol, but he didn't kill the man either.

Ngai studied the man for a moment, taking in the elegant Italian suit that had been custom fitted. "Who are you?"

"Garin Braden." The man smiled, showing perfect teeth. "I think you and I are going to be friends."

"What do you want?"

"To become your partner in your quest to find the City of Thieves."

"How do you know about that place?" Ngai asked.

Garin smiled. "I'm a student of history myself. Particularly when it pertains to treasure." He paused. "Is there some place we can talk?"

"I have an office upstairs."

"That would be ideal." Garin started to step inside the elevator.

Ji shoved him back outside. "The eighth floor. We'll meet you there."

Garin hung on to the elevator doors. Ngai knew that the man was on the verge of snapping, and he thought it would have been interesting to see who prevailed in such a situation. Garin seemed as much a warrior as Ji.

"Take your hand back." Ji flicked open a knife with a serrated blade. "Otherwise I will take your hand from you."

A brief, cold smile crossed Garin's lips. Ngai knew if the man had smiled at him in such a manner that he would feel threatened. The expression was as humorless as a shark's grin.

"The eighth floor then." Garin nodded and removed his hand from the doors. He looked at Ji. "Be glad you're working for Mr. Ngai."

The elevators closed.

"Do you know this man?" Ji didn't put his pistol away. He hid it behind his thigh.

"No." Ngai took out his phone and made a quick call. He said only Garin Braden's name.

Instantly the computer researcher on the other end of the line swung into motion. Before the elevator reached the eighth floor, the researcher knew something of Braden.

"Garin Braden is an entrepreneur from Berlin." The man's voice was calm and precise. "He's worth millions."

"Put together a full background check on him. I want it as soon as it's ready," Ngai said.

Ngai hung up and watched the floor counter. Suspicion and hope warred in his mind. The elevator doors opened.

24

Garin didn't go to the eighth floor as he'd been instructed. Orders of any kind irritated him, and his natural course of action was to disobey them. But he did want to meet with Ngai because the man had something he needed.

He just didn't want to appear desperate for it.

After living for five hundred years, he'd learned to be patient—sometimes. The brush-off he'd received from the security man still irked him. Another time, another place, and Garin knew he'd have killed the man for threatening him.

Instead, he put on sunglasses, then went to a small café across the street and ordered a coffee. While he was waiting, he called Ngai on his personal cell phone. The call was meant to throw Ngai off-balance and point out that Garin knew much more about him than he could have guessed.

"What is it?" Ngai sounded irritated.

Garin smiled. There was nothing like being in the

driver's seat. He paid the woman behind the counter and tipped her what probably amounted to a week's pay.

He spoke into the phone. "It's Garin Braden."

"What do you want?" Ngai's voice was harsh, but not too harsh, Garin noted.

Garin took his coffee and walked out to the street again. He gazed up at the tall office building, looking at the windows along the eighth floor. He knew that Ngai could hear the street noise around him over the phone connection. He also knew that the man's offices were in the front of the building.

"I want to talk to you," Garin said.

"An appointment was made."

Garin scanned the windows. A moment later, one of the curtains pulled to the side and he made out the security man's face. Garin hoisted his coffee cup in a salute.

"I'll be along in a minute." Garin sipped his coffee. "Tell your security man he owes me his life."

Ngai hesitated. "What do you mean?"

"If I'd wanted to hurt you, I'd have put a team with a rocket launcher on top of the Peace Hotel. By now, that office would be a fiery pit that would have swallowed you up." Garin sipped his coffee and looked at the Peace Hotel.

The hotel actually consisted of two buildings. The first building had been on the south side of Nanjing Road, and it had been built where the old International Settlement had been. Back when it had been built in the 1850s, it had been known as Central Hotel. Garin had stayed there right after it had opened.

The north building, the one where he would have placed an assault team if he'd been so inclined, had originally been called the Sassoon Building. Sir Victor Sassoon had constructed it in 1926. Garin had stayed there, as well, and had known the baron. The Chinese government had taken over the building in 1956 and renamed it the Peace Hotel. A distinctive green steeple capped the top of the building.

The security man's face disappeared from the window.

"Come up and talk to me," Ngai said.

"No. I don't think so." Garin grinned, knowing he had the man. "If you want to meet, you come see me."

There was a pause. "Where?"

"At the Dragon-Phoenix Restaurant in the Peace Hotel. I'll have a table waiting for us. I'll even buy." Garin closed the phone before Ngai could protest.

Feeling satisfied, Garin walked to the hotel. He already had a table reserved from the time his spy inside Ngai's organization had told him the man's private telephone number.

THE DRAGON-PHOENIX RESTAURANT was one of the tourist attractions at the Peace Hotel. As such, the decor was properly opulent. Circular red tables stood out like large islands against the dark floor. The color scheme was primarily cream and red, and the distinctive dragon and phoenix crest was displayed proudly.

Ngai Kuan-Yin arrived with his entourage only a few minutes after Garin's phone call. The hostess stopped them at the door, chatted briefly, then brought them to Garin's table.

After thanking the hostess, Ngai turned to Garin but didn't sit. "I don't like the way you do business," he stated.

Garin looked up at the man. "You don't have to like it, but you do have to respect it." He turned a hand toward a chair. "Have a seat. You're going to look foolish eating soup while standing."

"I didn't come here to eat," Ngai said.

"No, but by eating you won't draw so much attention."

The late afternoon crowd was sparse, mostly tourists and a handful of businessmen having a late lunch or an early dinner.

Garin smiled. "I'm buying. As an apology for meeting without a proper introduction."

It wasn't much, but it was a gesture to allow Ngai to save face. Usually introductions between two people of power were mitigated through a third party. Garin had purposely skipped that.

Showing obvious reluctance, Ngai sat.

The servers descended upon them, bringing soups and appetizers. They filled glasses with water and with tea.

Ngai's eyes never left Garin's. "What do you want, Mr. Braden?"

"By now you'll have called someone to find out who I am." Garin blew on his soup. "They'll have told you I'm an entrepreneur, and that I also dabble in archaeological collections."

Ngai nodded.

"I know about the belt plaque and I know about the City of Thieves." Garin saw the fear in the man's eyes and knew that Ngai was considering killing him. He thought that it was fair, though. If Garin had had time to get the information on the back of the belt plaque any other way, he'd have killed Ngai.

"Mere fables," Ngai said.

Garin smiled. "Do you think so? You had Suen Shikai killed for the artifact that he held."

"I don't know what you're talking about," Ngai said.

"Of course you don't," Garin continued. "A woman

killed the men who tortured and murdered Suen Shikai. Do you know who she was?"

"No," Ngai replied.

"She was his daughter," Garin stated.

New light dawned in Ngai's eyes.

"Now you understand why the artifact was not at Suen's home," Garin said.

"Suen left it for her."

Garin smiled again. "It's all about legacies in this country. Everyone is someone else's descendant or ancestor."

"Does she have the artifact Suen protected?"

"I believe so. There's a man named Tse Chu-yu. Do you know him?"

"Of course. He is a very dangerous man to cross," Ngai said.

"You knew he was a friend of Suen."

"I did. I never understood what they saw in each other."

"Both of them are fishermen, and they both loved and lost their wives. Sometimes it doesn't take much to bond people." Garin stared into Ngai's eyes and saw that the man had never bonded with anyone. He'd never had to.

Garin still remembered that cold winter morning his father had told him he would be riding away with Roux, that the old man was going to be his new master. *Master,* not father. For years they'd ridden together, and every year Roux swore that he would find some home to send him to, some orphanage that would keep him. And every year they kept riding together.

Then Roux had failed Joan of Arc.

Taking a breath, Garin pushed the memories away. He understood bonds between people in a way Ngai never could. He also knew how to take advantage of them.

"The point is, I believe Kelly Swan has the artifact her father protected."

"Where is she?" Ngai asked.

"Somewhere plotting to kill you, I suppose." Garin smirked at Ngai's discomfort.

The head of Ngai's security team leaned in. "That will never happen. Do you understand?"

Garin ignored the security man. "Do you even know who Kelly Swan is?"

Ngai hesitated. "No."

"She's a trained assassin."

Surprise showed in Ngai's eyes.

"She was trained in the United States." Garin stirred his soup. "By the CIA. She was going to be used in the Asian theater. She's an expert with handguns and a sniper rifle, familiar with demolitions. Very, very patient. Evidently even when the man she most wants to kill has murdered her father."

Ngai looked at his chief of security.

The man never took his eyes from Garin, but his face flushed.

"You can't blame your security chief. He wasn't in a position to know something like that," Garin said.

"It is his job."

"You know, I don't think replacing him right this minute is in your best interests." Garin turned his attention to the soup again.

"What would be in my best interests, Mr. Braden?" Ngai asked.

Garin mentally rubbed his hands together in anticipation. He loved making offers that couldn't be refused. "You make me your partner. For a percentage of the treasure."

"That's unacceptable. This treasure is something that my ancestor—"

"Betrayed and killed his friends for." Garin made his voice harsh. "I already know the story. I probably know more of it than you do." He took another spoonful of soup. "I also know that even if you succeed in finding the City of Thieves, which I doubt because you would have by now if you knew the secret, you won't make it past the dangers that lie ahead of you." He paused. "Your ancestor and the other thieves made the way difficult. Only one path will be clear. I know how to get you there."

Ngai remained quiet.

Garin tapped his watch. "Tick tock. While you're sitting there wasting time, another group—someone who has as much information as I do—is closing in to take that treasure away from you." He leaned back in his chair. "What's it going to be? Are you going to waste this excellent meal trying to find a way out of this? Or do we have a deal?"

25

Annja woke before Roux. Soft morning sunlight hit the loft's windows with rays of pink and gold. She listened intently, hearing the traffic sounds as the city came alive around her. Judging from the amount of light in the room, it was only a little after six. This was her favorite time of the morning.

From a short distance away, she heard Roux lightly snoring. Annja was surprised that he was still there. She wasn't sure how she'd have felt if he'd disappeared.

Because Roux was there, and because she didn't fully trust him, Annja reached into the otherwhere and drew the sword. She felt it hard and certain in her hand for a moment, then she pushed it back.

Sitting up quietly, she looked across to the sofa where Roux slept. She'd let him borrow one of her sleeping bags and a blanket because the building cooled off in the evenings and the temperatures had plunged during the night.

Looking across the street, she saw a fresh layer of

white on the roof. Delighted, Annja got up and looked outside. Her breath fogged the window. She loved winter in the city. Everything looked fresh and new. Of course, it didn't stay that way. The snow would be dirty within hours.

Grudgingly, feeling the chill of the day seeping into her, she retreated to the bathroom.

A SHORT WHILE LATER, HER HAIR wrapped in a towel and fresh from the shower, Annja raided the refrigerator. Roux had bought enough food to last for days. She set everything she wanted to one side and got started.

She put coffee on first, thinking the smell of it in the loft might wake Roux, then peeled a few potatoes, chopped them into chunks, and added onion. She mixed up a bowl of waffle batter and started frying bacon. She put a package of link sausages in a pan of water, covered it with a lid, and put it on a burner.

Roux got up as Annja opened up a carton of eggs. He looked tired and haggard in the pajamas he'd gotten from the suitcase he'd had his driver deliver.

"Scrambled or over easy?" Annja held up the eggs.

Roux's morning voice was a dry growl. "Benedict. We have muffins."

"We also have waffles."

Roux frowned. "Those are too sweet."

"You don't have to put syrup on them." Annja turned back to the stove and added another pan.

"You're up early," Roux said.

"We've got a lot to do," Annja said.

"Is the coffee ready?"

Reaching into the cupboard for a cup, Annja poured Roux a cup.

"Thank you."

"Sure." Annja felt relaxed making breakfast. She'd thought she'd have been self-conscious. Especially after Roux had dismissed the driver and stated his intentions about staying—in case her enemies decided to strike again.

Instead, nothing had happened but a good night's sleep.

"I'LL DO THE DISHES." Roux took the dirty dishes from Annja's tray.

"I can do them." Annja got up and started to help.

"No." Roux waved her back to her chair. "You did the dishes last night. It's the least I can do."

Annja watched as Roux went to the kitchen sink. It surprised her that Roux had demonstrated a softer side. Especially after nearly five hundred years of male chauvinism.

Annja retreated to her computer. "Where did you learn to be so domestic?"

"Back when I was on the road a lot, and Garin was just a boy, about the time I'd met Joan and knew that I was supposed to watch over her, there was no one else to take care of us. So I did."

Annja brought the computer online. "Were you poor in those days?"

Roux glanced at her as if wondering if she were sane. "No. We had money."

"Then why not hire servants?"

"Because someone traveling with servants was a clear target for brigands. It was better to pose as an old man and a boy with little material possessions. Although I can't remember the number of times we had to fight merely to keep our cook pots and horses."

"You could have stayed at inns."

"I had enemies." Roux frowned as he looked down into the dishwasher. "I've always had enemies. If Garin and I stayed at an inn, we'd have been found more easily."

Annja sorted through her e-mail. There were also a lot of fan letters from viewers of *Chasing History's Monsters.* She checked to see if anyone had posted anything new about the belt plaque.

She spotted one from Professor Michael Hu. Annja recognized the name from Michelle Kim's research while she'd been in California.

I'm a professor of Archaeological Studies at Peking University in Beijing, China. I'd like to confer with you if I may. You recently posted an image of a piece I'd be very interested in seeing.

If you would please, reply to this e-mail and I'd be happy to call you at my expense.
Sincerely,
Michael Hu

"Interesting." Roux stood at Annja's shoulder.

Annja checked the time and date on the message. It had been posted while she'd been asleep. She clicked on the attachment.

The image of the Scythian belt plaque filled the screen. The snarling tiger's savage face stared back at Annja in frozen silence.

If only you could talk, she thought. She sighed, then turned to Roux. "You came here about the thing Sha Wu Ying captured. Why is Professor Hu interested?"

"You'd have to ask him." Roux frowned. "There are too many people interested in the secret that lies behind that belt plaque."

"Could he know what you know?"

Roux considered that for a moment. "There are always whispers, legends, and half-truths." He spat a curse. "And, of course, there's no guessing whom Garin might have told. Over the years, he talked about a fair number of things that he shouldn't have talked about."

"Dr. Hu is working on a dig in Loulan City. It could be in our best interests to work with him. On some level," Annja said.

Scowling, Roux ran a hand over his face. "Unless this is a trap."

"There's two of us. Think they can trap us both?"

Roux smiled. "Did you know that ego was sometimes the best bait in any trap?"

Annja smiled back. "Whose ego? The trapper or the trappee?"

"Upon occasion, both." Roux paused. "I need to see the inscription that was on the back of the belt plaque."

After a moment's hesitation, Annja printed an enlarged image of the back of the belt plaque. Although she trusted Roux to an extent, she never knew what that extent was. He always seemed to know more than she did about the things he was interested in, and he only doled out what he reluctantly decided she had to know. Like the nature of whatever weapon it was that fell into Sha Wu Ying's hands.

Even if he took off with the image, though, she still had copies of it. He couldn't keep her from seeking the truth on her own. Surely there was someone in New York's Chinatown who would be able to interpret more of it than Harry Kim had been able to.

IT TOOK ANNJA ALMOST an hour to get through to Professor Hu. Most of that time was spent tracking down a graduate assistant who could give Annja a cell phone number to try.

It took three attempts before Annja got Hu to answer. He spoke in Chinese.

Annja replied in English. "I'm sorry, Professor Hu, I don't speak the language. My name is Annja Creed. You sent me a message about a Scythian belt plaque."

"Ah, Ms. Creed." The professor's English was accented. "Thank you for getting in touch with me, but I would have been happy to call you."

"This is fine. And I was anxious to contact you. The belt plaque has become quite a puzzle for me."

Roux sat at the dining room table with the image Annja had given him. He used a notebook and pen as he worked. Annja still didn't know what he was doing.

"How so?" The professor sounded curious.

"I'll get to that in a minute. I'd like to know how you became interested in it."

Hu hesitated only a moment, then launched into his reply like a true academic. "I specialize in the ancient history of my country. I leave the last thousand years or so for my contemporaries to argue and fight over. I'm more interested in the primitive cultures that sprang up before Emperor Qin conquered the Seven Warring States and created China. I'm presently in Loulan City—actually, I'm in what is left of Loulan City—digging for more artifacts."

"I'm familiar with your work there, and somewhat with that period," Annja said.

The professor sounded relieved. "That will save us some time."

Annja also heard the fatigue in Professor Hu's voice.

"As you know, the Scythians were great traders. Being

basically a nomadic culture, the Scythians traveled extensively. Archaeologists can trace their beginnings back to 3000 B.C. Generally it's believed that they were Iranian, although there are some who refuse to accept this. They roamed freely over Europe and Asia."

"They also conducted a lot of trade along the Silk Road," Annja said. She didn't want the conversation to turn into a lecture, which sometimes happened when talking to professors about a favorite or intriguing subject.

"Exactly." Professor Hu caught himself. "I suppose you're probably aware of a lot of the background on those people."

"Yes."

"Sorry. This dig is the first time I've gotten to do something I've wanted in a long time."

"Not a problem. I completely understand.

"But what is your interest in them there in Loulan City?" Annja asked.

"The history of their trade, of course, but there is more."

Annja waited, watching as Roux diligently worked.

"Do you know what the Scythian kurgan was?"

"A burial tomb." Annja remembered that from her reading.

"Precisely. Many of the kurgans were plain, but some were—for the time—elaborate affairs constructed with larchwood."

"The Scythians were thought to have believed the larchwood could bring about renewed life," Annja said.

"Yes. The Ice Maiden, the mummified remains of the woman in the Altay Mountains, came from such a kurgan. As far as we have discovered, no Scythian written language existed. Most of the history of that nomadic culture that we know today came from the writings of the Greeks."

"Some runes that were found in Eastern Europe and Central Asia are believed to be Scythian in origin." Annja had found references to that when she'd tried to decipher the writing on the back of the belt plaque.

"I don't know that I disagree with them, but until we actually find something more substantial, I'm going to remain somewhat skeptical," Hu replied.

"I understand." There were things Annja chose to remain skeptical about, as well.

"Have you heard of the Scythian *tamgas?*"

Annja had. "Tamgas are brand marks the Scythians left behind that allowed the various clan members to claim grazing rights to land tracts."

"You have been doing your homework, I see." Hu sounded pleased.

"Ever since I identified the belt plaque as potentially Scythian in origin."

"Brilliant. The *tamgas* have been extremely important in our understanding of the Scythian culture. Historians have been able to track the movements of the nomads, as well as get some ideas of generational progression. Many of the marks—not even close to becoming a rudimentary language in my opinion, however—remained similar over the years."

"But some scholars believe the *tamgas* are a written language," Annja said.

Roux looked up from his notebook at Annja's objection.

Hu took a breath. For the first time, he sounded a little testy, but Annja totally understood the cause. Each archaeologist—and specialist of any kind with leeway in the reconstruction of their particular field of study—had pet theories and basic beliefs they'd built for themselves. She had a few of her own. It was obvious that she was treading on toes by pointing out that possibility.

"I don't ascribe to that," Hu said.

Annja backed up. "The *tamgas* were used to claim pastoral lands."

"Yes." Hu relaxed a little. "They also marked treaties, community action, religious practices and affiliations between the clan members and other clans, as well. The *tamgas* didn't change for two thousand years."

"Even when clans died out, other clans would adopt their *tamgas*," Annja said.

"Yes. So we have a history of sorts regarding the movements, religious beliefs, and community bylaws developed by the Scythian people."

"But what does that have to do with the belt plaque I found?"

"That particular *tamga* was ascribed to a Scythian known as Tochardis."

"Tochardis. How do you spell that?"

From across the loft, Roux looked over at her with renewed interest. When he noticed she'd caught him, he scowled and bent his head back to his work.

Hu offered the spelling and reminded Annja that since there was no Scythian language or alphabet there was no correct spelling.

"Then how was Tochardis identified?"

"By his tamga. That belt plaque you have, Ms. Creed, bears Tochardis's *tamga*."

Annja pulled up the image of the belt plaque again. She studied the tiger image. "Tochardis's *tamga* was the tiger?"

"Tochardis's tamga was a tiger's shadow. Underscored by a sword."

Peering more closely at the belt plaque, Annja thought she could just barely make out the remnants of the sword and the dim outline of the tiger.

"The tiger motif was replicated," Hu said, "but many of the Scythians preferred mythological creatures. Dragons, griffins, and the like. They were borrowed from Greek and Chinese cultures. But no one replicated the three items from that belt plaque."

"The belt plaque is steatite. I could be wrong, but from everything I've studied, the Scythians worked in gold or bronze, not steatite or jade. If that is the case, then this belt plaque was made by a Chinese artisan, not a Scythian," Annja said.

"True, Ms. Creed. What you found was a copy of the original. The Chinese people also borrowed the rectangular shape of the belt plaque from the Scythians. But what you have is a copy of Tochardis's *tamga*. It shouldn't exist."

Annja studied the piece. "It's an anomaly."

"Yes. One I would very much wish to know more about."

"Why?"

"Because, although their culture seemed to promise such an occurrence, as far as I know Tochardis is the only Scythian to ever rise from the grave."

26

Roux stood at the ticket counter at La Guardia at six the next morning and booked a flight out for 8:10 a.m.

In line behind him, Annja looked around, tense and ready to do anything but sit on a plane. Having an extra day of Roux sitting around the apartment with her had been more than a little unnerving.

"Two tickets to Dunhuang, China." Roux's voice was loud over the hubbub around him.

Not exactly on stealth mode here, Annja thought. She knew she was being overly critical. She couldn't help it. She was still slightly paranoid about a potential warrant being out on her from California.

She'd been ignoring calls from Doug Morrell and Bart McGilley. She didn't trust Doug not to be more interested in getting news coverage of her arrest than in her continued freedom, and she didn't want to put Bart on the spot with his department.

So far, the media seemed to have dropped the story. She wasn't yet certain how she felt about that. On one hand, it was good not to be wanted, but on the other hand—she wasn't wanted.

The travel specialist quickly made arrangements for the flight to Dunhuang, routing them through Pudong Airport in Shanghai where a puddle-jumper would take them on to Dunhuang.

Roux offered a credit card at the end of the transaction. The airline representative quickly ran it and returned it, after looking at his identification. She offered the card and ID back. "Thank you for flying with us, Mr. Loftus. I hope you and your niece enjoy your trip."

After a brief inspection of Annja's documents, the representative checked the luggage. Annja claimed her backpack as carry-on, determined not to trust the computer to cargo handlers.

Once they were out of auditory range of the representative, Annja looked at Roux. "Mr. *Loftus?*"

Roux looked at her blandly. "Would you have preferred another name?" He handed her a ticket.

Looking inside the envelope, Annja found there was also a New York driver's license and passport in the name of Abigail Loftus inside. That explained where he'd gone when he'd left the apartment for a short time yesterday afternoon.

"Abigail?" Annja couldn't believe it.

"Abigail is a fine name."

"Is that ID going to pass inspection?" Annja didn't relish the idea of rotting away in a Chinese prison as a suspected spy.

The old man scowled at her. "Don't even pester me with questions like that. Of course it will. Give me your other ID."

After a brief moment of hesitation, Annja did.

Roux stopped at a courier service, asked for a protective envelope, then prepared to mail Annja's documents to the hotel where he had reservations in Dunhuang. "That way they'll be there if you need to prove who you are later. But for the moment, we're off the passenger manifests. In case anyone's looking."

The whole cloak-and-dagger scenario made Annja feel vulnerable. Still, she saw the reasoning behind it.

"Why are we flying commercial? Don't you have a private jet?"

Roux passed through the security area with ease. "Yes, but how much attention do you think we really need to attract?"

Annja knew. Roux had a point. As she started to pass through, the metal detector beeped and she was asked to step back. Trying to fly these days was exhausting.

"WHAT DO YOU KNOW about Tochardis?" Annja sat across from Roux at a small table in an airport restaurant. She picked at a salad with little enthusiasm. Roux made short work of a barbecue sandwich.

"Until today, I had never—"

Annja cut him off and heard the anger in her own voice. "Don't. Don't forget that I'm getting you into the Loulan City dig. If you could have done that on your own, you wouldn't have flown me across the country and met me in New York. Furthermore, don't forget that whoever Huangfu Cao works for is willing to kill to get whatever he's after."

For a moment, Roux held her gaze. Then he shrugged and smiled a little. "You are right."

"Were Sha Wu Ying and Tochardis related?"

"Before he was known as Sha Wu Ying, he was called Tochardis."

"Was either his real name?" Annja asked.

"No."

"Is he still alive?"

"I don't know."

"Was he dead somewhere in the middle of that?"

Roux thought for a moment. "I suppose so."

Annja couldn't believe it. "You *suppose* so? How can you suppose someone was dead?"

A few of the nearby patrons glanced in their direction. A mother with two small children got up from the table next to them and wandered out into the main hallway.

Scowling, Roux turned his attention back to his sandwich. "Maybe we could be a little more circumspect."

"Being a little more circumspect isn't going to fly. I need to know more of what you know."

"If I tell you too much, I ruin the chances of you reaching important conclusions all on your own."

"I'm willing to risk it. Did Tochardis rise from the grave?"

"From everything I've been able to learn, yes. Of course, he could have faked his own death. I've had to a number of times over the years. I've lived an extended life, but it's never been without risk. You wouldn't believe the number of times I woke with someone poised over me prepared to drive a stake through my heart."

"Why?"

"They believed that I was a vampire."

"Vampires aren't real."

"Neither are men who live hundreds of years." Roux grinned. "You'd be surprised to know what is real, my dear girl."

"Was Tochardis immortal? Or long-lived?"

"By your standards?" Roux waved his sauce-drenched fork aimlessly. "Yes. Of course he was."

"How long?"

Roux shook his head. "I don't know."

"Who was Tochardis?"

"In reality? I don't know. Maybe it would surprise you to learn this, Annja, but there's still a great deal I don't know. That's what keeps my life interesting after all these years."

The knowledge that there was a lot Roux didn't know was vaguely unsettling to Annja. She pushed the trepidation from her mind and concentrated on her line of thought. "Who was Tochardis to the Scythians?"

"A great warrior. One of their leaders."

"I don't recall the name in any of the studies I've done."

Roux smiled. "Men who live unnaturally long lives, I've found in my own experience, tend not to want to draw attention to that fact if they can help it. Tochardis worked in the—"

"Shadows," Annja said as she thought of the shadow that mirrored the great tiger on the belt plaque.

"Exactly. You're very good at what you do, you know."

Annja didn't know whether Roux was pleased about that, or worried. She wanted him to be worried, but she was surprised at how much she wanted him to be pleased, as well.

"Why didn't Tochardis stay with the Scythians?"

"He couldn't hold the Scythians together. They were, by nature, a group of wandering tribes. They built a few cities. One of the largest was Gelonus, the remains of which were identified by Boris Shramko."

"That's in the Ukraine."

"Yes. That was found in the last few years. There's still so much of the past that yet remains undiscovered," Roux said.

Annja was surprised at the wistful note in Roux's voice. She focused on the task at hand. They were due to begin boarding before long.

"When did Tochardis become Sha Wu Ying?"

Roux finished his sandwich and blotted his mouth. "Your guess about that would be as good as mine. Sometime after Tochardis was *killed*, Sha Wu Ying appeared on the scene."

"Why would he reinvent himself and ally with the Chinese?"

"Not the Chinese. To the Qin Dynasty. Remember, when Qin first came to power, there were only the Seven Warring States. I suspect what drew Tochardis to Qin was the potential for the new country Qin was assembling. What did Qin do?"

Annja only had to think about that briefly. "He conquered and united the seven countries—"

"Providing the potential for the largest army the world had ever seen."

"He declared a standard written language—"

"Providing for an ease of communications over long distances."

"Started building the Great Wall of China to keep out northern invaders and brigands—"

"Providing for stability and solidifying a base of operations. Not to mention cutting Tochardis off from any reprisal that might be forthcoming from the Scythians for taking whatever treasures he might have absconded with."

"Controlled the silk industry and—to a degree—the spice trade along the Silk Road—"

"Providing—"

"A large and stable economic base." Annja saw where Roux was headed with his thinking.

Roux beamed like a teacher pleased with a prized student. "Exactly. The way Tochardis would have looked at it, allying himself with Emperor Qin would have been the best thing he could have done at the time. By becoming the emperor's premier assassin, he was only a heartbeat away from world conquest."

Annja knew. China had been poised to extend its reach at that time. "Except that Emperor Qin was ultimately betrayed by other men who wanted the same power he had."

"Dissatisfaction among the ranks of intelligent men trusted with their leader's greatest secrets is probably the biggest risk any dictator faces," Roux stated.

Annja arched an eyebrow. "Is that little tidbit from personal experience?"

Roux leaned back in his chair. "I have never sought control over the lives of others. Ruling kingdoms—especially with the great, unwashed masses involved—is too hard and is often its own punishment for lofty thoughts of grandeur."

Maybe those are the words you're saying today, but was it always that way? Annja wondered. "What happened to Sha Wu Ying and what did you find out from the back of the belt plaque?"

At that moment, the airline announced the boarding call for their flight.

Roux stood. "Let's go. I've got to get a few things." He was in motion before Annja could grab her backpack.

Hurrying to catch up, Annja couldn't believe it when Roux entered a bookstore and chose four paperbacks from the popular fiction racks. He turned to her. "Did you want anything?"

"No."

"Are you certain? It's a long flight."

Annja knew it was a long flight. It was time that Garin Braden would be getting ahead of them. "I'm certain."

The older woman at the checkout desk rang up Roux's purchases. Annja stood at his side, irritated that he still hadn't revealed to her what he knew.

When she was finished with his credit card, the woman handed it back and smiled at Roux, then at Annja. "You have a beautiful granddaughter, Mr. Loftus."

An unexpected warmth gushed through Annja. She smiled back at the woman.

Roux signed the credit slip and slid it back to the woman. "Oh, she's not my granddaughter." He didn't bother to explain the situation any further.

The checkout clerk's smile froze on her face as she surmised what Annja's relationship with Roux might truly be.

Annja's short-lived feel-good melted. Roux was smirking at her from the doorway.

"I'm his caregiver," she said to the woman.

The clerk looked at the credit card slip.

"No. He's still legal to manage his finances." Annja lowered her voice. "It's his physical needs I have to attend to. But rehab will only go so far when you're dealing with old age. Once the bladder starts to go, not much can be done. Do you know if they sell Depends in the terminal?"

Roux scowled and left the bookshop while the clerk told Annja she wasn't certain.

Annja caught up to Roux outside the bookshop. The

boarding call for their flight echoed through the cavernous tunnel again.

Roux spoke without looking at her. "That was ludicrous. I'll have you know that my bladder is in fine shape." He sounded properly peeved.

Annja felt somewhat mollified because Roux was vain enough to be vulnerable.

"You'll wear the weak bladder stigma every time you assign me to the role of potential golddigger. It's bad enough people think that all on their own without you encouraging it."

"Point taken," Roux said.

"Now, what happened to Sha Wu Ying?"

"He died."

"How?" Annja asked.

"He was assassinated."

"I thought he was the assassin."

"There's always more than one assassin, Annja. Some families take up the trade. Look at the Medici of Florence. Some of those family members even had their own specially blended poisons made. Designer poisons." Roux smiled.

They joined the line of boarding passengers.

"Who had Sha Wu Ying assassinated?"

One of the waiting passengers looked at Annja.

"Perhaps, Professor Creed, we could continue this conversation on the plane. There's no reason to bore others with our thoughts on that paper." Roux's voice carried easily. He smiled and gave his papers to the waiting attendant, who hesitated, then relaxed and smiled back.

Annja did the same, then they stepped into the tunnel that would take them to the plane.

27

Annja stowed her backpack in the overhead compartment above her first-class seat. Then she sat down next to Roux. The old man read the backs of the novels he'd purchased, then put three of them away. From what Annja could see, Roux's tastes included fantasy, science fiction, Western, and thriller. None of it was especially mind-expanding.

After buckling into the seat, Annja turned to him. "Now you're going to tell me."

Roux sighed and spoke in Latin.

Annja made the transition effortlessly.

Roux asked her for a picture of the back of the belt plaque and she retrieved it from her bag.

When he had the image in his hands, Roux scanned it before he spoke. "The inscription on the back is a code."

"How do you know that?"

"What else could it be?"

"A family history. Just like it reads."

"But it's not. It's a trifle complicated, and you were

hampered by being unable to read Chinese. Mandarin, actually."

Annja blew out a breath of frustration. "The man I had translate it said it was Cantonese."

"You had someone translate this?" Roux frowned.

"Yes. I'd just seen Huangfu Cao gun down three men in cold blood. I was more than a little motivated to investigate."

"Did that man know what this pertained to?"

"No. He only knew part of the history. The belt plaque was rumored to be cursed."

"Knowing what I know about it, I have no doubt that it is."

"Maybe you could share."

"The inscription *is* in Cantonese. However, the code is written in Mandarin."

"It should be in Classical Chinese. That's the language Emperor Qin shifted everyone to when he conquered the Seven Warring States," Annja said.

"Yes. I have to admit, that confused me for a while, as well. I didn't see the message hidden within the other message." Roux shrugged. "But I think deviousness comes more effortlessly to me than to you." He touched a series of lines in the lower corner. "This is the key. It says, 'Even before the ashes in the burning pit became cold, riots had begun in Shandong. It turned out that Liu Bang and Xiang Yu were both uneducated.'" He paused. "I don't know what that means."

The inscription teased Annja's tired mind. Just when she was about to give up on identifying the reference, it suddenly came to her. "That's a poem."

Roux looked askance at the Chinese characters. "If you insist."

"It is. Let me get my computer and I'll look up the file." Annja started to release her seat belt.

Roux gripped her arm. "You're going to have to wait."

Only then did Annja realize the plane was in motion. She vaguely remembered the quick, professional pre-flight intro. She closed her eyes and thought back, managing to place the words on the computer screen in a mental image.

"It was written by a poet from the Tang Dynasty. Zhang Jie, I think. Something like that."

Roux shook his head and smiled. "I don't see how you can remember things like that."

"Because I've trained myself to." Whenever working on a project, Annja built a mental timeline for it and constantly added facts to it, shoehorning them in. She'd always had a near-photographic memory and hadn't had to study much to get through college.

"You said that poem is the key. The key to what?" Annja asked.

"To the characters in the inscription to pay attention to. When you have your printout, I'll show you."

ONLY A FEW MINUTES LATER, the plane leveled off. Annja unsnapped the seat belt and retrieved her computer. Placing it across her knees, she opened it and powered it up. A few clicks later, she had the obverse image of the belt plaque on the screen.

"Here is the key." Roux indicated the four Chinese characters in the lower right corner.

Annja had assumed they were the name of the artist or the name of a family.

"Now look at the placement of the fish icons." Roux pointed to the fish symbols standing on end that Michelle and Harry Kim had pointed out.

"They overlap different characters. How do you know which one a fish is indicating?"

"It's a matter of trial and error." Roux flagged down a flight attendant and ordered a whiskey sour. "Much as you would do a cryptoquote. If one of the characters didn't make sense, I threw it out. That's what took me so long this morning. Would you like anything?"

"Water." Annja remembered the sheets of paper Roux had filled while she'd talked to Professor Hu. "There is a message in the code?"

"Of course there's a message. That's how codes work."

The drinks arrived. Annja opened the bottled water and drank. "What does the message say?"

Settling into his plush seat, Roux frowned at the small screen that had flipped down in front of him. The screen showed an in-flight commercial, offering a free television show immediately afterward.

"The belt plaque belonged to a man who betrayed Sha Wu Ying."

"How was Sha Wu Ying betrayed?"

"The man who owned that belt plaque was one of Sha Wu Ying's most trusted assassins. Before that, he was a monk who lived in disgrace."

Annja was intrigued. "What kind of monk?"

"They were from Chang'an. Have you heard of them?"

"Yes." Annja was somewhat familiar with the order from her martial arts classes. "The name means *perpetual peace.*"

"I wouldn't know. I've never really fancied the history behind open-handed fighting. I've dabbled in it, of course. Anyone who's traveled as much as I have would be a fool not to."

Annja didn't bother to mention the health and mental

benefits derived from martial arts. "Chang'an was located near Xi'an."

Roux smiled. "That explains it then."

"What?"

"Xi'an was the easternmost end of the Silk Road. During different periods, the Chinese emperors called upon the various monasteries to provide warriors to protect them or wage war on their enemies."

"Why was the monk disgraced?"

"His name was Wan Shichong. He made the mistake of falling in love with a nun. Knowing they would never be allowed to live together, they ran. Eventually they went to Loulan City. There Wan Shichong took up employment with Sha Wu Ying."

"As an assassin?"

"The young monk was trained in martial arts. It was probably a good fit. At that time, war was everywhere. Qin Shi Huang was forcibly uniting the Seven Warring States. Eventually, though, Wan Shichong was torn trying to serve two masters. He had sworn loyalty to Emperor Qin, but he'd also sworn loyalty to Sha Wu Ying."

"He had to betray one of them."

Roux nodded. "In the end, he chose to betray Sha Wu Ying."

"Why?"

"Because he believed that Qin was the future of China, and his wife was pregnant with their first child. By this time, he'd also come to suspect that Sha Wu Ying was also Tochardis."

"What led him to that conclusion?"

"Artifacts that Sha Wu Ying had that had once belonged to the Scythians. The belt plaque Sha Wu Ying had chosen as a standard was another."

"So he betrayed Sha Wu Ying?"

"Yes. Wan Shichong went to Emperor Qin's court physicians and got exposed to a plague victim. At the monastery, he'd been trained in medicines that would help him stave off death."

"Plague? As in bubonic?"

"Or measles or smallpox. All were quite deadly."

The thought of the monk deliberately exposing himself to such a sickness sent a cold chill through Annja. "That's insane."

"Sha Wu Ying was a feared man. Desperate times required desperate measures."

"Did it work?"

"When Wan Shichong was certain he was sick with the illness, he returned to the City of Thieves. That was the other name for the City of the Sands. He went among the assassins and spread the plague. Evidently it didn't take long to manifest. The sick thieves wandered out into the desert and were cut down by Emperor Qin's men."

"Wan Shichong led the emperor's men to Sha Wu Ying's refuge?"

"Yes."

"Then how was the location of the City of the Sands lost?"

"All of this took place while Emperor Qin was out taking the last tour of his country."

"Sha Wu Ying had succeeded in bribing one of the emperor's closest advisors into poisoning him."

"What about the warriors who went with Wan Shichong?"

"They contracted the disease. The ones who didn't die in the desert were killed as soon as they reached the Imperial City. None of them made it through the gates."

"That wasn't exactly the payoff they'd planned on."

"By that time, news of Emperor Qin's death had spread and the country was in turmoil."

"What happened to Sha Wu Ying?"

"According to the inscription, he died inside that underground city."

"Did Wan Shichong survive?"

"He did. But he carried the disease home with him. His wife died from it, but his daughter survived. He lived out the end of his days and never told anyone where the City of Thieves was."

"There was no map?"

Roux frowned at her. "Did you see a map?"

"No, but I thought—"

"There was no map. I decoded the secret message. I suggest *you* figure out a way to find that hidden city."

Irritation bubbled up inside Annja. "Actually, if you just want to keep hidden whatever Sha Wu Ying took all those years ago, not finding the City of the Sands would serve the same purpose."

"Except that there is a map."

Annja took a deep breath and counted to ten. "You just said there was no map."

"Not on the belt plaque. But there is one. Wan Shichong left one for his daughter and told her she could find the hidden city if she ever wanted to."

"Where did he leave the map?"

"It's in the form of a toy. That's all I know."

A toy. Annja leaned back in her seat, sipped her water, and studied her notes on the computer.

Roux turned pages in the paperback Western. "I'm kind of sad that I missed this."

"That book?"

"The time period. The Wild West. I stayed in Europe during those years. I always imagined what it would be like to meet a cowboy. It was a very interesting period of colonial expansion, you know."

Ignoring him, Annja opened files and started sifting through her research. She brought up maps of Loulan City, both present and past, and started trying to think like Sha Wu Ying, the Dancing Shadow of Death.

28

Garin Braden sat inside the bar and looked over the crowd of tourists and Chinese businessmen. The Silk Road Dunhuang Hotel was a four-star establishment on Dunyue Road almost three miles south of the city. It was a little over two miles from the center of the city and twelve miles from the airport. The bar was a good place for a patient man to wait.

Ngai Yuan-Kim wasn't as patient. He sat across the table from Garin and talked on the phone.

I need to really consider who I take on as partners in the future. Garin thought as he signaled the cocktail waitress for another round.

Closing the phone, Ngai glared at Garin. "We should not be here."

Garin grinned. "Really? And where should we be?"

"Out there. In Loulan City. With Professor Hu."

"Do you think he's hiding the City of Thieves? Or purposefully not finding it to spite us?" Garin couldn't decide whether he was amused or angry.

"You said you could find it."

"I can. When the time is right."

The waitress returned with Garin's drink. He signed the bill and tipped her generously. Ngai was paying all expenses.

"When will the time be right, Mr. Braden?" Ngai's words were menacing.

Garin shifted in the booth. Ngai's three bodyguards mirrored his movements. Their constant presence was wearing on Garin's nerves.

"Look. You don't know what you're up against."

"One old man and a young woman."

That wasn't exactly how Garin would have summed up Roux and Annja Creed, but he knew he wasn't going to convince his new partner any differently.

"They can cause considerable difficulties."

"Just two people?"

"Your boy Huangfu Cao couldn't put Annja Creed away." Even as he said that, Garin had to wonder how he'd have felt if the man had killed Annja. Garin didn't necessarily want her dead—not if the sword could be destroyed or shattered without that. And he'd discovered he had mixed feelings about her. If she wasn't in his way from time to time, as she was now, he might have liked her even more.

Ngai waved the comment away. "That was nothing."

"On top of that, somebody shot your men out in the desert while they were spying on the dig. We still don't know what that's about."

"We can hardly resolve that by sitting here."

"Yes, it would be much better if you were out there in the desert acting as a target."

Ngai pursed his lips.

"We've got people watching the dig." Garin kept his voice calm. "If Hu discovers something, we'll know. And when Annja Creed and Roux arrive there, we'll know that, too."

"Perhaps they're not coming," Ngai said.

Garin considered that. Roux knew what was in the City of Thieves. Nothing would keep the old man away with that much raw power on the line.

If the legend is true. That was the part that Garin had no way of knowing. There were always more lies than truths, and there was no way to find out which was which without going to see.

"They're coming," Garin said and turned to peer out the window at the harsh expanse of desert. They were coming. He could feel it in his bones.

"IS YOUR GRANDFATHER DOING all right?"

Annja glanced up at the male flight attendant. He was slim and good-looking, maybe thirty. She looked over to Roux.

The old man slept soundly. While he'd been awake, he'd read constantly and conducted short, cryptic phone calls that meant nothing to her. His latest paperback, some kind of fantasy novel with a garish cover and a woman in scanty clothing, lay closed on his chest under his folded hands.

He'd finished the book over an hour ago, laughing uproariously from time to time and reading aloud to her different sections that he'd found hilarious.

"He's fine." Annja thanked the flight attendant and he moved down the row, getting everyone ready for the coming descent.

Annja looked at Roux and thought about how vulnerable the old man looked. The desert was going to be hard on him. She wondered if he would be up to the task.

Then she settled back and wondered if she would. The City of Thieves wasn't actually a city. It was just a few rooms that supposedly held a vast treasure trove—and whatever it was Roux was looking for.

Beneath a shifting sea of sand.

Annja sighed. Sha Wu Ying and his followers couldn't have built even a few rooms in the shifting sand. They needed bedrock for that.

And she thought she knew where to start looking.

By THE TIME THEY LANDED at Pudong International Airport, Annja had been in the air almost twenty hours.

The pilot Roux had arranged met them in the terminal. He was a slim, well-built Australian who had married into a Chinese family that had pulled enough strings to get him a work visa. He was talkative and boisterous, which Roux seemed to enjoy.

He walked them out to a small plane that he assured them would make it to Dunhuang. As soon as they claimed their baggage they taxied onto the runway and were almost instantly cleared for takeoff.

A RENTAL AGENCY HAD A Land Rover waiting for them. Roux squared the bill and they were ready to get underway by the time Annja and the Australian pilot had loaded the luggage.

Roux drove and Annja was glad to let him.

Everywhere she looked, gold and tan sand covered the countryside, filling it with dunes and planes. Stubborn scrub brush and scraggly trees shoved up through the baked crust and loose powder of the Gobi Desert.

"It's beautiful," Annja said.

"It is beautiful. Like another world." Glancing up through the windshield, Roux pointed to a circling vulture. "But this world is also unforgiving. Don't make any mistakes about that."

"I won't." Annja drank from the bottled water she'd bought from a vendor at the airport.

ROUX PULLED THE Land Rover up in front of the Grand Sun Hotel and let the valet take care of the vehicle. Bellboys brought out a rack for the luggage.

Annja shouldered her backpack. While checking through customs at Pudong, she'd changed into light-weight khaki pants and a sapphire blue cotton T-shirt.

Inside, the hotel held all the modern conveniences. The air-conditioning provided welcome relief but she knew that she'd better enjoy it because there wouldn't be any at the dig.

Roux took care of the rooms and retrieved the package he'd had couriered to the hotel.

The suite was done in lacquered woods with plenty of red and black in the color scheme. Instead of a dressing room, it had a long folding wall with a green and yellow dragon stretched across the panels.

Roux had the adjoining room.

With the bellboys out of the way, Annja called Professor Hu.

Hu answered in Chinese.

"It's Annja Creed. We've arrived."

"Splendid. I thought I saw you drive up. The hotel has a coffee shop. Why don't you meet me there?"

Annja said that she would, then hung up and went to tell Roux.

"MISS CREED." PROFESSOR HU, dressed in khaki attire, stood near one of the tables in the back. He smiled brightly.

Annja walked over to the man and held out her hand. She introduced Roux and they sat at the table.

Hu turned his attention to Roux. "I know Miss Creed's field is archaeology, but what is your specialty?"

Roux gave an expansive smile and spread his hands. "I'm more of a dabbler, I'm afraid." His French accent was suddenly pronounced. "At my age, I tend to gravitate to whatever excites me. Miss Creed's interest in this whole mystery behind the belt plaque fanned my own interest."

The server came and took their order.

"If you don't mind my asking, Mr. Roux, where did you study?"

"At the Sorbonne. I was somewhat eclectic in my studies. I picked up several courses in art, languages and literature."

Annja wondered if that were true, then realized that even if she checked there was the possibility that Roux might have attended under another name.

The server returned with three large coffee mugs and put them in front of everyone.

Hu blew on his coffee. "If you don't mind my asking…" He let the question hang, awaiting permission to continue.

"Of course." Roux loaded his coffee with cream and sugar.

"What interested you in Loulan City?"

"The story about Sha Wu Ying, of course." Roux's blue eyes twinkled in excitement. "An emperor's assassin who turned on the hand that fed him in a bid for power. You've got to admit, it's a powerful story."

Hu was taken aback for an instant. "You know that those stories might only be myth."

"I do." Roux nodded agreeably. "But I also know that you were interested in the belt plaque Annja located as the result of a subterfuge. That tells me you're also interested in this *myth.*"

Hu grinned. "I am interested in it. The rumors of Sha Wu Ying have never been verified, but I feel certain they're based in some kind of fact. If the City of the Sands existed, if some of it—any piece of it—still exists, such a find could make a career."

"Or might make a man rich," Roux said.

29

At Roux's bold statement, the smile left Hu's face. "That's not why I do this kind of work. If it was, I could make a very comfortable living in the black market. I want to learn from what's out there. China is one of the oldest civilizations and there's so much history that's been lost and forgotten over the years." He frowned. "Or has been rewritten by those in power. I hope you're not here just for some treasure hunting expedition."

"No." Roux waved the idea away as if it was ridiculous. "However, I would like to take part in the search for whatever secrets the belt plaque holds. If we're successful, I believe Miss Creed is going to feature it on her television show. My financing her efforts here wouldn't have to be philanthropic then. I might end up helping to produce that segment of her show."

Hu tried not to grimace but failed. "Forgive me, Miss Creed, but that program doesn't appeal to me."

Annja nodded. "I understand. There are days that it doesn't appeal to me. However, the show does fund some of the other research work that I do. People aren't standing in line to hand out money for archaeologists, but that television production company does allow me some leeway in what I do."

"Was the belt plaque part of a television assignment?" Hu asked.

Realizing then that she hadn't told Hu the exact nature of the events leading up to her discovery of the belt plaque, Annja told the story again, this time including all the information about Huangfu Cao.

Hu frowned and looked uneasy. "I've heard of that man. I've even had dealings with him."

Suspicion dampened Annja's excitement. "What kind of dealings?"

"He and his men have broken into my office and home searching for information about the City of Thieves. I had only just come across Sha Wu Ying's name in some of the research I was doing." Hu took a breath. "Only a couple days ago, I found two men that I believe belong to Huangfu Cao's criminal organization."

Roux sat up a little straighter, a little more attentive. "Have you confirmed that?"

Hu shook his head. "No. When I found them, one of the men was dead. The other died before we could get him here to Dunhuang."

"What happened?"

"They were shot." Hu glanced into the depths of his coffee cup for a moment, then looked up. "The man who lived for a short time talked. Briefly. He said that they were attacked by a fox spirit."

That interested Annja immediately.

"I don't think that's what happened, of course, but word got around to some of the people in camp. I lost a few of the more superstitious among the crew. I think they got bored, got stoned, and shot each other. When I arrived in the cave where they'd camped, I got a contact high from whatever they'd been smoking."

"Did you see any drug paraphernalia?" Annja asked.

Hu shook his head. "To tell you the truth, I didn't look. Finding that dead man and the other one wounded, it was all a bit much."

"It would be." Annja reached into her backpack and brought out her computer. "You're sure you got a contact high while you were inside that cave?"

"Yes." Hu looked a little embarrassed.

Annja opened the computer and powered it up. "You've heard of Dr. Sven Hedin?"

Hu nodded. "Of course. He's credited, by some, for the rediscovery of Loulan City while traveling along the Silk Road for the studies he was doing."

"What about Dr. Heinrich Lehmann?"

Hu shook his head. "I've never heard of him."

"Dr. Lehmann was a casualty on Dr. Hedin's expedition." Annja tapped a few keys and brought up the copies of the documents she'd found regarding Loulan City. "There was a sandstorm in the area at about the time Loulan was discovered."

"Those happen with astonishing regularity out there."

"A few days after the discovery of Loulan, some men from Hedin's work crew found Lehmann a few miles away." Annja pulled up the news story of Lehmann. She'd tracked it to a Berlin newspaper after finding out about the death in the reports she'd read about Hedin's discovery.

The black-and-white picture of Lehmann showed a young, gawky man with round-lensed glasses. He wore a simple black business suit.

Hu studied the picture and the article. "I'm afraid I don't read German."

"Neither do I. But I had a friend translate it for me." Annja brought up another page that had the translation. "The news story talks mostly about Lehmann, his education and his family. But it talks about his death, as well."

"How did he die?"

"From dehydration. But before he died, he was raving about having found a system of underground chambers filled with gold and gems. He also said he was attacked by a fox spirit."

Hu sat back in his chair. "I haven't heard of any of this."

"I wouldn't have, either, if I hadn't found Dr. Lehmann's name on one of Professor Hedin's reports."

"Annja can be quite meticulous once she gets started." Roux's voice took on a note of pride that Annja reminded herself was false. We're just playing a game. Just creating an illusion for Hu. But it would have felt good if she'd known Roux actually meant what he said.

"Do you know where Lehmann's body was found?" Hu asked.

Annja nodded. "One of the other men, also a German, kept a journal. He noted Lehmann's death, and even made a map of where they found him.

Hu licked his lips. "It seems to me that a man in the state that Lehmann was in wouldn't be able to walk very far."

"I don't think so, either."

"Did Hedin's team search for the underground chambers?"

"They did. But they came up empty-handed. Hedin didn't put much stock in Lehmann's story."

Hu let out a sigh. "They could simply have been the ravings of a man out of his head with thirst."

"The man who wrote about Lehmann's death was a medical doctor. Archaeology was a hobby."

"Save us from the hobbyists." Hu glanced quickly at Roux. "I mean no disrespect."

Roux smiled and shrugged. "None taken."

"The doctor also believed that Lehmann was under the effects of a hallucinogen," Annja went on.

Hu's eyebrows raised. "A hallucinogen?"

Roux studied Annja.

Annja knew she'd surprised him, too, because she hadn't mentioned that to him before.

"Opium was in common use back then." Hu stroked his jaw thoughtfully. "But that tends to discredit Lehmann's claims."

"According to the journal, Lehmann smoked cigarettes but didn't use opium."

"You believe Lehmann was suffering from exposure to some drug," Roux said.

"I do. One of the things that the myths about Sha Wu Ying agree on was that he was an expert herbalist."

"He was reputed to be a healer among the Scythians," Hu added. "When he was known as Tochardis."

"In the City of Thieves," Annja asked, "would it have been out of line to assume they might have stock-piled poison?"

"Not at all." Roux smiled coldly. "In a water-poor environment such as that around Loulan, poisoning a water source would have been a good tactic to drive an entrenched enemy away."

"You think those men I found were exposed to the same hallucinogen?" Hu looked incredulous.

"Yes. And you, as well."

"A hallucinogen that was still viable—after two thousand years?"

"More than two thousand years," Annja agreed. "The dryness of the desert has preserved bodies, mummies, that were over four thousand years old. A burial tomb wouldn't be that different from an underground chamber. Back in the 1960s, the Chinese government experimented with nuclear weapons. Maybe one of those shock waves fractured some of the passageways near the storerooms. They might have opened a crack."

Hu shook his head. "You must forgive me if I offend you, Miss Creed. But that's quite a stretch."

"If I'm wrong," Annja said, "we should know it soon enough."

IT WAS ALMOST DUSK when Annja arrived at the Loulan City dig site. She stared out over the small tent town, then up into the foothills of the nearby mountains.

Roux parked the Land Rover in the motor pool next to the camels. Stepping out, Annja felt the heat slam into her. Her sunglasses blunted most of the residual brightness, but there was no way she could avoid the drastic change in temperature.

She looked back along the way they'd come. Heat shimmered over the desert sand.

"What is it?" Roux asked in French.

"Nothing. Not really." Annja jerked her attention back to the camp. "I just had the feeling we were being followed."

"I watched," Roux said. "I didn't notice anyone. Out here, you can't hide."

Annja reluctantly agreed. Still, she couldn't shake the feeling that someone was out there.

KELLY SWAN WATCHED the new arrivals with interest and more than a little paranoia. For the past few months, men and women had hunted her for the price the CIA had put on her head. Although it was unlikely they could have traced her here, she couldn't discount that possibility.

She sat outside her tent and ate mechanically, hardly tasting the food. Dinner consisted of meat and steamed vegetables.

Even though she was in excellent shape, Kelly felt worn-out. The work at the dig was hard and never ended.

One of Professor Hu's assistants went through the camp, talking with different workers. Observing him, Kelly saw that he only talked to the younger men and women among the laborers.

She finished her meal, then drank water till she couldn't hold any more. By that time the assistant approached her.

"Good evening." He stood before her, shining his flashlight to one side so the reflected light illuminated the immediate area but didn't shine it into her eyes.

Kelly responded in kind. She was known as a woman who kept to herself. A few of the men had hit on her, but she'd politely and consistently refused their advances. There were already a few who suspected she wasn't a local and she knew she couldn't hide there much longer. She hoped Ngai Kuan-Yin would put in an appearance soon.

"Professor Hu is putting together a special expedition," the assistant said. "He's looking for volunteers." He held his clipboard expectantly, pen poised.

Kelly almost said no. When undercover it was best not to draw attention. Volunteering was all about drawing attention. "Expedition to where?" she asked.

The assistant pointed up into the mountains. "There are some caves Professor Hu wants to investigate."

"Why?"

"I don't know."

That didn't make any sense. Loulan was *here*. The work they were doing was here. She looked at the young man. "Are the new people going?"

The assistant shrugged. "I don't know. Maybe. Does it matter?"

Does it? Kelly didn't know. Either way, she'd left the men—one dead and one alive—up in those mountains. She felt she had better find out what was going on.

"Well?" The assistant sounded impatient.

"I'll go."

He took the name she was going by, jotted it on his list, and kept moving through the camp.

After taking her plate and cup back to the camp mess, she washed them and put them away. Then she got a bedroll and walked outside the camp, easily slipping by the sentries posted to watch out for bandits.

Once in the shadows, she made her way to the place where she'd buried her weapons and the bag of bones her father had left for her. She'd finally figured out the secret of the bones, and she was ashamed that she hadn't discovered it earlier.

Sheltered by a dune, steeped in shadows, she took the ball from the bag. All of the bones had been cunningly cut and shaped. If she'd studied them more back in Shanghai, she might have seen then what the bones truly were. Once she'd divined their nature, she'd put them together.

When they were all in place, each piece interlocking with the next, they'd formed a spherical, three-dimensional interlocking puzzle. When she'd been little, she'd been fascinated by such things.

But thinking about those times now, she wasn't sure if she'd been interested in them or if her father had trained her to play them so she would be ready for his "gift."

Each of the bones held an inscription. But they were nonsense written in Cantonese. And they had designs that she couldn't fathom and had never seen anywhere before.

After a while, she put the ball back into the bag, then took out her weapons. She wrapped the pistols in the bedroll, folding it so the weapons wouldn't fall out.

Whatever happened in the morning, she would be ready.

THE PHONE RANG, WAKING Garin Braden from a tangle of slender female arms and legs. Struggling with a hangover, he cursed Ngai. He'd only gotten drunk so he wouldn't have to listen to the man complain anymore. Garin grabbed the cell phone from the nightstand.

"Mr. Braden, they're moving," a voice said.

"Where are they going?"

"Toward the mountains."

That was unexpected. "Are the woman and the old man together?"

"Yes, sir."

That, at least, meant something. If Annja and Roux were in an agreement on how to proceed they had to know more than he did at the moment. "Is the helicopter ready?"

"Yes, sir."

Garin smiled as he walked to the window and looked out across the desert. Darkness from an approaching wall of stormclouds smudged the horizon. "Good. Wake Mr. Ngai and let him know."

"Yes, sir."

Closing the phone, Garin leaned against the window. The coming heat was already warming the glass. Morning was barely dawning. *They're up and moving early.* He knew that may have meant only that they wanted to escape the heat of the day.

Still, Garin couldn't help wondering if Roux's bones or his were going to bleach in the desert before the sun set.

30

The sun rose shortly before seven. Annja had been awake since five, worked through a set of t'ai chi forms, and took an abbreviated shower in one of the camp's portable units. She checked her computer and digital camera, then hauled out her working journal and caught up on the entries.

Roux had risen at six and grumbled about the bad coffee. His attire surprised Annja. He wore khakis, hiking boots, and a broad-brimmed hat with a leopard print scarf tied around it.

"The hat's a bit much, don't you think?" Annja tried to hide her grin and failed. She'd known Roux had arranged for clothing, but she hadn't had a clue what the wardrobe would be like.

"Say whatever you must," Roux growled. "Get it out of your system." He clapped the hat on his head. "It's hot out here and the hat protects my head. I hope you brought something suitable."

Annja reached behind her and grabbed the replica

Brooklyn Dodgers baseball cap she'd packed. She pulled her chestnut hair into a ponytail and threaded it through the opening in the cap.

Roux grumbled. "You won't get much protection from that." He stomped off without another word.

ANNJA AND ROUX SHARED a silent breakfast of rice and pork and some fresh fruit while the rest of the camp came awake around them. Professor Hu approached them while they were cleaning their dishes.

"I've got ten people accompanying us." Hu took his hat off and mopped his brow. "If Miss Creed's predictions are accurate and we do find evidence of the City of the Sands up there, we may need help."

Annja looked at the people saddling camels near the motor pool. "Do they know why we're going up there?"

"No. My assistant simply told them this was to be an ancillary expedition."

"You do realize that you may have a spy somewhere in your ranks?" Roux asked.

"Other than myself, two assistants, and six graduate students, there's no one here I've met before. I don't want to take all of my experienced people with us. Work here will come to a standstill. And if we need help, I'd rather not have all of my people exposed to any danger."

Annja knew that was a good plan. Under the circumstances, it was probably the best that they could do.

"Are you ready?" Hu asked.

Annja nodded.

"Ever ridden a camel before, Miss Creed?"

"A few times." Annja went to the corral and picked out one of the belligerent beasts.

The camel smelled bad and loudly complained at her urging it to its feet so she could secure the saddle. She used a riding crop to make it kneel again so she could mount.

Seated in the saddle, Annja tugged on the reins and commanded the camel to its huge, disc-shaped feet. It surged, pushing up on its hindquarters first, then on the front legs. She sat, very high off the ground and waited for Roux.

He'd gone back inside his tent for a moment. He re-emerged wearing a large pistol strapped to his thigh and a heavy hunting rifle slung over his shoulder.

The weapons caused a stir among the workers, but Roux ignored it as he saddled and mounted his camel. He bobbed off-balance as the animal stood.

Roux cursed. "I've always hated these foul-tempered beasts." He spoke in Latin, making Annja wonder again if that language rather than French was his native tongue.

"You've ridden them before?" Annja asked.

"More times than I care to remember."

"Where?" Annja wanted to ask *when* but doubted she'd get an answer.

"Here. A time or two." Before she could ask anything further, Roux whipped the camel into a trot, falling in behind Professor Hu.

Annja followed, already feeling perspiration coating her back and dripping between her breasts. By midday it was going to be insufferable. She hoped most of their work would continue in the caves.

As she rode to join Roux, hoping to coax a few more answers from him, Annja noticed one of the women in the group staring at her.

She was a Chinese woman about Annja's age. She held Annja's gaze for just a moment, then looked away.

Annja rode on, rocking to and fro with the camel's awkward gait.

WHEN THEY REACHED the cave less than an hour later, Annja asked Professor Hu to order everyone to stay back and to remain upwind.

Even Roux stayed back, though his stiff body language clearly marked him as not happy with the idea. But he didn't try to be bullheaded about the situation.

Annja and Hu went on alone. They wore surgical face masks the professor had brought at Annja's suggestion. She hoped that the mask would help keep any hallucinogenic dust—if there was any—out of their lungs.

Adrenaline pumped through Annja as she thought about all the stories she'd read, and what Roux had told her about Sha Wu Ying. With the timelessness of the desert spread out all around them, it didn't take much effort for her to imagine what it would have been like two thousand years earlier.

Vultures rode the slow air currents under the sun. With Loulan's remains in view, she could imagine what the city would have looked like in its heyday. Remnants of walls marked the city's boundaries.

To the south, though, angry black clouds filled the sky. They'd moved much closer in the past hour.

"Is it supposed to storm?" The mask muffled Annja's voice as she followed Hu up the incline to the cave mouth.

"There's a possibility." Hu's words sounded garbled and forced. "Storms out here come up quickly, Miss Creed. Usually there's no rain. Only the wind."

"That's good. If we go subterranean with this, we don't want to risk getting drowned in a flash flood."

"The sand is just as risky. It's as fine as powder. If water will flow there, so will the sand."

Terror touched Annja for a moment. She'd thought about drowning before, had almost had situations come to that before, but being buried alive in sand? The idea of slowly suffocating was horrifying.

Once on a dig in New Mexico, she'd helped unearth two bodies that had been buried in a cave-in. The heat and the environment had mummified them. Annja knew she'd never forget their dead faces. Their mouths, eyes and ears had been packed with sand.

INSIDE THE CAVE, ANNJA TOOK out her flashlight and peered around. Remnants of the two men's gear lay strewn about the cave. Evidently whoever the professor had sent up to collect their things hadn't been tidy about the cleanup.

"What about our eyes?"

Drawn by Hu's voice, Annja looked at the professor.

Hu pointed to his eyes. "Can't the drug affect us through our eyes?"

"I don't think so. The poison Sha Wu Ying and his followers used was probably *datura*. Are you familiar with that?"

Hu nodded. "It was supposed to have been brought over from the Americas and isn't native to China."

"There are just as many botanists who will disagree with that," Annja said.

Hu shrugged as he scoured the ground with his flashlight. "Datura was known to the stone age people. It was used as a painkiller and to trigger vision quests by shamans. I first read about that in *The Clan of the Cave Bear.*"

Annja smiled. "You read popular fiction?"

Hu's eyes crinkled as he glanced back at her. "Whenever I can. Popular fiction allows me time to think about concepts, let them gel with other things I've learned." He followed the flashlight beam into the back recesses of the cave.

Trailing after the professor, her boots shuffling through the loose sand that had blown into the cave, Annja realized something. She felt foolish for not having thought of the possibility earlier. "The sand."

Hu turned to look at her.

"The wind blows the sand into the cave," Annja explained. "If there is a crack in here, it may have been buried."

Hu gazed around. "What do you suggest?"

"Sweep the floor with trenching tools."

"That could take hours."

"If we do it by ourselves."

"What do you propose?"

"Put masks on everyone else and bring them inside. You and I aren't feeling any effects from anything."

Hu hesitated. "That may be because the crack the powder was coming through is filled up. If we uncover it—"

"We came here to uncover it."

IT TOOK LESS THAN ONE HOUR. And the crack wasn't where they'd been looking after all.

Annja used one of the square-bladed trenching tools, dragging it across the uneven cave floor as she searched for a tiny fracture that had let the dust up into the cave.

The grating noise was deafening. In the enclosed sweltering environment of the cave, her clothes were immediately soaked with perspiration.

Roux tapped her on the shoulder. He was covered with sand and his beard and hair looked unkempt from the heat and sweat.

"What?" Annja suddenly realized that she was the only one still scraping the floor. She'd been so focused on the effort that she hadn't noticed the others.

Hu and the others stood looking away from her. They were focused on a section of the wall at the back of the cave.

"The crack wasn't in the floor," Roux said.

Annja walked to the rear of the cave. The mask across her lower face felt heavy and stiff from grit that had accumulated there as wet muck. She aimed her flashlight at the wall and spotted the thin crack that ran five feet across the solid plane of rock.

"Get everyone out of the cave," Annja said. "We'll need a chisel and a sledge."

"WE SHOULD GO IN NOW."

Seated on the cargo bay of the helicopter, Garin looked at Ngai and tried to hide his disdain for the Chinese businessman. He wasn't altogether certain he was successful. "It's not time yet."

Impatience tightened Ngai's features. "It's past time."

Garin sighed and it was all he could do not to reach for the .45 holstered under his arm and put a bullet through Ngai's head. "Let them find their way into the labyrinth first."

"I'm not even sure the underground passages you say exist are truly there."

Smiling, Garin pinned the man with his gaze. "If they're not there, then what's the hurry?"

Ngai didn't have an answer for that.

"Annja Creed is good at what she does," Garin said. "If the City of Thieves is there, she'll find it."

They sat little more than a mile from the mountains where Ngai's spy had informed them the expedition had gone. Ngai's guards had spread a sand-colored canvas over the helicopter, hiding it from distant viewers and providing some relief from the unbearable heat.

Garin was willing to wager an egg could be fried on the sand even in the shade. He took out another water bottle from the supplies and drank. The cold liquid rushed down his parched throat. But immediately his body started leaking it out again.

"We could go in there and take possession of the area." Ngai sounded bitterly frustrated.

"And if the City of Thieves isn't there?"

"We force her to tell us."

Garin shook his head. "That woman doesn't work like that. She's made of sterner stuff. If she hasn't sniffed it out by now, we need to let her run with it."

"You said you could find the City of Thieves." Ngai glared at him.

"If I have to, I can." However, Garin wasn't sure he could. He'd translated the back of the belt plaque, even seen through the confusion of the surface message to find the deeper one buried within.

But he didn't have the map of the interior. That was promised in some kind of child's toy. He hadn't figured out what that meant yet.

His phone rang and he answered before it could ring again.

"Braden," Garin said.

"Mr. Braden," the male voice at the other end of the line said.

"Yes."

"She's found it."

"Are you certain?"

"Yes. There's a passageway behind the wall at the back of the cave."

"Be ready." Garin closed the phone, then called Ngai's shock troops into action as he turned to the businessman. "Now."

Ngai cried encouragement to his men as they swept the canvas from the helicopter. By the time they had the canvas packed away, the rotors were churning at full speed, tossing sand in all directions.

Garin hauled himself into the copilot's seat as Ngai's men clambered aboard. Less than a minute later, Garin flashed the pilot a thumbs-up and the helicopter surged into the air.

31

Annja drew the sledgehammer back for another strike. Perspiration streamed down her body. Dust, fine as talcum powder, stuck to her exposed skin and drenched clothing.

Hu closed his eyes and turned his head away. His left hand was wrapped around the chisel poised at the center of the crack. The professor hadn't wanted the responsibility of swinging the sledgehammer while someone else held the chisel, so he'd volunteered for that task. But he couldn't watch.

"Steady," Annja said.

"I am." Hu's hand wasn't trembling as much as it had the first time. It was almost still.

Behind and to Annja's side, Roux and Hu's assistant held high-beam lights that splashed over the wall. So far she'd struck the chisel three times. The crack they'd discovered had grown wider. Dust swirled from the chamber on the other side of the wall.

Setting herself, Annja swung the hammer again. Metal crashed against metal, a sharp noise that rung inside the cave. Sparks flashed and died before they hit the ground.

This time the chisel sank into the wall several inches. The crack split, fragmenting in different directions. Stone splinters peppered Annja's face.

The cave wall held. More powder whirled into the air.

Hu tried to withdraw the chisel but couldn't get it to move. "It's stuck."

"Do we have another chisel?" Annja breathed deeply, hoping the mask was protection against whatever poison might be seeping from the room on the other side of the wall.

"Not one that big." Hu's assistant knelt at the toolbox they'd brought in. He held up a much smaller chisel.

"That's too small." Frustration chafed at Annja. She couldn't wait to see whatever was on the other side of the wall.

This was what she lived for, what she studied and why she researched and put in countless hours—the find. There was no drug like it. No other feeling she'd experienced came close to what she was feeling. Adrenaline, hot and insistent, pounded through her.

"Stand back." Annja lifted the sledgehammer to her shoulder again, set herself, and swung, putting all of her weight and muscle behind the effort.

The sledge hammered the wall. The fractures deepened and grew longer.

She drew back and hit again and again, turning into an automaton, not stopping until she couldn't lift the hammer any more. A pile of pebbles, stone splinters, and the powder collected where the wall met the cavern floor.

Breathing hard, the caked mask impeding her, Annja stepped back and dropped the sledge. She held her arms over her head to open her rib cage and let her lungs work more easily.

"It's all broken," Hu said, examining the wall, "but the weight is keeping the pieces locked in place." He turned to Annja. "We could send for some dynamite or plastic explosive."

"You have those at the camp?"

Hu shook his head.

That frustrated Annja even more. Getting those things would take too much time.

She turned her attention to the toolbox and found a long crowbar, bent like a shepherd's crook at one end and slanted at the other. Returning to the wall, she looked at the pieces like they were a jigsaw puzzle.

Somewhere in there, there's a rock that will give. A piece that will allow the others to fall. Annja ran her hand over the cracked mass bound together by its own weight. She made a selection near the top, extending her hands well above her head. Then she tightened her grip on the crowbar and slammed the slanted end into the crack beside the rock she'd chosen.

Rock and steel met in a loud, grating rasp. The crowbar sank into the crack a few inches.

Annja tried wiggling the crowbar and didn't feel much give at first. She focused and concentrated, drawing all the strength she had. In her mind, she felt for her sword, almost touching it. She felt stronger then, and she pulled even harder.

With a grumbling crush of noise, a rock the size of Annja's head tumbled from the wall.

Powder swirled for a moment, then poured to the floor.

Roux moved his flashlight beam to the hole Annja's efforts had made. "You're through." He walked forward, shining the light into the chamber beyond.

The room was small, and it seemed to be—as Annja had guessed—a storeroom. Cloth bags sat heaped in arranged stacks.

"If that's all poison," Roux said in French, "Sha Wu Ying had been planning to kill a lot of people."

"What did you say?" Hu joined them.

Annja interpreted for the professor. "It may not all be datura powder," she went on. "They could be other herbs, as well."

Some of the bags did look different.

"Look." Hu redirected his light. "There's a door."

Peering through the darkness, Annja spotted the door leading from the chamber.

She wondered what lay beyond.

HU BROUGHT THE WORK CREW in and set them to the task of carefully clearing away the powder and debris. They used shovels and wheelbarrows to haul it outside and dump it down the front of the mountainside.

Annja worked at the opening, digging more and more rock out of the way. It was hard work, but she wouldn't back off and let anyone else do it.

She monitored her own feelings, though, alert to any change in her perceptions. There was no sign of anyone succumbing to the hallucinogen's effects.

In just a few minutes, although it certainly felt longer, the opening was large enough to crawl through. Annja stepped back and put the crowbar down.

"Where do you think it goes?" Roux asked.

"It could be just a few rooms," Annja answered. "But

if the legend was right, if this really was a city of thieves, then I'll bet it goes deep underground and stretches back toward Loulan."

"Why Loulan?" Hu asked.

"Because they'd have needed a source of water. Loulan had the canal that supported the city."

"They could have dug wells," Roux said.

Annja nodded. "That's a possibility. But Tarim Basin dried up. It was primarily created by collected rainwater, not an underground river or reservoir. I doubt there's much groundwater in this area." She felt certain she was right.

"There's a helicopter," one of the workers shouted.

Wary at once, remembering there had been no sign of Garin Braden or Ngai Kuan-Yin so far, Annja went to the cave's mouth and peered up into the sky. She used a hand to shade her eyes against the bright sun.

Looking waspish, the aircraft swooped in low, coming in from the dark cloudbank that was now almost upon the mountains. The gathering wind swept across the open desert, bringing dust devils to life and causing the helicopter to bob in the air.

STRAPPED INTO THE PASSENGER seat, Garin cursed the windstorm that had swirled into being around him. If he didn't know better, if he hadn't learned to get over so many of his superstitions, he would have sworn that the fates had decided to intervene.

The helicopter closed in on the mountainside. Garin watched as one of the workers dumped another wheelbarrow full of detritus over the side.

Ngai's voice came over the headset. "Kill them."

Angered, Garin turned to look into the back, intend-

ing on arguing the point. Instead, whatever attempts he
might have made to forestall the wholesale slaughter
died as the pilot opened fire.

Once they'd arrived in the desert outside the Loulan
dig site, Ngai's men had mounted machine guns under
the helicopter and a digital weapons system had been
added that fed directly to the pilot's controls.

Furious, Garin considered drawing his pistol and
shooting Ngai through the heart. But he knew Ngai's
men wouldn't have allowed him to escape.

The heavy machine-gun bullets chopped into the
camels and the people who were tending to them. Most
of the camels went down at once, huge bloody holes torn
in them, sagging on legs that would no longer hold their
weight. Two men ran, but they didn't get far.

Then the pilot pulled his craft up, taking aim on the
cave mouth.

KELLY SWAN ACTED ON instinct as the sounds of the
heavy machine-gun fire echoed around her, reverberat-
ing in the cave and mixing with the sounds of the continued assault. She scrambled for her bedroll, watching
from the corner of her eye as the helicopter came up to
address the cave as she knew it would.

They were trapped in the cave, there was nowhere to
go. She knew the machine guns would chop them to
rags if they tried to flee down the mountainside.

Diving to the ground, Kelly yanked the bedroll open.
It didn't matter who knew her secrets now. They were
all about to die.

In her haste, she spilled her pistols from the bedroll.
They slid across the exposed rock and dust collected on
the cave floor. The bag of bones skittered free, as well,

and the ivory sphere tumbled free of the cloth bag, landing in plain sight.

A hand reached out and caught the bone sphere.

For a moment, Annja Creed locked eyes with Kelly. Kelly knew instantly that the archaeologist realized she wasn't just a laborer picked up in Dunhuang.

Move! Kelly told herself. There's nothing you can do about that now!

Sliding forward Kelly grabbed both of her pistols, flipped the safeties off, and charged toward the cave mouth. Two of the workers stood frozen in the opening, staring at what was happening in stunned disbelief.

Kelly threw herself at the two men, hitting them at knee level and knocking them to the ground. She yelled at them, cursed at them, telling them to get moving. Then she pushed herself up from their midst, throwing her pistols before her as the helicopter swelled to fill her vision.

She pulled the triggers, aiming almost point-blank.

GARIN SAW THE WOMAN in the cave opening before the pilot did. In the bright light, he couldn't see the muzzle flashes of her pistols, but he knew they had to be there when the Plexiglas nose of the helicopter suddenly spiderwebbed.

Most of the bullets glanced off the rounded surface, but two or three of them tore through. One of them cut by Garin's head and stuffing exploded from his seat.

"Get us out of here!" he roared at the pilot.

The machine guns silenced as the pilot jerked the yoke back and brought the tail section sharply around. Ngai's men slid the cargo door open.

Wind howled into the helicopter, jostling the craft even more. A few of the men fired and the hot shell casings ricocheted inside the helicopter. Ngai cursed them and sank into his seat, taking cover.

Glancing across the pilot, at the cave mouth, Garin saw the woman duck back inside. "She's out of bullets. Quickly. Turn the helicopter—"

He stopped speaking as he saw Roux step from the cave with a hunting rifle in his arms. The old man took aim. Garin knew from experience how deadly Roux could be in a fight.

"Get out of here!" Garin yelled.

The pilot's head disappeared in a rush of blood and bone that sprayed the inside of the Plexiglas. Garin felt the sticky heat spread over his face and tasted the salt of the man's blood. His left eye went dark. He didn't know if the bullet had hit him in the eye or if it had just filled with blood.

With a sickening lurch, the helicopter swerved out of control as the corpse draped the yoke.

32

Garin's world turned into a kaleidoscope of movement. He shoved the pilot's corpse away and switched off the helicopter's engines. The vision in his left eye improved as he continued to blink, so he felt certain Roux's bullet hadn't caught him when it had passed through the pilot.

He hoped that shutting off the helicopter's engines would save them. He'd been on board one that had lost power before, and he'd panicked. But the pilot at the time had remained calm and told him that the aircraft's design gave it a fighting chance to survive impact. The rotors still turned enough, powered by the descent, to slow the fall somewhat.

Time slowed. Garin watched the approach of the desert floor coming up at them. Evidently Roux kept firing, because holes appeared in the left side of the helicopter and at least one of Ngai's warriors was hit.

When the helicopter hit the ground, everything went too fast again. Garin fell hard against the strap but was restrained. He was certain his upper body would be covered with bruises by nightfall. But he was alive.

He tried to breathe and couldn't. Panic surged through him. After five hundred years of a life filled with death and danger, though, he calmed himself and relaxed. A moment later, his lungs opened up and he took a breath.

Confusion filled the helicopter's interior. Men yelled and cursed, amazed to be alive. The smell of gas mixed with the air, whipped by the storm's growing ferocity.

Then a hole opened up in the helicopter's side and slammed a man against the opposite cargo bulkhead. The sound of the high-powered rifle crack reached them shortly afterward.

Garin cursed. Roux hadn't given up on killing them.

"Out," he ordered. "It's the old man. Stay in the helicopter and he'll kill you."

He pulled at his seat restraint and found that it was locked and wouldn't release. Reaching into his right boot, he pulled out a fighting knife and slashed the restraint. He rocked forward, barely clearing the seat before another high-powered round slammed through the helicopter and opened another hole he could almost put his fist through.

Kicking the door open, Garin dropped to the sand outside. He didn't pull his pistol. He knew the bullets would never have reached Roux in the cave mouth.

Racing to the cargo area, Garin helped yank the door open, then reached in and jerked Ngai's warriors from the death trap the helicopter had become.

One stray spark and this whole thing will blow up in your face, he told himself grimly.

Five of the men were down. Dead, dying, or

wounded, they weren't going to be of any use and would only hold the group back.

"Out of the helicopter!" Garin shouted. "Out of the helicopter before it explodes!" He leaned in and seized an AK-74 from one of the dead men. Another swipe netted him the ammo bandolier.

Ngai got out of the helicopter under his own power. Despite his impatience and self-imposed sense of worth, the man moved like a fighter, powerful and quick.

Roux continued targeting the helicopter. One of the surviving men stepped into the old man's line of sight. A bullet punched through his chest and tore out his backbone. He was dead before he hit the ground, falling first to his knees then to his face.

"Away from the helicopter," Garin ordered. "Follow me." He ran, heading for a sand dune that offered some shelter.

Bullets from Roux's rifle tore dish-sized divots from the sand, but the whipping winds quickly filled them in again.

Garin threw himself behind the dune, fell into a prone position, then took aim with the AK-74. He fired on semiautomatic, pumping round after round at Roux. Garin saw that he didn't have the distance right. He adjusted the sighting screws and took aim again. Before he could squeeze the trigger, a bullet plowed into the sand in front of him, then cut through the sand and burned across his neck.

Realizing that the bullet had nearly taken his head off, Garin ducked down. Sand filled his eyes, bringing an onslaught of blinding pain.

Damn you, old man! Garin called for a canteen, hoping that the sand didn't cut his eyes before he could get it out. Assault rifles around him chugged on fully automatic.

STUNNED, HER ATTENTION TORN between the bone
sphere in her hand, Roux standing in the cave mouth
with his rifle to his shoulder, and the woman who was
reloading her pistols with spare clips from the bedroll,
Annja didn't know where to look.

Once her weapons were recharged, the woman
pointed the pistols at Annja's chest. "Give that back to
me." Her voice was flat and hard.

Hu and the others had thrown themselves to the
cave floor when the shooting had started. They looked
on in amazement.

"What is this?" Annja asked.

"None of your business."

Turning the ball over in her hands, Annja spotted
Scythian *tamgas* cut into the surface of the bones. She
realized then that the ball was made from several different bones that fit together.

Annja looked at the woman. "Who are you?"

Throughout the encounter, the sound of Roux's
hunting rifle came with metronomic regularity.

Deliberately, the woman pointed one of the pistols
at Annja's right eye. "If I have to ask again, I'll kill you."

Bullets suddenly sprayed against the front of the
cave. A few of them entered the cave, ricocheted, and
somehow didn't hit anyone.

Roux bolted back from the cave mouth, cursing flam-
boyantly in a variety of languages. He pressed himself
against the scant protection offered by the wall and
started feeding shells into the rifle. Then he saw the
woman with her weapons trained on Annja.

"What's going on?" Roux snapped in Latin.

"I don't know." Replying in the same language, Annja

didn't take her eyes from the woman. "But the ball I'm holding seems somehow connected to all of this."

"Let me see it," Roux said.

The gunfire from outside continued.

"If I try to hand it to you, I think she'll shoot me." Annja reached for her sword.

"You can't just give it to her," Roux protested.

"We're not exactly at the negotiating table on this one." Annja handed the ball to the woman with her left hand. She had her right firmly around the sword, ready to pull it into the cave with her.

The woman reached for the ball.

Annja twisted, drawing the sword and striking the woman's gun arm aside the flat of the blade. Swinging again, taking some satisfaction from the look of surprise on the woman's face, Annja caught her with the flat of the blade again, this time whipping her on the temple.

Dazed, the woman dropped to her knees.

Annja plucked the ball from the woman's hand, then kicked her pistols toward Roux. Surging, the woman pulled a knife from her boot and lunged for Annja's throat. Annja barely got the sword up in time to deflect the surprise strike. Metal rasped on metal.

The woman sprang backward, throwing a round-house kick. Annja ducked under the kick and took the sword's handle in both hands.

Roux's bolt-action ratcheting in the cave sounded loud against the sudden silence as the outside guns fell idle. From the corner of her eye, Annja saw that Roux had aimed squarely at the woman's chest.

Roux spoke English, rapidly and harsh.

With a look of pained disgust and maybe a little embarrassment, the woman threw the knife down.

"Now then," Roux said, never moving the rifle, "let's look at the facts. That little bauble you've been carrying means that your presence here isn't a mistake or by chance."

"No," the woman agreed. "I came here to kill Ngai Kuan-Yin." Her eyes looked blank and hard above the dirt-encrusted surgical mask.

"Well, that certainly gives us common ground. If I haven't killed him, I'd be more than happy to have another go at it."

"Roux!"

Annja recognized Garin's voice.

"You don't have to die in there," Garin bellowed. "You can still walk away from this."

Roux looked at Annja. "Do you think we can trust him?" he asked.

"No."

"Neither do I." Roux turned his attention to the woman. "What's your name?"

The woman hesitated. "Kelly."

"Why do you want to kill Ngai?" Roux asked.

"He had my father murdered."

"I saw how you handle those pistols of yours. You've had training."

Kelly didn't say anything.

"You knew Ngai would come here."

"Yes."

"How?"

"Ngai is looking for the City of Thieves."

Annja held up the ball. "Where did you get this?"

"That's for me to know."

"What you know," Roux said forcefully, "is important. We can hear you out, or we can figure it out on our own. Guess which way you get to live?"

A chill passed through Annja. She had the distinct impression that Roux really would kill the woman if she didn't talk. *That's just a ruse. Isn't it?* She suddenly wasn't sure.

"I don't know what it is." Kelly seemed embarrassed. "My father left it for me. Until a few days ago, I'd never seen it."

"Roux! Don't be foolish!" Garin's voice sounded loud and impatient.

Garin just doesn't want to risk his own neck, Annja thought.

"Is the ball important?" Roux asked.

"There are *tamgas* on the pieces," Annja replied.

Roux sighed. "I hate having to make a lot of decisions all at once. I don't know whether to trust her or not."

Annja willed the sword away, then knelt and picked up the nearest pistol. She handed the ball and the pistol to Kelly. "Fine. I'll make this call. You figure out whether we should trust Garin."

Kelly seemed surprised. The pistol jerked automatically in her hand, almost coming up despite the fact that Roux still had her covered.

"We're in this together," Annja said. "Ngai and Garin aren't going to give you a free pass out of here."

"I don't want one." Kelly tossed the ball back to Annja. "I can't figure that out." She retrieved her other pistol, then held them both up. "I'm better with these."

Annja nodded.

Roux sighed with disgust. "How do you know she won't put a bullet in the back of your head the first chance she gets?"

"It's my amazing woman powers," Annja said.

Kelly nodded back at her. "As long as we understand each other. I came here to kill the man who killed my father."

Annja looked at the ball. "Oh, I think we all have our agendas."

"Roux! Answer me!" Garin shouted.

"I don't think we're going to get out of here without putting some of them to rest." Annja walked to the cave mouth and carefully peered down. A couple hundred or so yards away, Garin, Ngai, and fifteen armed men occupied positions behind sand dunes.

"*Annja!* Talk some sense into—"

Roux rolled out of hiding and fired, swiftly working the bolt-action and firing again.

The first bullet missed Garin by inches. The second struck the helicopter's gas tank, exploding it. The helicopter flew from the ground with a convulsive shudder, then broke apart and caught fire. Black smoke roiled up to mix with the thick, ominous clouds that swirled in the sky.

Garin and his newfound friends ducked for cover.

"So much for negotiations," Annja muttered.

"It would only have been a waste of time." Roux stepped back from the cave mouth and nodded at the passageway they'd uncovered. "We have a way out."

If it goes anywhere, Annja thought. But, in the end, they really didn't have a choice.

The archaeology crew climbed through the hole in the cave wall and stepped into the waiting darkness.

33

Outside the storeroom, which had obviously been designed to stand apart from the rest of the underground structure, Annja followed a corkscrew spiral staircase that had been carved from solid stone. The amount of work involved told her that the subterranean complex must have taken years to construct.

She followed her flashlight beam, but the beams of the crew behind her wavered and flashed through the darkness, as well. Knowing that Garin and Ngai wouldn't waste any time pursuing them, she went as quickly as she could.

The steps went on and on leaving a feeling of vertigo swirling in Annja's skull. Several of the people following her had started to bump up against the rough-hewn walls. She hoped no one would fall, because it would have a domino effect.

Finally reaching the bottom of the steps, Annja discovered a hallway ran to the left and to the right.

She waved her flashlight at the wall in front of her,

hoping for some kind of help that would explain where she was. She transferred the bone sphere to her backpack, as everyone gathered.

"Do you know where we are?" Kelly stood behind Annja, breathing as regularly as if she'd been on a stroll.

Definitely not your common dig worker, Annja noted.

"Maybe eighty or a hundred feet below the surface." Annja looked at the ground, hoping the wear on the stone would indicate which way most of the pedestrian traffic went. She figured that heavier wear would indicate the shortest path to an exit.

Don't get your hopes up. Whatever exit might have been there two thousand years ago may not exist now, she reminded herself. Doubt ran through Annja's mind. Suddenly a new thought occurred to her. It's only been a hundred years. Lehmann claimed to have gotten down into the City of Thieves.

Her hope shored a little, Annja knelt and ran her fingers across the stone. She felt the deep grooves in the rock caused by frequent trips of those who had lived underground.

"Do you have maps of this place?" Kelly asked.

"Unfortunately, no. Hold them back for a moment. Until I decide which way we're going."

Kelly blocked the doorway, holding back the line of people. She held one of her pistols in her fist. Stopping traffic was no problem.

"What's going on?" Roux demanded from the end of the line. He'd chosen to bring up the rear.

Annja ignored the question. She started back along the hallway in the other direction. The stone was worn more heavily there. A trench occupied the center of the corridor, deep and smooth.

She stood and pointed the flashlight ahead of her. "This way." She took off at once, stooped just a little because the corridor's ceiling was low.

Kelly followed her, matching Annja's pace but leaving her room to work. "That was a neat trick with the sword. How did you do that?"

"Sleight of hand," Annja replied. "I always loved David Copperfield's performances."

"You'll have to show me some time."

"A good magician never reveals her secrets," Annja said.

GARIN PAUSED AT the cave mouth, resting his AK-74 on his hip and listening intently. It was hard to hear anything. The storm's fury had worsened. The wind picked up sand and spun it hard enough to sting exposed skin, even through light fabric. He'd slid his sunglasses on to protect his eyes.

Ngai's men were in line behind him.

"Go," Ngai ordered impatiently from the rear of the line. "They're going to get away."

Get away where? Garin wondered. But since he heard nothing, he entered the cave mouth and peered inside.

He spotted the opening in the cave wall at once. Piles of rock had tumbled before it. Lead smears from the bullets they'd fired into the area streaked the walls.

"They're gone." Ngai was furious. Color reddened his face. He addressed Garin like he was to blame.

Garin swallowed his anger. There would be a time for reckoning later.

"They're inside the underground city. They found the City of Thieves." Garin felt certain that's what had been located. "They haven't gotten away. We're just going to hunt them down like rats in a maze." He grinned. "Now, I need a flashlight."

One of Ngai's warriors handed him a light.

Taking the flashlight, Garin switched it on and stepped through the opening, taking up pursuit.

WHEN ANNJA FELT the section of floor tremble underfoot, she threw herself against Kelly and yelled, "Back!"

The two women moved, dropping to the floor and bouncing off Professor Hu and the men behind him. Annja hoped they'd gotten clear.

Stone grated and a dozen metal spikes suddenly thrust out of the wall to the right and chipped stone from the opposite side of the hallway. Sparks flew like tiny fireflies and quickly died out.

Some of the local workers cried out in fear, calling on their ancestors for blessings.

Annja got to her feet and eased up to the pressure plate that had tripped the trap. Two thousand years old and it works like a Swiss watch she thought with admiration.

"That was close." Kelly was at Annja's side.

Annja used a small crowbar from her backpack to pry the pressure plate back into place. The iron spikes retracted into the stone wall with a grinding noise.

"So what do you do when you're not dodging death traps in lost and forbidden underground cities?"

Kelly seemed to consider the question for a time before she answered. "Espionage."

"Chinese?"

"American."

"Interesting. That's what brought you over here?"

"Actually, the agency that I used to work for and I have a hand's-off policy we're following with each other. I was coming to visit my father when I found him murdered by Ngai's thugs."

Annja grimaced. "Oh. Sorry." She searched the ground and found four small rocks that fit up under the pressure plate. Annja wedged them in tight.

Bracing herself, she put pressure on the plate and found she'd managed to keep it from making contact with the tripping mechanism. She turned to the group of people behind her.

"Give me room to work. If there was a trap here, there'll be others." Annja pointed to the pressure plate. "I've jammed this one, but you should still step over it if you can." Her surgical mask had slipped off during the exertion. She took a deep breath. There was nothing but the scent of stale air, and no effects from the datura powder that she could feel. "I think we'll be fine without the masks at this point."

As the others moved on, Kelly hung back.

When she checked on her charges a short time later, Annja saw Kelly kneeling by the pressure plate. The woman carefully pried out the rocks Annja had wedged in. When she stood, the trap was set again.

Standing nearby, Roux looked at Kelly and grinned in approval. "I like the way you think," he said.

"There's no sense in letting a perfectly good trap go unused," Kelly replied.

"That might not be such a good move if we have to come back this way," Annja said.

"We haven't found a true exit yet," Roux retorted. "The way we came in was through a room, not a door."

Annja had to admit that was true.

"And," Roux added, "going back into superior fire-power isn't a good plan."

Also true, Annja agreed. Then she took up the lead again, easing through the darkness.

AT THE BOTTOM OF THE spiral stairs, Garin hunkered down to survey the floor.

"What are you doing?" Ngai demanded.

"Looking to see which way they went." Garin played the flashlight over the rock and dust.

"They went this way." One of Ngai's warriors stepped forward impatiently. He indicated the footprints in the dust. "Any fool can see that."

Unless Annja or Roux faked those footprints for a time and dragged a shirt over the dust in the other direction to mask their trail, Garin thought that. He didn't say anything.

"Go," Ngai ordered.

The warrior ran, following the hallway.

Garin stood and looked at Ngai. "How many underground cities have you been in before?"

Ngai ignored him.

"Station a couple men here," Garin said, "to keep them from doubling back and escaping."

With terse commands, Ngai assigned two men to guard the stairs. Then he followed his men.

Garin trailed after them, knowing they were too eager. Like hounds on a scent. He knew they were thinking about the fact that only Roux and the woman had fired back, suggesting that their prey was virtually helpless.

They didn't see the dangers posed by the unknown terrain they traveled.

Only a short distance ahead, Garin heard a distinctive clicking sound. He froze in his tracks. He'd been on far too many tomb robberies not to pay attention to such things.

Then iron spikes suddenly jetted from the wall, slamming into the lead warrior and impaling him. Incredibly, the spikes didn't kill the man outright. He hung there, pinned against the stone wall like an insect on a collector's board.

The man screamed in pain, but the sound was as much a gurgle as shriek. At least one of his lungs had been punctured. Garin figured probably both.

The other warriors stood back from the dying man. They were used to street violence, not something so unexpected.

The man begged and mewled for help, growing weaker by the second.

Garin muscled his way to the front of the stunned men and looked at the wounded warrior. There was nothing to be done to save him. Kneeling, Garin took out his knife and lifted the pressure plate that had sprung the trap.

The bars withdrew, pulling back through the man's body and dropping him to the ground. He flailed his arms helplessly, no longer able to move his legs.

Garin guessed that the man's spine had been severed. Blood spread in an ever-widening pool beneath him, but it would be some time before he died from blood loss.

Turning to Ngai, Garin said, "Maybe I could lead now. You can bet this isn't going to be the only trap in this place. Sha Wu Ying and his people probably littered this place with death traps. I might be able to keep more of your men alive."

Ngai said nothing, then slowly nodded.

Drawing his pistol, Garin put the barrel against the dying man's head. The man's eyes widened as he realized what was going to happen. Somehow he found the strength to yell even louder.

Garin pulled the trigger and the pistol bucked in his fist.

34

At first, Annja had thought the cries of pain that had filled the corridor behind them had been horrible. But they didn't compare to the sudden silence that followed the last ringing echoes of the gunshot.

She knew that the trap they'd left behind had claimed at least one victim. That knowledge didn't make her feel good—or safe.

In the last fifteen feet, she'd disabled two more traps. She made her way to the doorway ahead. When she reached it, she paused, shining her flashlight around.

"What is it?" Kelly asked her.

The woman's question echoed inside the massive vault before them.

"Whatever it is, it's big." Annja moved her flashlight around. The darkness effortlessly absorbed the light, like a great ocean of blackness. She turned to Hu's assistant. "I need the flare gun from the emergency kit."

The young man dropped to his knees and opened the pack. He reached inside and brought out the flare gun.

Chambering one of the fat rounds, Annja aimed the flare gun at the ceiling above them. She couldn't see it, only knew that it had to be there. Drawing a breath, squinting her eyes, she squeezed the trigger.

The flare took flight with a muffled sound! It smacked into the ceiling some twenty feet overhead, sending a colony of bats into panicked flight.

Bats, Annja thought. She watched them for a moment. If bats have found a way in, there has to be a way out. That didn't mean that way out was big enough for human beings, though.

The flare bounced from the ceiling, then deployed its parachute. Burning a pallid ruby and trailing smoke, the flare floated toward the ground.

The chamber was at least a hundred and fifty or two hundred yards across. To Annja's right and dead ahead of her, doors opened into rooms built into the ground. The chamber floor was covered in rock quarried in alabaster-colored flat slabs a foot to two feet across, fitted and mortared together.

"There are steps cut into the wall over here," Professor Hu said.

Before the flare winked out, Annja looked at the wall and saw the steps. They curled around the chamber, gradually leading up, vanishing in the darkness again before she could see where they ended.

"It has to be the way out," Hu said hopefully.

At least at one time, Annja thought. Nothing else made sense. But there had been nuclear testing over the Lop Nur area, and two thousand years of history.

Annja took a deep breath. She wanted to stay and explore the buildings cut into the chamber side, but knew she couldn't with Garin and Ngai hot on their heels.

"All right," Annja said. "Let's see where it takes us." She took the lead, playing her flashlight over the steep steps.

MINUTES LATER, THEY REACHED the top of the stairs. A tumbled-down mass of rocks blocked the way.

Annja couldn't tell if there had been a doorway under the debris or if the stairs had merely fed into another corridor. She felt air on her face, cool against the perspiration.

Reaching into her pocket, she took out the lighter she habitually carried for starting fires. She struck the igniter, sparks flared to life, and the wick caught. A bright yellow-blue flame danced to life.

Immediately, the flame shimmied, pulled by the invisible air currents that Annja felt. Airflow meant there was a gap somewhere. She moved the lighter close to the chamber wall, knowing that air had a tendency to follow solid surfaces, the same principle that allowed an airplane's wing to achieve lift.

Sliding the lighter's flame within inches of the wall, Annja discovered that the air flowed through the wall at different places. Training her flashlight on the wall, she searched for cracks.

"Here." Kelly traced her forefinger along a too-straight crack that ran along the wall. That crack met three others, all at right angles to each other, framing a rectangle.

"It's a door," Roux said.

The sound of approaching footsteps echoed from below.

"They're coming," Professor Hu whispered.

As a group, the other members of the archaeological party shrank back against the wall, acting as if they could pull the shadows over themselves and stay hidden.

Annja handed her flashlight to Kelly, then ran her hands along the wall. *If it's a door, there has to be a means to open it.*

Her questing fingers found a dust-covered rock that jutted out a little from the wall and felt too smooth to be natural.

Annja pulled and twisted, and finally pushed, on the rock. It slid a quarter-inch. Something clicked.

Abruptly, the rectangle set in the wall recessed, then swung inward.

Kelly shined the flashlight into the new hallway. It went on a short distance, then steps cut into the stone descended again.

"We want to go *up,* not down," Kelly whispered.

The footsteps had almost reached the chamber, growing louder and more threatening.

"We want to get out of here first." Annja took her flashlight, then took the lead.

When everyone was inside, she watched as Roux closed the door behind them. Light flared around the edges of the door.

"Lights off," she ordered. "They'll see us."

Reluctantly, everyone turned off their flashlights.

"Wait to move until I tell you to move. I'm going to explore ahead." Cautiously, Annja trailed a hand along the wall and crept forward, all her other senses alert.

One of the steps clicked underfoot. She threw herself backward as mechanical rumblings sounded ahead of her. Something whisked by overhead. She landed with bruising, bone-jarring force.

"Annja!" Roux cried.

"I'm okay." Annja breathed out, tasting the alkaline dust that caked the floor. She'd made that announcement to herself as much as to Roux. She wondered which of them was more surprised.

She risked a brief flicker of the flashlight and saw three sword blades that had arced overhead and bit into the wall above her. They'd probably only missed her by inches. She saw no rust on the blades, another indication of how the dry environment had preserved everything.

She went more slowly and finally reached the bottom of fourteen steps without further incident. "Fourteen steps," she called out to the others. "There are swords in the wall to your right, but the edges are turned in. You'll be all right."

Only a short distance ahead, the passageway turned to her left and went down again. Unwilling to venture forward without benefit of a light and trusting that the bends would mask her flashlight, Annja switched it on.

The yellow cone of illumination strobed the darkness, revealing a short flight of carved stone steps. Beyond the steps the mummified remains of several men hung in a variety of torture devices.

GARIN LED THE WAY INTO the large chamber. Everyone, Ngai included, was willing to follow his lead now. The two rooms carved out of the walls interested him at once. Excitement thrummed within him. There was nothing like raiding someone else's treasure vaults.

"Where are they?" Ngai asked.

"Maybe in the rooms." Garin held his pistol. He wouldn't have minded if Annja and Roux had escaped. The old man had only tried to kill him because he knew Garin would have tried to do the same. It really wasn't anything personal.

Garin played his flashlight beam over the chamber,

spotting the stairs carved into the chamber's side immediately.

"Get a team up there," he directed. Thoughts of the big hunting rifle in Roux's capable hands weren't pleasant. "Find out where that goes."

Three men split off and trotted up the steps.

Garin watched them.

A moment later they stopped. "The way is blocked," one of the men called back.

"Maintain your positions there," Garin ordered. "You've got a clear field of fire from there." That would help in case they needed to retreat or fall back. If Roux and Annja hadn't escaped, that meant they had to be close by. "The rest of you watch the entrances of those rooms."

Cautiously, Garin approached the first space, expecting to feel a bullet slap into him at any time.

The doorway to the first chamber was narrow and functional, not ornate like the second one. A quick inspection revealed that it was a barracks. Dead men filled the beds.

Garin played his light over the corpses and remembered the stories he'd heard of Sha Wu Ying's betrayal. A momentary fear trickled along his spine when he wondered if the sickness that had claimed so many lives might still be active in the room. Some illnesses hid as spores for years, waiting for the right moment to reactivate.

In five hundred years, Garin had never been sick. He'd convalesced from wounds, of course, and almost died from a few of them. But he'd never been sick. He'd been in London when the Black Death had broken out, had seen the carts roll by filled with corpses.

Now that Joan's sword was whole again, he didn't know how it would affect him. Would he be susceptible to disease?

"Mr. Braden."

The man's voice broke into Garin's reverie. He looked up to find one of Ngai's warriors standing in the doorway. "What?" he snapped.

"You must come to the other room. Quickly."

Cursing, Garin walked out of the barracks and over to the other room.

Ngai stood outside.

"I thought we'd agreed that you would let me lead this," Garin growled.

"We needed to secure this building," Ngai stated calmly. "If the archaeological crew was inside, if Annja Creed and the old man were inside, we needed to know. I acted in both our interests."

It made sense, and it was too late to do anything about it.

"There is a problem." Ngai pointed into the building.

35

Garin shined his flashlight into the darkness. A short distance in, a ten-foot section of a corridor had turned sideways, revealing a gap in the floor.

"What happened?" Garin asked.

Ngai looked unhappy. "Two of the men went forward into the corridor. It twisted and turned before they got halfway. They fell."

It was, Garin thought, a well-devised trap.

"Where are those men now?" Garin asked.

Ngai shook his head. "I don't know."

"I'll check," one of the warriors said.

Garin glanced at the man and smiled. "You want to go in there?"

The warrior drew himself up belligerently. "I'm not afraid. Chan was my friend."

"Well, then, by all means go get him." Garin waved the man inside the corridor.

After a brief hesitation, the man walked in. "The trap has already been sprung. There's nothing to be afraid of."

Garin didn't say anything, knowing the man was suddenly more desirous of convincing himself than in convincing anyone else. Garin watched and waited.

The warrior reached the edge of the opening. In the next instant, iron spears spaced six inches apart rocketed from the ceiling along the edge. Three of the spears pierced the warrior. One slid neatly through his skull.

"The first trap set the second one." Garin spoke as calmly as though lecturing a class. "Whoever designed this spent considerable effort at it. Getting through it is going to take time." He looked at Ngai and the remaining members of the security force. "Anybody else in a hurry?"

ANNJA PLAYED HER FLASHLIGHT beam over the horrific scene before her.

Manacled to the wall, missing limbs, bound in iron cages, strung upside down from chains, strapped in impossible positions, the corpses were frozen in horror, pain, and despair.

Professor Hu gasped and spoke in Chinese. Several of the dig workers cursed and backed away.

Steeling herself, knowing they couldn't go back the way they'd come without risking discovery, Annja walked into the room. She'd seen things like this before, but they were usually in illustrations.

She took her digital camera from her pack and started taking pictures. Annja couldn't help thinking, *Doug, I've got a story for you.* The scene was something the audience for *Chasing History's Monsters* would love.

"Looks like Sha Wu Ying built his own private chamber of horrors," Roux said solemnly. "He never did have much use for enemies." He paused, reaching out to touch the remains of a man who'd had both eyes pierced by long iron needles. "Except as diversions, of course."

Annja kept going forward, passing horror after gruesome horror, until she reached the other side of the big room. There were no doors, no way out.

"Well," Roux stated calmly, "I'd say it looks like we're at a dead end."

Annja looked at him in the reflection of the flashlight beams.

"I thought it was time for a little levity," Roux said.

"No," Annja told him. "I'll let you know when it's time."

Roux switched to Latin. "We can't leave this place until that item I've come for is secured. Or I know it's destroyed."

"I've got to get these people out of here. Before they get killed down here, either murdered by Ngai's people or some death trap," Annja replied.

Roux nodded, but he clearly wasn't happy about it.

Annja turned to the group. "We'll rest here. At the moment we're safe. Professor Hu, find out how much water we're carrying. We'll need to ration it out, but I want people to get a drink right now." It was important that they feel like they were in control of their situation instead of at its mercy.

Shrugging out of her backpack, Annja tried her phone but wasn't surprised when she couldn't get a signal. Placing her flashlight on the floor beside her, she took out the bone sphere Kelly had been carrying.

After inspecting it, she took it apart.

"What are you doing?" Kelly asked.

"This is a puzzle, right?"

"Yes. When my father left it for me, it was just a collection of loose bones. When I was a little girl, he used to have me put interlocking puzzles together. I figured out the secret of the bones."

"And learned what?"

Kelly looked at her, then sank to the ground opposite her with her legs crossed. She wore her pistols in a double shoulder holster now. "That they would fit together to make a ball."

"Maybe that's because you thought it should," Annja said. "It merely met your expectation." She dropped the freed pieces of shaped bone on the ground in front of her. "What I have found in my research is that often puzzles—truly complicated puzzles that are meant to stymie—have more than one solution. Sometimes they have several. But only one is correct."

Annja spread the pieces, turning them up so the Scythian *tamgas* stood revealed. She pushed the pieces around and tried to forget that their lives could depend on her ingenuity. I need to take at least long enough to figure out if there's anything here or if I'm wasting time, she thought.

Roux stood behind her, the hunting rifle resting on its butt plate. He peered over her shoulder. "What are you thinking?"

"That there's a reason Sha Wu Ying—Tochardis—hung on to his Scythian heritage."

"If the symbols are linked," Kelly said, "there has to be a progression. A key that unlocks the encryption system."

Annja looked at her.

Kelly shrugged. "I have a little experience with codes."

Excited, Annja brought out her computer and powered it up. She brought up the research she'd done and hoped that her batteries would last. She'd charged it before leaving camp. Then she also hoped the batteries in the flashlights held up.

When she had the page of the known *tamgas,* Annja read through them. The pile of bones before her had thirty different symbols. She smiled.

Roux looked at her and grinned a little. "What do you think you know?"

"The *tamgas* collected here cover a generational span. Each one came into being at a different time." Annja pointed to the list. "The research might not be exact, there may be some differences, but that has to be the answer."

Returning her attention to the piles, Annja found one of the oldest *tamgas.* Then she found one of the next *tamgas* in line. It didn't fit. Neither did the next three. But the one after that did. After years spent reassembling broken pottery, skeletons, and other artifacts that had almost been lost to hard use, ill care, and time, Annja's brain, eyes and hands moved quickly.

By the time she got the fourth piece locked into place, she knew the final design wasn't going to be a sphere.

GARIN TOOK THE CORRIDOR inch by bloody inch. When he was halfway to the dead man transfixed by the spears, he found yet another pressure plate that triggered a third response.

He skirted it and moved on, arriving at the spears thrust down from the ceiling. With them every six inches apart, he couldn't squeeze through. He played his light into the hole under the trick corridor section and saw the rod in the left end that formed a hinge. Recessed areas on the right held spokes that had withdrawn and allowed the section to fall.

It was rather ingenious and Garin had never seen the like. But he couldn't get at a proper angle to see down into the hole.

"Are you down there?" he called out in Chinese. He repeated himself more loudly.

There was no response.

Moving carefully, he turned his attention to the spears that blocked forward passage. He pushed and pulled on them to no avail.

He'd come prepared for such an eventuality. This wasn't the first tomb he'd raided, and he was careful enough to plan that it wouldn't be the last.

He returned to the arched doorway. "I need the cutting torch from the equipment cases."

Most of the equipment had survived the destruction of the helicopter. The explosion had thrown the cargo free.

Ngai wasn't happy. "That will take time to retrieve."

"Then it will take time," Garin said. "If you rush now, you're going to die."

Cursing, Ngai ordered two of his men to get the torch.

ANNJA KEPT CLICKING BONES together. Once it was big enough, Roux and Kelly helped her, sorting pieces for her and starting smaller sections that she clicked into the bigger one.

The finished piece was nearly three feet long and three-dimensional. It forked like a plant in a few areas, but stayed to a central stalk.

When Annja pieced the tallest bit together, one that had a circular assemblage of bones, she knew what the pieces made.

Everyone was quiet, looking at it.

"There must be some mistake," Roux said after a short time. "That isn't anything."

Annja grinned. "Actually, it is."

"What?"

Annja touched the tallest piece, the one with the circular assembly. "It's a map."

"Impossible," Roux said.

"Not impossible. Quite clever, actually. I don't know that I've ever seen anything like it." Annja tapped the circular assembly. "This is the spiral staircase we came down. The storeroom was atop it." She traced the hallway in the direction they hadn't taken. "There's an exit here, I would guess from the way it looks, but I doubt it's still functional. If I'm oriented right, this one probably came up in Loulan City."

"We've never found evidence of a tunnel like that," Professor Hu said.

"That's why I'm betting it's no longer functional." Annja traced the linked bones the other way, pointing out the large assembly that had to be the chamber they'd found. "This represents the staircase we followed to come up here, with another exit, also blocked. And this is the hallway that led us to this room."

Roux leaned in closer. "If that's right, then what's this?" He tapped a line of bones that led from the room on the opposite wall.

Those bones spiraled around, too, then led to a line that curved around and went to the bigger of the two spaces in the large chamber.

"That," Annja said, "should be another hidden door."

36

Annja pushed herself up, put her computer away, and shrugged into her backpack. Excitement buzzed through her and wouldn't be denied despite the fact that they were in hostile surroundings.

Crossing to the back of the room, she felt along the wall. Roux and Kelly joined her, adding their flashlights to hers.

"This passageway doesn't lead out." Professor Hu pointed at the bone assembly Annja had constructed. "According to this 'map,' it only leads into the center of that big building. We need a way to escape."

"We have a way." Annja continued feeling along the wall and thought she detected a crack. "We can go back out the way we came in."

"Except that Ngai will have posted guards," Kelly said. "Not to mention that we'd have to get through the large chamber unseen. And I don't hold out a lot of hope for that."

"Ngai isn't after us," Hu said. "He wants what's in the building out there. If he gets it, perhaps he'll leave."

"And perhaps he'll take time to kill witnesses," Roux pointed out.

Hu fell silent.

"Either way," Annja said, "it's in our best interest to cut down the odds some. You keep the others safe here, Professor. Roux and I will—"

"I'm not going to be left out of this," Kelly interrupted. "Ngai had my father killed."

"The three of us," Annja amended, "will do what we can to eliminate some of the risk." She took the flare gun and extra flares from the emergency kit. Roux and Kelly had the only firearms. Annja preferred her sword anyway, and she thought if there was any fighting in the large space it would all be up close and personal.

"I found the release." Roux pressed against a spot on the wall.

A section of the wall opened up, revealing a small corridor beyond.

"Stay here," Annja told the professor and the others. "Until we come for you—or you know we *won't* be coming."

Hu nodded and wished them well.

Stepping into the darkness, flashlight in one hand, Annja reached into the otherwhere and pulled out the sword. Reflected light gleamed along the blade.

"You've really got to show me how you do that," Kelly said quietly.

Annja smiled grimly and continued on.

EMBERS FROM THE IMPURITIES in the iron flew in all directions as Garin cut through the spears. The metal glowed red-hot. He wore welder's goggles to protect his eyes and heavy gloves to protect his hands, but the embers burned his face and forearms. His clothing smoldered and he frequently had to stop cutting long enough to put out the biting fires.

When he cut through the fourth spear, he judged there was enough room to get through. If he could get through, the other men definitely could.

He tossed the torch aside, added the goggles and the gloves, then waited.

"What is the problem?" Ngai asked.

Garin knew the man was impatient. So was he. But Garin had been alive long enough to know that impatience killed a man as quickly as a knife to the throat.

"I'm letting the metal cool a bit," Garin replied. "And I want my vision somewhere near normal before I proceed."

"Let someone else—"

"Letting someone else go first is just going to let someone else get killed."

Ngai fell silent, but Garin knew there'd be no lasting partnership after this was over. He was beginning to doubt Ngai would let him out of the desert alive. Garin realized he'd seriously underestimated the situation and the man he was dealing with.

If Garin had known men who would stay bought, he would have brought them. Everyone he knew would have been bought out by Ngai the first time they took a water break.

Taking a pistol in hand, Garin eased through the opening between the bars. He reached the edge of the floor section that had twisted.

Using his flashlight, he peered down into the dark depths. The two men Ngai had sent on ahead lay impaled by four-foot high iron stakes.

What was it with Sha Wu Ying? Garin wondered. The man had a total fixation on piercing unsuspecting people.

Garin called two of Ngai's men to his side. Together, they righted the tilted corridor section and locked it back in place. Garin also found the lever inset in the wall that locked the spikes into place so the floor would remain in position.

Still, even though he assured the men the corridor would hold, they wouldn't cross until Garin did. He deactivated two more traps along the way, then felt heartened when he saw the door ahead of him.

His good mood evaporated at once when he saw light shining through the cracks around the door. He didn't know how, but he was certain Roux and Annja had beaten them inside the room.

DESPITE THE DESPERATE NATURE of their circumstances, Annja couldn't help grinning as she played the flashlight around the big room. They'd entered from the secret passageway.

The room was huge and round as a pie plate. The architecture caught Annja's eye and made her curious about why it was made that way. But it was the contents of the room that amazed her.

Chests of gold and gems filled shelves and floor space. Beautiful tapestries—some with images of warriors fighting dragons or other impossible creatures—hung on the walls. Casks held what Annja believed was probably oil and myrrh. A king's ransom occupied the room, leaving little space for the statue of a man in the center of the room.

The statue stretched from the floor to the ceiling, at least twenty feet. Made of stone, it had been meticulously carved into the likeness of a grim warrior dressed in Chinese leather armor. His face was hard and unforgiving. His right hand rested on the hilt of a curved, cruel sword. A fierce mustache covered his upper lip.

"Is that Sha Wu Ying?" Annja asked.

"I don't know. Perhaps." Roux sounded distracted as he walked among the piles of treasure. "Unless Sha Wu Ying developed a fascination for someone other than himself."

Annja joined him. She had to step over the mummified remains of a man in leather armor similar to that of the statue. Along with all the treasure, there were several dead men in the room.

Roux kicked one of the mummified bodies. "I'd feel better if I saw Sha Wu Ying's body here somewhere."

"You don't think he survived?" Annja asked.

After a brief pause, Roux shook his head. "He couldn't have survived."

"Because nobody lives two thousand years?"

Roux caught up a fistful of gold coins and let them trickle through his fingers. "Because he wouldn't have left all this behind." The last coin clinked against the pile. "No, if anyone had escaped this place, it would have been looted long ago."

"What are you looking for?" Annja was all too conscious that they didn't have much time before Garin and Ngai arrived.

Roux tucked the hunting rifle under his arm for a moment and held his hands about a foot apart. "A jade figurine about this tall. It's an ogre with a man's body and the head of a baboon."

"Something as unique as that shouldn't be hard to find," Annja said. Of course, there is a lot to sift through.

As she walked through the piles of wealth, Annja couldn't help wondering what Roux wanted with the statue. He'd talked about it being powerful and dangerous.

She joined Kelly at the shelves. They shined their flashlights along the loot piled on the shelves. Together, they hauled down large chests and opened them on the floor.

"My father told me about this place." Kelly used a slim-bladed knife to open the locks. "He didn't have many stories about it, but he'd tell them over and over." She shook her head. "I always thought they were just stories."

"Your father gave you the bag of bones?" Annja asked.

"Yes."

"Did he ever tell you their secret?"

"No. That's why I'd made a sphere of them. It was all I knew how to do."

"Sha Wu Ying had fallen out of favor with Emperor Qin," Annja said as they sifted through coins and gems. "He'd decided to assassinate the emperor and become ruler himself. The problem was, there were a lot of ambitious men around Emperor Qin. And Sha Wu Ying had a young monk in his league of assassins who couldn't bear the thought of all the deaths Sha Wu Ying intended on his way to power."

Kelly reached for another chest and Annja helped her.

"The monk decided he would bring a sickness back to the City of Thieves," Annja said. "To spread it among the assassins and kill them all. He died, either of the sickness or for his betrayal. Before he did, though, he left behind a child's toy that mapped the underground city."

Kelly looked at her, understanding then. "The puzzle."

Annja nodded. "I think so."

"My father said it had been in our family for generations." Wonder widened Kelly's eyes. "The monk was my ancestor?"

"He had to have been."

"What about the spirit fox? The one that was said to be the curse hanging over the belt plaque?" Kelly asked.

"Your ancestor's daughter was trained in martial arts. Maybe she came out here seeking vengeance against the thieves and used the superstitions to be more fearsome. Maybe she knew how the puzzle worked, but she couldn't find the city. Maybe she was afraid of the sickness her father had spread throughout the city and remained in the area to keep people from searching for the place. Maybe something happened to her before she was able to pass the secret of the sphere to her own child. Perhaps she felt the gold was tainted, not something that should be kept." Annja sighed. "We may never know. It's like that sometimes. You get most of the story, but not all of it."

Kelly looked around at the dead warriors. "One of these men could be my ancestor."

"Possibly."

Kelly was silent for a moment. "If we can, I'd like to find his body and bring him home to a better resting place. My father would have liked that."

Annja seriously doubted that would happen any time soon. They had to make their escape first.

A few minutes passed in silence. They worked frantically. There was so much treasure that Annja couldn't even process it anymore. Nearly everything in the treasure room spoke volumes of history, untold stories that they might never come by another way. She was overwhelmed.

Suddenly the door opened and Garin Braden walked into the room, backed by Ngai Kuan-Yin and his warriors.

"Ah, Annja." Garin smiled in the darkness, his face highlighted by the flashlights around him. "Long time no see." He raised the AK-74 in his arms. "I'd really prefer not to have to hurt you. I'd rather you just—"

Beside him, Ngai spoke. "Kill them."

The warriors opened fire.

37

Annja dove, reaching for Kelly, but the other woman had already reached for her, as well. Both of them were intent on rescuing the other. As a result they made it to cover in an awkward sprawl as bullets sprayed the chests and shelves.

Trapped in the room, the gunfire sounded deafening. Then the sharp, rattling reports were punctuated by loud booming sounds. One of Ngai's warriors went down, fluttering like a broken kite. Another swiftly followed.

Roux, Annja realized, recognizing the basso reports of the heavy hunting rifle. She reached for her sword.

Ngai's warriors turned, seeking Roux, thinking him to be the most dangerous threat. Some of them scattered, looking for places to hide. Garin and Ngai were among them, moving swiftly as they slid across the stone floor, slipping on coins and gems and the mummified remains of long-dead warriors.

Roux's rifle blasted again. This time Annja tracked the muzzle flash that accompanied the shot. So did several of Ngai's warriors. Their bullets chewed into the tapestries Roux had hidden behind.

Annja tried not to think about all the irreplaceable history that was being destroyed. She groaned inside. Beside her, Kelly opened fire with both pistols in a swiftly measured cadence that spoke of years of experience with the weapons.

Abruptly, the room *shifted*.

Sparks flared along the ceiling.

Gold coins slid down hills of gold coins and toppled from open chests. The sound of mocking laughter filled the treasure room, but it sounded strangely non-human, like something nightmarish wrung from a monstrous throat.

For a moment primitive fear trailed icy fingers down Annja's spine. It's a trick. There's nothing supernatural about that laugh. But part of her wasn't sure. She was holding on to a very good reason to believe in unexplainable things.

The sparks caught fire and ran along grooves that followed the walls, leaving blazing flames that suddenly reached to the floor. The darkness peeled away. The gold coins gleamed as they reflected the surging flames.

"It's another trap," Ngai shouted.

The battle was temporarily forgotten by Ngai's warriors as they watched the racing flames. Annja was watching, as well. But Roux and Kelly both took advantage of the distraction and each killed another man.

Annja objected to the cold-blooded nature of their efforts, but she knew their foes would have done the same thing if they hadn't been so distracted.

The deaths of their comrades quickly brought their attention back to the fight. Scarcely had the dead men hit the floor before the remaining warriors opened fire again. With the addition of the flames clinging to the walls, their aim improved considerably. They raced forward, assault rifles chattering in their arms.

The door that Garin and Ngai had come through closed with a grim finality, a thunderous boom that rocked the treasure room.

Taking advantage of the new distraction, Annja pushed herself up and ran behind a row of marble statutes. They looked Grecian or Roman, and she had to wonder if they were treasures that Sha Wu Ying had brought with him from his days as Tochardis.

In the next moment it didn't matter and she guessed that she would never know. Bullets knocked off huge chunks of the statues, chopping away arms and legs.

When the gunman got close enough, Annja slammed her body against the statue and toppled it over him. The man didn't have time to move. The falling statue pinned him against the floor, crushing his chest.

Annja kept moving, gunfire blazing all around her. Bullets passed only inches from her head. She ran behind the shelves ahead of her, a gunman on her heels. The wood chipped and split as she ducked behind it.

She stopped as soon as she was out of sight, then watched as a row of bullet holes suddenly opened up in the shelves ahead of her.

Whirling, Annja set off in pursuit. The gunman was only a few feet in front of her. He turned to bring his weapon to bear.

Annja put away the civilized part of herself and concentrated on survival. She whipped the sword through the rifle, knocking it from the man's hands, then brought the blade through her opponent's neck on the return movement. The man toppled to the ground.

Turning at once, knowing that the battle still raged, Annja spotted another man running toward her. She threw herself forward as he opened fire, managing to crash to the floor behind a huge vase.

Bullets smashed the vase into a thousand pieces but were deflected by the gold coins and bars and gems inside. Released from the shattered container, the contents scattered across the floor. Some of them skittered under the running man's feet and he went sprawling.

Annja recognized Huangfu Cao, the man she'd guided to the grave in California. His face was a mask of rage in the fiery light. Lying on his back, he tried to lift the assault rifle.

Throwing herself forward, sliding on her knees, Annja swung at the rifle and smashed it. She swung again, aiming at the man's neck, but Huangfu Cao rolled away. As he got to his feet, he picked up a spear from the nearby weapons rack. The spear was six feet long and topped with eighteen inches of sharp iron, a foot soldier's weapon capable of bringing down a charging horse or the rider.

Huangfu attacked at once, driving the spear at Annja's face. Sidestepping, Annja blocked the spear with her sword but the impact trapped her arm against her side. Stepping forward, Huangfu swung the spear's butt up and into her face. Annja barely had time to roll her head forward so she caught the blow across her forehead instead of in the eyes and nose.

Pulling a leg up, Annja snap-kicked Huangfu in the chest, knocking him away from her. But his greater weight drove her backward, sending her skidding across the loose coins and gems underfoot. Her back foot shot out from under her. Giving in to the motion, wanting to gain control over her movements, she went down in the splits.

Huangfu roared and came at her again, driving the spear down at her.

Rolling to the side, Annja caught hold of the spear just behind the blade and pulled the weapon down. The point caught on the stone floor. She whipped her legs around and kicked her attacker's feet out from under him. Still holding on to the spear, he arced over her head.

She spun on the ground, slashing out at him with the sword. But he wasn't there. Huangfu tucked himself into a roll, bringing the spear across his chest and coming to his feet. He whirled with the spear tucked under one arm, using it like a bo staff.

With her sword out before her as it was, Annja lacked the strength to hang on to it. The weapon shot out of her grip and skittered across the floor.

Grinning in triumph, seeing that she was on her back on the ground, Huangfu launched himself at her, driving the spear at her heart.

Annja slid backward, reaching for the spear with her left hand and willing the sword with her right. It materialized in her hand, bound to her by whatever forces she still couldn't explain, and she thrust it as Huangfu came down on top of her.

His victorious look melted into one of surprise. His face only inches from Annja's, he looked at the sword between them. It had gone cleanly through his heart. He opened his mouth, then slumped as death claimed him.

Pushing the dead man away, steeling herself, Annja pulled the sword from Huangfu's chest. She stared around the treasure room battlefield, amazed to see that only Garin, Ngai, and a couple of warriors survived.

Kelly was bleeding from a head wound, but she was swapping out magazines in her pistols, so Annja knew the woman was well enough.

Garin was a short distance from Ngai, taking cover.

The gunfire had died away, but the mocking near-laughter still pealed.

The rumbling in the room grew louder. A section opened up in the ceiling and a dais dropped through. The upper and lower sections of the dais were identical and were connected by iron bars, making it look something like an hourglass in construction. The upper disk effectively replaced the bottom disk that had slid through the ceiling.

However, instead of glass and sand in the familiar narrow-waisted shape, a man in resplendent robes sat on an ornate throne. A crown sat atop his mummified head. His ivory grin mocked them all. The ghoulish laughter came from some kind of mechanical device under the throne.

"Sha Wu Ying," Ngai said. His voice was hoarse with fear and wonder.

Annja didn't blame the man. The sight was definitely eerie, and the laughter gave her goose bumps. She realized then that the device had to have been spring-loaded and been wound by the same mechanism that had put the room into motion.

But it wasn't the room that was in motion, she realized. It was the ceiling. Inch by inch, the ceiling was lowering, coming down to meet the floor.

With the flames licking the walls, filling the room with an oily black smoke that burned Annja's lungs, she was able to see the line of demarcation that separated the ceiling from the walls. They'd been fitted together with the precision of a drum cylinder.

Now that the ceiling was in motion, she noticed the channels in the walls that allowed the immense stone slab to descend. The architects had to have cut the slab from the mountain, using the original ceiling and cutting it free.

The spring-loaded near-laughter finally ended. Either it had run its course or the device had broken.

The skeletal remains of Sha Wu Ying regarded them from his throne suspended only a few feet from the ground. A sword and jewel-encrusted scabbard lay at his mummified feet. A jade statue of a baboon-headed ogre lay across his lap.

Slowly, the ceiling descended.

Annja remained behind cover, not trusting Ngai or his men. Evidently Garin didn't trust them, either, because he hadn't moved from his spot.

This is some standoff, Annja thought disgustedly. She knew it was possible the ceiling would stop when it reached the piles of gold, but there was no way they were going to get out of the treasure room. It would become their tomb.

Ngai shouted commands to his men. One of them ran toward the door. Kelly picked him off with two quick shots at the same time Roux broke cover and ran toward the jade ogre.

Ngai and one of his men took aim at Roux.

"No!" Annja shouted the warning, but she knew she was going to be too late.

38

The old man swung the hunting rifle over his shoulder as he churned across the loose gems and coins. He nearly fell twice.

By then Annja was in full motion, streaking for her backpack. She reached inside for the flare gun, brought it up, and took aim. Kelly was exchanging fire with Ngai's remaining two men. One of them fell as Annja squeezed the trigger.

The flare leapt from the emergency pistol, streaking across the intervening distance like a flaming arrow. Annja had aimed at the center of Ngai's chest, but the flare veered off-course and slammed into the face of the man beside him.

Annja rushed forward as the wounded man screamed and swiped at his burning face. The flare had caught him in the mouth, breaking teeth and lodging inside. His screams sounded strangled. As he jerked, he smashed into Ngai.

Before Ngai could recover, Annja was on him. He

tried to bring up his pistol, but she slashed his hand and forearm with one swipe. She followed that with a deadly blow. Then she realized she'd seen Roux go down.

Feeling scared and helpless, Annja turned toward the old man.

Roux was dragging himself onto Sha Wu Ying's throne, grabbing the bony knees for support. Blood covered his lower back and one of his legs.

Garin stood, the assault rifle dangling at his side. His face held disbelief and pain as he looked at Roux.

Stubbornly, Roux reached for the jade ogre. He wrapped his arm around it and fell backward, coming to a seated position at the foot of the throne. He clasped his bloody hands over the statue's head, like he was keeping it from hearing anything he said.

"Garin!" Roux's voice was loud and commanding.

Annja stepped in front of Garin, holding the sword within inches of his face. "Stay back," she ordered.

The ceiling continued to drop.

Angrily, Garin spat fierce curses. For a moment Annja though he was going to go for the assault rifle hanging at his side.

"Annja," Roux cried. "Let him through. I need him."

"He tried to kill you," Annja argued. "More than once." But she didn't know if she would be able to shoot him if it came to that.

Roux cursed loudly. "We don't have a choice."

Suddenly aware of a frightful green glow taking shape behind her, Annja glanced over her shoulder.

Roux held the jade ogre tightly. Light leaked through his hands and arms. "It's activated, Garin. We have to stop it."

"That's not my problem, Roux," Garin snarled. "You

knew it was going to activate the instant you touched it. If anyone's to blame, it's you."

"You're the only one who can help me," Roux said.

"I was your apprentice once, old man. You don't own me now."

The jade ogre smoked and smoldered, and Annja thought it had to be hot enough to scald or burn Roux. Still, the old man hung on to it. Blood smeared over the statue.

"If you don't help me, it's going to kill us all," Roux said.

"Let it." Garin switched his attention back to Annja. "Kill me or let me go. Either way I'm not going to stay here and be crushed."

Annja didn't know what to do. She fully expected Garin to try to pull the assault rifle into position. If he did she'd have to kill him. She had no choice.

Slowly, Garin turned to go.

Only a few feet away, Kelly pointed both of her weapons at him.

"No," Annja said. "Let him go."

The light from the ogre grew stronger. The ceiling was within leaping distance. Annja knew they didn't have much time.

"Garin," Roux called. "Please. In memory of the boy I took from his father's cold hearth and gave as much of a life to as I knew how."

For a moment, the words hung in the room in spite of the grinding going on around them.

Garin froze, then turned to face Roux. "You owe me, old man. Swear on your life and your black soul that you owe me."

Roux hesitated. "I swear to you, Garin. You shall one day have my favor."

Without another word, Garin ran to Roux. Together they put their hands on the jade ogre and started chanting words that Annja couldn't understand. The light coming from within the ogre alternately grew stronger and weaker, pulsing faster and faster.

In the next instant, the statue exploded.

The detonation rendered Annja deaf for a moment, and the flash blinded her. Disoriented, her head swimming, she lost her grip on the sword and sank to her knees. She thought she'd blacked out. Then the shrill grinding of the ceiling continuing its downward spiral ate through the cottony deafness in her ears.

Annja forced her eyes open. Ahead of her, Roux and Garin were slumped on the floor. Pushing herself up, Annja looked around, then saw that Kelly was rising, as well. Both of them had been out of the main blast radius.

Going to Roux first, Annja found the old man unconscious. She tried to rouse him and couldn't get him to acknowledge her.

"Is he all right?"

Glancing over her shoulder, Annja saw Garin forcing himself up. "He's breathing," she said. "Other than that, I don't know."

Garin stumbled over to Roux's side and pressed his fingers against the old man's neck.

Annja reached for her sword and felt it in her hand.

"I wouldn't hurt him." Garin didn't look at her when he spoke. "There'd be no honor in that."

Annja didn't see Garin as an honorable person. But maybe he was talking about a more personal level of physical combat rather than life in general.

"He needs a doctor," Annja said.

"I know. You're going to have to get one for him when we get out of here."

Annja thought Garin's plans for them getting out of there needed serious review.

"The front door is jammed," Kelly said, "but there's the secret entrance we came through."

Annja squatted and tried to pull Roux to his feet. The old man never made a sound, just lolled helplessly.

Stooping, Garin scooped the old man up in his arms. He was so tall and broad that Roux looked tiny and frail in his arms. "Go," Garin growled. "I've got him." He could no longer stand fully upright under the descending rock slab.

With the walls losing height, the flames in the channels weren't enough to light the heart of the treasure room. Or maybe whatever fueled them was running out. Annja didn't know.

She took a flashlight from the ground and charged toward the back of the room. The secret passageway was half-closed from the descending ceiling. Annja crawled through, then turned to help Garin pull Roux through the opening.

Once they were through, Garin hoisted Roux once again.

"Where does this go?" Garin asked.

"Back to the main chamber eventually." Annja took off. Garin and Kelly followed.

THEY MADE GOOD TIME, winding up back at the torture chamber in short order. There was brief consternation when Professor Hu and his crew recognized Garin as an enemy.

Before they could get into an argument or discussion

about who was on whose side, one of the workmen pointed to the top of the stairs. "Look! There's sand coming down through the hallway!"

Several flashlights aimed at the doorway to the torture chamber. As Annja watched, puffs of dust roiled into the room.

"Quickly," she ordered. "Let's go." She led the way out.

IN THE MAIN CHAMBER, a solid column of desert sand poured onto the middle of the floor. The deluge pushed treasure chests and mummified bodies in all directions. The sand kept coming.

"That's what pushed the ceiling down after it was freed," Garin said. "There's no telling how much is going to come through."

Across the room, the sand began to lap at the door to the hallway. With both exits that she knew of blocked, Annja knew there was only one way out.

"Let's go." She set out at a brisk pace, running down the steps as fleetly as she could.

Once she reached the floor, she headed for the doorway. Her feet sank into the powdery sand and running became harder, but she pushed herself.

"Did you leave any traps intact back the way you came?" she asked Garin.

"Nothing."

Good, Annja thought. They didn't need anything else to slow them down.

The sand came faster, and Annja had to believe that wherever it was coming from, it had to be draining the entire Lop Nur. She felt it pounding at the backs of her legs.

Two of Ngai's men guarded the doorway that led to

the spiral stairs. They unlimbered their weapons, but they froze, stunned by the approaching wall of sand.

Kelly didn't wait for them to recognize the threat for what it was. She pointed her weapons and opened fire. The bullets knocked the men down, spilling them across the hallway.

At the doorway, Annja stepped to the side and urged Kelly on. "Take the lead. In case there are any more of them."

Kelly nodded. She entered and started running.

Annja wished she had another surgical mask—anything to keep the choking dust out of her lungs. Her mouth and throat felt raw and dry.

Garin carried Roux up next.

Annja waited until Professor Hu and his team were safely up into the spiral staircase. By that time the sand was swimming around her knees. It had washed over the two corpses and hid them from view.

Hacking and gagging, Annja followed the last man up into the spiral staircase. Starving for air, head swimming, she went as quickly as she could, dizzy from the lack of air and the constant circling.

She kept the person in front of her in sight, making certain she didn't run up their back. Briefly, she flicked the flashlight down and made certain the sand wasn't rising any higher. It had peaked far below.

Only a few minutes later, Annja was stumbling through the entrance they'd made in the cave's side. Garin still held Roux, looking down at the old man as if he were gravely concerned.

"Is he all right?" Annja asked.

Garin nodded.

"What did the two of you do to the ogre statue?"

Garin sighed. "We destroyed it. Something so full of power, and now it no longer exists."

"The sword returned to the world."

Smiling at her, Garin said, "Some things don't, Annja. That statue was one of them."

"What did it do?"

Garin shook his head. "I don't know. I would have kept it and found out."

epilogue

A beep woke Annja, but it was accompanied by the very definite feeling she was being watched. Blearily, she shifted in the chair and cracked her eyes open, wanting to check on Roux.

For the last three days, she'd been his constant companion in the hospital. She was irritated because she thought she'd have been used to all the beeps from the hospital machinery by now.

During those three days, Roux hadn't woken at all. Not even for a minute. Garin had left them at the dig site, before the emergency medical people had arrived. He'd told her that Roux would be fine, that he'd seen the old man survive worse.

But the doctors had told Annja that Roux had lost so much blood—in addition to a broken leg and internal injuries—that they didn't know if he would come out of the coma.

At first there'd been a lot of questions asked by the Chinese police in Shanghai after Roux had been trans-

ferred to the hospital. Then an attorney who claimed he
represented Roux arrived and made all the questions go
away. He spoke with Annja, too, explaining how to get
hold of him if she needed anything.

For the last two days, everyone at the hospital had left
her alone. Annja was happy with that. She didn't know
what to say anyhow. Professor Hu had most of the story
and had interfaced with the police.

When she looked at Roux, she expected him to be
sleeping comfortably. Instead he was staring right at her.
A look of apprehension tightened his features.

Roux glared at all the medical equipment around
him. He cursed. "You'd think someone had been hurt."

Relieved at the fighting spirit so evident in Roux's
voice, Annja laughed.

"I think they thought you were going to die," she said.

"Fools. It's going to take more than a few bullets
to kill me."

How much more? Annja couldn't help thinking.

"Did they say when I could get out of here?" Roux
demanded.

"No."

"Well, we'll have to see about that, won't we?"

"If you try to get out of that bed, I'm going to kick
your skinny butt."

"Oh, so that's how it's going to be."

"Yes."

Roux looked around the room. "I seem to have a
shortage of visitors."

"I think Garin would be here if he could. There were
going to be too many questions from the police."

Roux closed his eyes and breathed deeply. When he
spoke, his voice was soft. "I judged him too harshly."

"When you needed him, he was there. Garin carried you out of the City of Thieves. He could havĕ left you." That had amazed Annja, and she'd spent considerable time thinking about that when she wasn't worrying about Roux.

"No, he couldn't have. He got me to agree to a favor for him. He won't squander that," Roux said.

Annja had been wondering about that, too, trying to figure out how much trouble that might cause.

"Well, I suppose everybody's rich now," Roux said glumly. "At least, the Chinese government should be richer."

"Actually, no." Annja explained about the desert sand that had poured into the underground complex. "It's going to take a lot of money and effort to dig everything out."

"They will," Roux said unkindly. "After all, there's gold and gems down there. Men can't stay away from such things."

Annja knew that was true.

"What about you?" Roux asked.

"I'm fine."

Roux looked away from her. "You didn't have to stay. Obviously I was well taken care of, and I had an attorney standing by for just such an occasion."

"He was here."

"I presume he took care of everything?"

Annja nodded.

"What about the young woman who was with us?"

"She got out, too."

Roux smiled. "She seemed quite capable. I liked her."

"So did I," Annja said.

"Do you think she's seeing anyone?"

Annja slumped back in her chair and shook her head. "You," she said distinctly, "are a goat."

Roux smiled. "Women who can take care of themselves are exciting, attractive and refreshing in this day and age. You don't find many."

"She's gone."

"Pity. Is she going to be all right?"

"I think so. I gave her one of your cards. And mine. I told her that if she needed help, we would do what we could. Of course, I also told her that you can do her more good than I can."

"Maybe she'll call," Roux said with a grin.

Annja didn't think so. Kelly seemed very complete and self-reliant.

Silence filled the room for a time, interrupted only by the wheezing and beeping of the hospital equipment.

"You didn't have to stay," Roux said again, more quietly than before.

"I know."

Roux stared at the ceiling. "I have to admit, there was a time there that I was worried." He raised his right hand and opened his thumb and forefinger a fraction of an inch. "A little."

"About what?"

"I thought I might not make it back this time. Things are different now. The sword is back." Roux looked at her. "And it's in good hands. There's a possibility that the world doesn't need me anymore."

"Wow," Annja said, "self-centered much?"

Roux grinned at her. "We are all interested in our own lives. We can't help it. It's just how things are for most people." He paused. "But a few of us, sadly a very few of us, can look beyond our own lives to the lives of others. I want to thank you for staying."

"You're welcome." Annja thought about Kelly. For a while the woman had stayed with her. She'd talked about how hard it was to lose her father, how close they'd been when she was younger, before she'd been sent away to the United States to go to school. Before she'd been lured into working for the CIA.

"You should get out of here," Roux said. "Surely there's something else you can do. I'm going to be fine."

"I've got a hotel room I haven't seen since we checked in. A shower. A change of clothes. I'm going to go but I'll be back." Annja stood. "Is there anything you want?"

"You're coming back?" Roux looked vulnerable in that moment.

Annja had to wonder how many people the old man had lost. For that brief instant, she saw the pain in his face. He's afraid of losing me, she realized. He's afraid I'm going to end up like Joan.

That was part of why he treated her so brusquely. She thought of how things had been in her apartment when he'd stayed with her while they figured out what to do. It had seemed natural, not uncomfortable. Two travelers sharing the road.

"I am," Annja said.

"Do you play poker?"

"No. The nuns at the orphanage wouldn't allow it."

Roux looked more interested, almost like a fox in a henhouse. "You've never played?"

"Not ever."

"Bring back a deck of cards and some chips. I'll show you how to play."

"Okay." Annja leaned over the bed and kissed his

forehead. Then she left quickly, while Roux was still so surprised he didn't know what to say, and before he could say something that would embarrass them both or infuriate her to no end.

Knowing Roux as she did, it could have gone either way.

She'd lied about the poker. Bart McGilley had taught her to play and she'd learned a lot about bluffing from his fellow cops in several all-night tournaments.

Who knew? Maybe before Roux got out of the hospital he'd owe her a favor, too.

James Axler
Outlanders®

SKULL THRONE

RADIANT EVIL

Buried deep in the Mayan jungle amidst a civilization of lost survivors and emissaries of the dead, lies a relic that hides secrets to the prize—planet Earth. In sinister hands, it guarantees complete and absolute power. Kane and the rebels have just one chance to stop a rogue overlord from seizing glory, but must face an old enemy to stop him.

Available May 2007, wherever you buy books.

Or order your copy now by sending your name, address, zip or postal code, along with a check or money order (please do not send cash) for $6.50 for each book ordered ($7.99 in Canada), plus 75¢ postage and handling ($1.00 in Canada), payable to Gold Eagle Books, to:

In the U.S.	In Canada
Gold Eagle Books	Gold Eagle Books
3010 Walden Avenue	P.O. Box 636
P.O. Box 9077	Fort Erie, Ontario
Buffalo, NY 14269-9077	L2A 5X3

Please specify book title with your order.
Canadian residents add applicable federal and provincial taxes.

GOLD EAGLE®

GOUT41